PRAISE FOR THE AUTHOR

"Atmosphere, setting, plot and style combine in a compelling tale" *Sherlock Holmes Journal*

"Designed to entertain" *Kirkus*

"I can't imagine a cozier new book for fans of classic mysteries to curl up with" *Library Journal (starred review)*

"Compelling and inherently fascinating...a must read" *Midwest Book Review*

"James Lovegrove has become to the 21st century what JG Ballard was to the 20th" *The Bookseller*

"Not only is this an entertaining and atmospheric classic Holmes-esque story, but it's also a beautiful book that you'll want to revisit year after year" *Culturefly*

"Lovegrove proves once more that he can capture an authentic sense of the originals and still create a compelling tale" *SFBook*

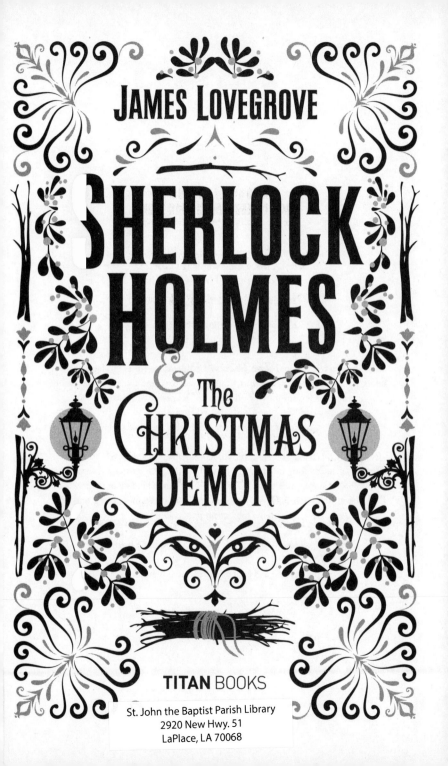

JAMES LOVEGROVE

SHERLOCK HOLMES

& The CHRISTMAS DEMON

TITAN BOOKS

Sherlock Holmes and the Christmas Demon
Paperback edition ISBN: 9781785658044
Electronic edition ISBN: 9781785658037

Published by Titan Books
A division of Titan Publishing Group Ltd
144 Southwark St, London SE1 0UP
www.titanbooks.com

First paperback edition: October 2020
2 4 6 8 10 9 7 5 3 1

A CIP catalogue record for this title is available from the British Library.

Printed and bound in the United States.

Respectfully dedicated to

SIR ARTHUR CONAN DOYLE
THE MASTER

whose fictional creations have brought delight to so many and in whose footsteps I proudly, if trepidatiously, tread

SHERLOCK HOLMES

& The CHRISTMAS DEMON

Chapter One

A FELONIOUS FATHER CHRISTMAS

"Father Christmas! Halt right there!"

These words were delivered by Sherlock Holmes in his most stentorian and authoritative tone of voice.

The object of his command, however, did not heed it. On the contrary, the festively clad fugitive lowered his head and increased his speed.

The ground floor of Burgh and Harmondswyke, the noted Oxford Street department store, was crowded with shoppers, for it was December 19th and all of London, it seemed, was out buying gifts and other seasonal essentials. There were shouts of consternation and the occasional shriek of alarm as the man dressed as Father Christmas, complete with ivy-green robe and mistletoe crown, hurtled through the milling throng. Those who did not get out of his way of their own volition, he barged aside with a ruthless thrust of the forearm. Several men and women, and even a child, found themselves on the receiving end of such rough treatment.

Holmes was hard on his heels and would have overtaken him halfway across the haberdashery department, had a shop clerk not intervened. The young fellow, dressed in an apron with the characters "B & H" emblazoned on the pocket, misread the situation and identified Holmes as the villain of the piece. Boldly he stepped into my friend's path and made strenuous efforts to waylay him. With as much delicacy as the situation permitted, Holmes disentangled himself from the clerk's clutches and continued after his quarry.

The delay cost him precious seconds, however, and now Father Christmas was nearing one of the sets of doors that afforded access to the street. Naught lay between him and freedom, save for one thing: me.

I had been guarding the door for the past half an hour. Inspector Lestrade and a number of police constables, all in plain clothes, were likewise stationed at the other points of egress around the building. As luck would have it, the onus of intercepting our felon now rested upon me.

It was not a task I relished, since the man was nothing short of a giant: six feet seven tall if he was an inch, and broad as a barrel around the chest. He weighed, I would estimate, in the region of seventeen stone and, to judge by his speed, was possessed of considerable strength and vitality, not to mention a determination to evade capture that bordered on desperation.

I braced myself as he approached, feeling the way a matador must when confronted with a charging bull. Father Christmas's cheeks, above his bushy white beard, were crimson with exertion. His eyes, beneath the mistletoe crown, glared like a madman's. His nostrils flared.

I had faced men of similar stature on the rugby pitch, and duly adopted a half-crouch, as one might when preparing to tackle an oncoming flanker.

Father Christmas, on seeing me, did not falter. If anything, he accelerated.

"Watson!" Holmes called out from behind him. "He is yours! Deal with him, would you? There's a good fellow."

All might have been well, had I not in the heat of the moment made a crucial mistake, namely leading with my injured shoulder. When playing rugby, I was always at pains to tackle an opponent using my good shoulder, the one that had not received a bullet from a jezail rifle wielded by a Ghazi sniper in Afghanistan. On this occasion, I neglected to take the precaution. I drove the bad shoulder hard into Father Christmas's midriff. The collision saw both of us tumble to the floor, and the wind was certainly knocked out of Father Christmas's sails, and for that matter his lungs; but alas, I myself was rendered helpless too. My wounded shoulder seized up from the impact, feeling as though it were suddenly gripped in a vice. I could do nothing but roll on my back, clutch the offending area and clench my teeth, hissing with pain.

Giving vent to a roar of indignation, Father Christmas regained his feet.

At that moment, Holmes at last caught up. Without hesitation he pounced, driving the giant back down to the floor. There followed a brief struggle, which ended with Holmes enfolding his opponent in a complicated baritsu wrestling hold. His arms were wrapped around Father Christmas's neck, fingers interlaced, while one knee pressed into the small of the man's back and the other leg locked around his thighs.

"Submit," he hissed in the miscreant's ear, "or I will choke you into insensibility. The choice is yours."

There was further resistance, but Holmes merely tightened his grasp, and soon the fellow was choking, gasping for breath. He slapped the floor, indicating surrender. Holmes obligingly released him.

By now, the commotion had drawn Lestrade and his fellow Scotland Yarders. They swarmed around Father Christmas, and in no time he was in handcuffs, cursing hoarsely but volubly.

"Watson, are you well?" Holmes enquired with the

utmost solicitude. He extended a hand to me, helping me to my feet.

"I have been better, Holmes," I replied, rolling my shoulder in a gingerly manner. "I feel such a fool. In attempting to incapacitate the man, I ended up incapacitating myself."

"Nonsense! You performed admirably. You stopped him. He is in irons. What more could one want?"

"An explanation," Inspector Lestrade interjected in that rather testy way of his. "That is what *I* want, Mr Holmes. You prevailed upon me to assist you with the apprehension of a notorious jewel thief, and who do I now have in custody but good old Saint Nicholas?"

"Ah, but, Lestrade, that is where you are mistaken." Holmes reached for Father Christmas's bushy beard and gave it a firm, forthright tug. It peeled away, revealing itself to be false. "Tell me, whom do you see now?"

"Why, bless me!" declared the sallow-skinned, weasel-featured official. "If it isn't Barney O'Brien!"

"Indeed," said Holmes. "A criminal taker of treasures posing as a jolly giver of gifts. Barney O'Brien, newly released from Pentonville and already up to his old tricks again."

"Damn you, you dog," growled the man called O'Brien, adding a few less salubrious oaths and curses.

"A very pretty scheme you concocted, O'Brien," said my friend, unperturbed. "Something of a step up from your usual housebreaking. I salute you. Oh, by the way, Lestrade, have one of your men go to the jewellery department and arrest a certain female assistant there. Her name, I believe, is Clarice. She shouldn't be hard to recognise. Russet hair. Freckles. She is O'Brien's accomplice."

Having despatched a subordinate as requested, Lestrade said, "So where is the booty? You told me, Mr Holmes, that we would seize the culprit *in flagrante*. I suppose I am to rummage through his pockets in order to find his ill-gotten gains?"

"No need." Holmes plucked the mistletoe crown from O'Brien's head. He turned it in his hands, examining it until at last his eye alighted upon that which he sought. "You see, Lestrade? What you are looking for is right here."

He passed the crown to Lestrade, who cast his gaze over it. "All I see are leaves and berries."

"Look closer. All is not as it appears."

The official peered at the item of plant-based millinery with such furrowed-browed concentration, I thought his forehead might crack. "No," he said eventually. "I must confess myself baffled. I see nothing out of the ordinary."

For my own part, I was in agreement with him. The mistletoe crown appeared to be nothing other than a mistletoe crown.

"Great heavens above, the berries!" Holmes snapped. "Here." He took the crown back from Lestrade and dug thumb and forefinger into the wreaths of mistletoe. He plucked out what seemed at first glance to be an ordinary white berry. Only when he held it up to the light did I observe that it bore a distinctive nacreous lustre.

"A pearl," I said.

"Precisely. And there are two more wedged into the crown's interstices, here, and here. As for the others that O'Brien has spirited off the premises over the past few days, I daresay they are stashed at whatever lodging he calls home. If, that is, they have not already been sold on to a third party."

He thrust the mistletoe crown back into Lestrade's hands.

"Come, Watson," he said. "Our work is done. Friend Lestrade will tidy up the last few loose ends, will you not, Lestrade? I feel Watson and I are no longer needed."

"As you wish, Mr Holmes," Lestrade said, with some resignation. "And am I to mention your name, when the time comes to write my report?"

"It is up to you. You may take full credit if you like. Messrs Burgh and Harmondswyke have retained my services for a handsome fee. That, from my perspective, is more than sufficient reward for my trouble. Besides, if I know my Watson, this episode will no doubt form the basis for one of his stories, and so the general public will someday come to learn of the affair and my involvement in it."

We took our leave, donning hats, gloves and scarves and wrapping our greatcoats around us as we headed outdoors. Snow lay thickly piled on the pavements, here and there compacted to treacherous ice by the passage of countless feet, while the roadways were lined with churned-up brown sludge that was crisscrossed with wheel ruts. The afternoon sky was clear, the air bitterly sharp. That December was already proving to be colder than any in living memory, and indeed the winter of late 1890 and early 1891 is on record as one of the severest ever.

We walked a short way west along Oxford Street and thence southward into Soho, where we found a coffee house. Soon we were warming ourselves with hot drinks, and I felt the stiffness and pain in my shoulder gradually begin to abate.

"Now then, Holmes," I said, slipping notebook and pen from my pocket, "perhaps you would care to divulge some of the finer points of the case upon which we have just been engaged."

"While you take notes? It would be my pleasure. You did come in somewhat late in the proceedings, after all, and are not apprised of the full details."

"Until lunchtime today I did not even know there *was* a case."

"Well, it was a trifling but nonetheless enlivening matter. Put simply, it had come to the attention of the store's owners, Mr Burgh and Mr Harmondswyke, that pearls were disappearing from the jewellery department. Not in great numbers, but incrementally, two or three at a time. They were loose gems that had not yet been strung in a necklace or bracelet or set into a ring. The department would conduct its usual stocktake at the end of each day before consigning the valuables to a safe, and always when they tallied up the pearls, they would come up short.

"At first it was assumed a shoplifter was responsible, but close observation of customers disproved the supposition. Mr Burgh and Mr Harmondswyke then hit upon the notion that the culprit must be a member of staff, and so took the step of conducting a thorough search of all the clerks in the jewellery department daily as they left at close of business. When that did not stem the outflow of pearls, they instituted a regular search of *all* members of staff throughout the store. Still pearls continued to vanish. That was when I was hired to investigate.

"I spent a couple of days wandering the store in various disguises. You know my penchant for such masquerades, and you will be familiar with a couple of the personae I adopted. One was an asthmatic master mariner, another a rather guileless Nonconformist clergyman. I also essayed a new role, that of a venerable Italian priest, which, I will admit, remains a work in progress but which I hold out high hopes for. Watson? Are you paying attention? Your note-taking has tailed off somewhat."

"What's that, Holmes? Sorry. I was distracted. Pray go on."

The cause of my distraction was a smartly dressed and rather comely-looking young woman who had entered the coffee house shortly after us and now sat two tables away. I had caught her eyeing me in a quizzical fashion and had returned her curiosity with an amiable smile.

Holmes crooked an eyebrow and continued. "As I was saying, I visited the store several times over the course of two days, on each occasion in a different disguise, and made a careful study of the comings and goings in the jewellery department. It was mid-afternoon on the second day, yesterday, when I saw our Father Christmas enter and start greeting all and sundry in a hearty manner, customers and staff alike. A Christmas grotto has been erected in the toy department – a sizeable construction made of wood and papier mâché, designed to resemble an ice cave – wherein a Father Christmas impersonator might entertain youngsters and dispense cheap gewgaws. The gentleman, it transpires, was also under instruction to amble around the rest of the store, spreading yuletide cheer wherever he went. He whiled some time in the jewellery department chatting with the shopgirl whom I described to Lestrade."

"Russet hair. Freckles."

"The very one. Well remembered. The two appeared on cordial terms, to the point of clasping hands at one stage, and I inferred some sort of relationship between them. By means of a casual enquiry to the floor manager I learned that this girl, Clarice by name, had been with Burgh and Harmondswyke for several months and was regarded as a good, diligent worker. Not only that but she had recommended an intimate of hers for the job of Father Christmas, which had come vacant. She had described him as a close friend and given his name as Seamus Flynn. Physically he fit the bill, being large and ruddy-cheeked, and he even had his own costume, saving the store the trouble and expense of providing him with one.

"Already I was beginning to formulate a conjecture. Why was it only pearls that were disappearing? Why not some other, more valuable form of precious stone, of which the department had ample specimens? And by what method were the pearls being smuggled out? I rapidly hit upon the solution. Father Christmas's mistletoe crown was the key. Even if inspected closely, a pearl might easily pass for a mistletoe berry. It was a fairly ingenious stratagem.

"I was also aware – through the auspices of the *Police Gazette*, whose pages are a boon to the criminal specialist – that a certain Barney O'Brien had lately been released from prison, having served three years for stealing the Baroness Willoughby-Cavendish's diamond tiara."

"Yes," I said, "I recall the trial. He would have been detained for longer had the tiara itself actually been found. As it was, there was only circumstantial evidence connecting him to the crime, and so he received a more lenient sentence than he otherwise might."

Again, I caught the young woman's eyes upon me. She averted her gaze and resumed her business, namely scribbling industriously in a small journal. Nevertheless I had the impression that she found me interesting, and were I not a happily married man, I might have paid her the compliment of a brief word or two after Holmes and I were finished with our coffees.

"It was no great leap in logic," Holmes said, "to deduce that Seamus Flynn and Barney O'Brien were one and the same person. I knew of the latter's considerable height and girth, which were matched by the former's. I even had a strong suspicion that during his brief exchange of words with russet-haired Clarice, she could have surreptitiously passed a pearl or two to him, which he had then palmed with a view to inserting them into his crown later, when no one was looking.

"To prove this beyond a shred of doubt, however, I would actually have to observe the swap taking place. Hence I returned to the store today, this time as myself, and again shadowed Father Christmas on his perambulations. In the jewellery department I watched closely as he spoke to the shopgirl. There it was! Subtle but clearly visible to one who was looking for it. A glimpse of tiny, pale objects moving from her hand to his.

"I decided to wait until after he had secreted the pearls

inside his mistletoe crown. In this, I was indulging my theatrical streak somewhat. I wished to provide a dramatic dénouement to the case, by exposing not just the villain's identity but his modus operandi, in one fell swoop."

"Much as you did."

"Yes, but it was nearly not to be. As O'Brien was leaving the jewellery department, I saw him pause and remove the crown as though to make some small adjustment to it. It was then that he stealthily inserted the pearls in amongst the mistletoe fronds, before returning the crown to his head. I, spying my chance, pounced.

"'You scoundrel!' I declared. 'I have you now!'

"Unfortunately, I had underestimated the full extent of his strength and he was able to give me the slip. I gave chase, secure in the knowledge that he would not be able to leave the building unimpeded, since I had taken the precaution of enlisting the aid of Lestrade and his men – and yours too, of course – and the exits were covered. All the same, I feared I was to be denied my moment of glory. It was a close-run thing!"

"What about the shopgirl?" I said.

"As to her, she will doubtless confess her complicity in the crime in due course."

"Do you think O'Brien duped or coerced her into it?"

"Neither. On the contrary, my feeling is that Clarice was actually the mastermind and O'Brien her willing foil.

O'Brien has in the past not shown himself to be the shrewdest of operators. He is a skilled enough burglar but not what one would call cunning. Clarice already had the job at Burgh and Harmondswyke. She was the one who put O'Brien forward, under a pseudonym, as a candidate for Father Christmas. She could well have worked out a means of stealing the pearls and then simply inveigled O'Brien into participating in her scheme. It would not have been difficult for her. She is not unattractive."

"Nor would O'Brien have taken much persuasion, I'd have thought, an inveterate larcenist like him."

"Indeed. And now you have the long and the short of it, Watson. Let us congratulate ourselves. We have scored a notable success, doing our bit to ensure that this remains a time of peace on earth and goodwill to all men."

With this ironical flourish, my friend completed his disquisition, and I put away my notebook.

Lowering his voice, Holmes then said, "That young woman who has been proving so diverting to you – do you recognise her?"

"What young woman?"

"Come now, old friend. I have seen where your eyes keep straying."

"Well, I… I mean… *She* is the one whose eyes keep straying."

"And how could any female resist a square-jawed,

well-whiskered fellow such as yourself? Yet I regret to inform you that it is the both of us who fascinate the girl, not just you, for some of her glances have been directed at me. Moreover, we have seen the lass before."

"We have?"

"She was a customer in the stationery department at Burgh and Harmondswyke. I noticed her watching us during our exchange with Lestrade. Her scrutiny was quite intense. I am surprised you were not aware of it then. And now she has followed us to this coffee house, which I cannot believe to be a coincidence, and indeed, even as I speak, she is standing up and approaching our table."

Sure enough, the young woman was making her way towards us with a certain nervously resolute air, as though after a period of prevarication she had made up her mind to introduce herself.

"Please forgive the intrusion, gentlemen," she said. "You are, am I right in thinking, Mr Sherlock Holmes and his companion Dr John Watson?"

"None other," said Holmes.

"Your servant, madam," said I, rising a little from my chair and bowing. "But you have us at a disadvantage. You are…?"

"Eve Allerthorpe. I would never normally be so forward, but when I saw the two of you in action at Burgh and Harmondswyke, and heard you address each other by name, I said to myself, 'This is fate, Eve. Here I am, on a visit to

London, and who should I chance upon amid all the millions in this city but the celebrated detective Mr Holmes, in the flesh. A rare chance has presented itself, and you must take it, girl.' And that, after some inward debate, is what I am doing."

"Please, have my seat," I said, ushering her to it.

"You are too kind, Doctor. I don't rightly know whether I should trouble you with my predicament or not. Sometimes it seems ridiculous even to me, while at other times it seems the deadliest and most serious set of circumstances and I fear that my sanity, even my very life, might… might be…"

All at once, Miss Eve Allerthorpe broke down in tears. I tendered her my handkerchief and she sobbed into it copiously. A few inquisitive glances came our way from other patrons of the coffee house, and I offered them a reassuring wave of the hand, as if to say all was well.

"Oh, I vowed I would not give in to my emotions," the young woman said after her crying fit had run its course. "It's just that I have been under such strain lately. You can hardly begin to imagine what it has been like. First my mother dying, and now this…"

"I think," said Holmes, "that Watson and I should escort you to my rooms at Baker Street, Miss Allerthorpe, and there, away from prying eyes and eavesdropping ears, you may feel at liberty to unburden yourself to us in full."

Chapter Two

THE ALLERTHORPES OF FELLSCAR KEEP

Not half an hour later, we three were ensconced in the first-floor drawing room at 221B. Mrs Hudson had banked up a roaring fire, which did much to dispel the chill, and had drawn the curtains against the onset of dusk. I had relieved Miss Allerthorpe of her overcoat, mantle and sable muff and pressed a glass of brandy into her hand.

Now Holmes, having allowed the young woman a few moments to compose herself, embarked upon a gentle interrogation.

"Miss Allerthorpe," said he, "am I to take it that you hail from that distinguished clan whose family seat is Fellscar Keep, in the East Riding?"

"You would be correct in that assumption," she replied with a nod.

I saw Holmes bristle somewhat at her use of the word "assumption". It was a particular source of pride to him that he never *assumed* anything. However, tact and his customary politeness towards the gentler sex prevented him from upbraiding her.

In the event, the woman herself realised she had committed a solecism. "But of course, I am familiar enough with Dr Watson's writings to know that you possess a knack for gleaning information about a person upon first acquaintance, much as though reading a page of a book. That was the case here, was it not?"

"The trace of a Yorkshire accent was a clue," Holmes said. "Those flattened vowels, discernible even in one who is otherwise well-spoken. But also the surname Allerthorpe is an uncommon one, and given your evident affluence, it seemed more than likely that you are one of *those* Allerthorpes."

"Our renown has obviously spread further than I thought."

"It would be hard not to have heard of one of the richest families in the north, if not all of England, whose collective wealth derives from coal mining and wool, in which trades Allerthorpes became preeminent during the Industrial Revolution."

"I wonder what else you can tell about me," Miss Allerthorpe said. "Something more obscure, perhaps."

"Well, since you have thrown down the gauntlet, madam,

allow me to accommodate you. Judging by your youth – you can be no more than twenty years of age – you belong to the most recent generation of the Allerthorpe dynasty. You are as yet unmarried, as you wear no wedding ring. You are also fond of poetry."

Miss Allerthorpe's eyes widened. "How on earth can you know that? Outside of my immediate circle of acquaintance, there can be no one aware that poetry is my passion."

Holmes flapped a dismissive hand. "As Watson took your overcoat and hung it up, I spied the slim, well-thumbed volume of Keats protruding from the pocket. That was all the evidence necessary. You write poems of your own, what is more."

Her surprise at his deduction was this time not as great. "I suppose that is obvious. The odds are high that those who read poetry are versifiers themselves."

"Odds have nothing to do with it," said Holmes. "I observed you at your table in the coffee house. Thanks to our relative positions I could not see precisely what you were writing in your journal, but the distance your pen covered when moving from left to right was shorter than the full breadth of the page by some margin. Short lines customarily denote poetry. Added to that, you crossed out and rewrote several times, actions suggestive of someone in the throes of creative composition."

"I see. Anything further?"

"I would submit that you are in a state of high tension and have been for some days."

"I already told you that I am under great strain."

"And it is plain not only in the slight tremble that attends your every gesture, but in your recent significant weight loss."

"It is true I haven't had much of an appetite in the past few months," Miss Allerthorpe confessed. "I scarcely dare ask how you divined that."

"Your blouse has been recently taken in, as is evident from the thickness of the new seams. A woman of your means and background would not wear an item of clothing that was not tailored to her figure. Her blouse would neither be borrowed nor hand-me-down. Yours has been altered because it no longer fits you as once it did, a state of affairs which must be recent, else you would by now have purchased a whole new wardrobe better suited to the slimmer you. And would I be mistaken in inferring that you have a younger sibling? A brother?"

"I do. Erasmus."

"I thought as much."

"Perhaps you have read about him in the society pages. Raz has been known for his boisterous activities, reports of which sometimes appear in the gossip columns."

"No, I had not the faintest idea about his existence until I observed the small scar on your face."

"You mean here?" Miss Allerthorpe's hand went to her left eyebrow, just above which lay a small, all but imperceptible blemish.

"The very one. Its faintness bespeaks a wound sustained some years ago, in other words in your early youth, when, as the good Doctor here will attest, the body heals more quickly and efficiently than in adulthood. Your brother is the one who inflicted it upon you during a bout of horseplay."

"It is absurd that you could know that."

"I will admit I was somewhat chancing my arm with the deduction," said Holmes. "I felt moved to venture it regardless, and the gamble paid off. You see, my own brother, Mycroft, has a very similar scar in almost the exact same spot, and I was the culprit. I gashed him with the tip of a wooden sword while we were playing at pirates one afternoon. It seemed at least plausible that your wound was inflicted in a similar manner. It tends to be younger brothers who are to blame for such malfeasances, and older siblings their victims."

"I was ten, Erasmus eight," Miss Allerthorpe said. "He was pretending to be Saint George, riding a hobby horse and wielding, like you, a wooden sword. I was saddled with the role of the dragon he was bent on slaying. Raz was always a bumptious boy, lacking in self-restraint, and his enthusiasm for the game got the better of him. He has marred my features but I have forgiven him."

"Hardly marred!" I declared. "Why, if Holmes had not mentioned the scar, Miss Allerthorpe, I would never even have realised it was there. Your looks are quite undiminished for its presence."

"Thank you for saying so, sir."

"Watson's gallantry exceeds mine," said Holmes, feigning chagrin. "Consider me rebuked for my temerity in raising the subject at all. But now that I have discharged my duty by making these few small observations about you, Miss Allerthorpe, perhaps you are ready to expand upon the nature of this 'deadliest and most serious set of circumstances' in which you find yourself."

"Where to begin, Mr Holmes?"

It was a rhetorical question but Holmes answered it anyway. "You mentioned that your mother is dead and that this heralded the onset of your woes. There might be a good place to start."

Eve Allerthorpe steeled herself with a sip of brandy and commenced her narrative.

"My mother passed away a year ago almost to the day," said she. "She was never what one would call the most stable of characters. Her temperament was mercurial, her mood as changeable as the weather over the Yorkshire Moors. Some might even go so far as to call her mad. She could be angry and vituperative, downright venomous at times. Yet she could also be tender and loving, and on the whole was devoted both to Papa and to her two children. That made her death in one sense surprising and in another sense not surprising at all."

"How so?"

"Mama took her own life, you see." Miss Allerthorpe faltered. "Even now it is difficult for me to discuss."

"I understand. Take your time."

"Our home – Fellscar Keep, as you have said – is an immense, rambling edifice of towers, wings and battlements, perched on an island in the middle of a lake. One evening last December, my mother was in a particularly volatile frame of mind. She had endured some minor setback during the day – a maidservant had, as I recall, accidentally scorched one of her favourite dresses with the smoothing iron – and it threw her into a fit of rage and recrimination, as such things were apt to. Her anger, though it could often be visited upon others, was just as often visited upon herself, and so it was in this instance. Mama somehow blamed herself for the damaged dress, saying that it was no better than she deserved and that a wretch like her should not expect anything ever to go her way. All my father's efforts to placate her were to no avail. Eventually she went to her room and locked herself in."

"Her own bedroom? She and your father slept separately?"

"She was a restless sleeper. Papa preferred his slumber not to be disturbed by her wakefulness. At any rate, from past experience we knew we were unlikely to see any more of her until the following morning, when she would doubtless emerge all smiles and laughter, as though nothing untoward had occurred. Around midnight, however, she was heard rushing along the corridors of the castle, wailing at the top of her voice, and..."

Miss Allerthorpe strove to maintain her poise.

"And then," she said, "she took herself to the top of the tallest tower, which lies in the castle's east wing, opened a window and threw herself out, into the lake. The servants dragged the water all night, under Papa's supervision, but it wasn't until first light that the... that the body was eventually recovered."

I made sympathetic noises, while Holmes quietly steepled his long fingers and pressed their tips to the groove above his upper lip.

"You can well imagine the horror of the incident," Miss Allerthorpe said, "and the shock Mama's death wrought upon us. Erasmus and I, in particular, were distraught with grief. Our mother would never have abandoned us in this way if the equilibrium of her mind had not been seriously disturbed, we knew that. But looking back, we had perhaps known all along that it was not unlikely she might meet such an end. Often when Mama's depressions became profound, she would cause harm to her own person, by pricking her arms with a hatpin, for instance, and raking her fingernails down her cheek. My father had consulted the best alienists in Harley Street, to no avail. There seemed no cure, no hope of change. All any of us could do was accept and endure. Yet it was never wholly bad. There were happy times, too. When she was in one of her 'up' phases, my mother had the sunniest of dispositions and there was nobody whose company I would rather have kept."

"A tragedy is no less appalling when one can see it looming," I said.

"Quite the opposite, Doctor. The inevitability makes it worse. I will not say that my present difficulties stem directly from Mama's suicide. I will say, though, that the death has cast a pall over the household, which has yet to lift fully. Put simply, none of us has been the same since. Papa, always a rather remote person, has become positively aloof, and his temperament, once equable, now tends towards the irascible. Erasmus... Well, his behaviour was troublesome to begin with, and has done anything but improve. It was hoped, though, that this Christmas might bring about a change in our fortunes."

"Why should that be?" asked Holmes.

"If there is one thing that unites the Allerthorpes, Mr Holmes, it is a love of Christmas. At this time of year, the wider family travels from near and far, converging on Fellscar Keep to celebrate the season. It is a tradition going back a good five decades, instituted by my grandfather,

Alpheus Allerthorpe, and rigorously, one might even say religiously, maintained ever since. The castle opens its doors and plays host to a week-long revel. There is feasting, carolling, gift-giving. There is also an opportunity to renew family ties and mend any fences that might need mending. Only once has the event ever been cancelled."

"Last December, in the wake of your mother's death."

"Precisely. This year, it is hoped we may resume as before. Or rather, it *was* hoped. But before I get to that, Mr Holmes, I must furnish you with one last detail which may or may not be of relevance."

"Pray do."

"As you surmised, I am twenty years old. My twenty-first birthday falls this coming Wednesday."

"Christmas Eve," I said.

"That is right. I was born on Christmas Eve."

"Hence your first name."

"Again, that is right."

"Watson," Holmes remarked to me superciliously, "never let it be said that your powers of deduction are not at least the equal of mine."

I rewarded him with a dusty stare.

"When I turn twenty-one," Miss Allerthorpe said, "I am in line for a sizeable inheritance. It is a legacy left me by my aunt Jocasta. She died when I was very young. I hardly remember her, beyond a few vague impressions.

Mostly I recall a rather formidable woman, brusque but well-meaning, with a voice that could be heard several rooms away. Although she was my mother's sister, her senior by just over a year, the two of them could scarcely have been less alike. Mama, as I have made clear, was anxious and neurotic. Aunt Jocasta was as down-to-earth and dependable as they come. In terms of physique, Mama was tall, thin and brittle-seeming; Jocasta was short and sturdily built, practically as wide as she was tall. Mama did not concern herself with matters beyond the domestic sphere, whereas Jocasta was engaged in politics and a staunch advocate of the rights of women. She believed that women should be educated as men are and given the vote, and she was not afraid to voice her opinions. I am told she once stormed a general election campaign meeting being held by her local Member of Parliament and chanted demands for universal suffrage. Her protest caused disarray and brought the proceedings to a premature halt, resulting in her forcible eviction and an arrest for breach of the peace. I cannot attest to the truth of that. It may just be a family fable. I do know that Jocasta was reviled as a troublemaker in some quarters, and in others considered a radical heroine."

"And you are the sole beneficiary of her will?"

"Yes. Her husband was a prominent sugar plantation owner, Sir Cyril Keele, who died a few years into their marriage. He contracted typhus while visiting one of his estates in the Caribbean. Upon being widowed, Aunt Jocasta sold off his holdings and invested the capital in stocks, living very comfortably thereafter on the interest. She was childless, and her portfolio and cash savings have been held in trust for me since her death. Everything, minus a few small disbursements to charities, will become mine in just a few days' time."

"It is unusual for a legacy to be passed down the distaff line," said Holmes. "Yet, if your aunt was as favourable towards the advancement of her own sex as you say, then it makes sense. You, I imagine, are her nearest female kin, aside from her late sister."

Miss Allerthorpe nodded. "Jocasta, by all accounts, regarded my mother as sufficiently well-off already, for she had married into the Allerthorpe family. She knew, moreover, that my father, as husband, would gain control of the money if it went to Mama, and Mama herself might derive no direct benefit from it at all. She chose to confer it on me instead. You must appreciate that, as a daughter, I will profit in no way whatsoever from Papa's estate. Upon his death, his money will be passed to my brother in its entirety, as will the title to the castle and Allerthorpe lands, which are extensive. Jocasta felt I ought to be of independent means, beholden to no one – no *man* – for my living. I believe there is an additional reason, too, why she did not regard my mother as a suitable recipient for the legacy. It is implied by a codicil in the will."

"Which stipulates…?"

"That I am to receive the money only if, upon reaching the age of twenty-one, I am 'sound in mind'. Otherwise, I do not see a single penny."

"She deemed your mother not 'sound in mind', then."

"With some justification. And it would seem she feared the possibility that I might follow in Mama's footsteps. Madness is often hereditary, is it not?"

Miss Allerthorpe aimed this question at me. I replied, "Current medical thinking has moved on from the belief that mental aberration arises from social background and 'sinful' behaviour. According to Henry Maudsley, the eminent psychiatrist, just as a propensity towards certain diseases may be passed on through the blood, so may a propensity towards certain abnormal mental traits. It is not axiomatically the case, however, that the child of a mad person will likewise become mad. The trait may stay dormant."

"Aunt Jocasta would certainly seem to have made provision for the possibility that, in me, the trait is not dormant," said Miss Allerthorpe. "I imagine she felt that if I ended up like my mother, I would be incapable of properly handling my newfound wealth and thus lay myself open to criticism and exploitation. It would set a bad example if a woman were seen to lack the wherewithal to manage large sums of money. It would undermine all that Jocasta strove to prove during her life."

"What would happen to the legacy if, heaven forfend, you were to be certified *un*sound in mind?" said Holmes.

"In that instance, the totality is to be apportioned equally amongst family members of my generation. That comprises a number of my cousins and, of course, Erasmus. Each would receive currency and shares worth in the region of four thousand pounds."

Holmes gave a low whistle. "A tidy sum. Yet, with just five days remaining, it does not strike me as likely that you will be considered unfit to receive your legacy, Miss Allerthorpe. Although at the coffee house you implied that your sanity is imperilled, I see scant sign of it myself. You are anxious and agitated, yes. But mad? Hardly."

"Little do you realise, Mr Holmes, how close I am to losing my wits," said the young woman, her hand fluttering to her throat. "There have been times over the past few days when I have truly doubted the evidence of my own eyes, and on one occasion I have been visited by such terror that I can barely bring myself to think about it, let alone talk about it."

"Yet you must talk about it, if I am to help you."

"I know. Dr Watson, would you be so kind as to recharge my glass?"

I helped Miss Allerthorpe to more brandy, which she drank almost to the bottom before carrying on.

"When I relate to you now, gentlemen, the series of incidents that have lately befallen me," she said, "you will perhaps be incredulous and dismiss it all as nonsense. If, on the other hand, you believe me, then you could be forgiven for thinking that I have indeed taken leave of my senses. I am being haunted, you see. Doubly haunted."

"By a ghost?" said Holmes.

"By a ghost, and by a creature from nightmares."

Chapter Three

THE BLACK THURRICK

I could see Holmes doing his best to mask his scepticism. In his view, ghosts did not exist, nor any other form of paranormal phenomenon. He was adamant that that which purported to be otherworldly would, when subjected to proper analysis, invariably be exposed as a misapprehension of the data, a hitherto undiscovered natural occurrence, or a downright falsehood. As far as he was concerned, the bright, hard light of empiricism could disperse all shadows.

I myself was less confident when it came to such matters. To me there seemed plenty of room in this world for mysteries that science and logic could not explain. Human understanding only reached so far before it ran up against the ineffable and the irrational, and without that extra, unknown dimension, life would truly be a poor, drab affair.

At any rate, where Miss Allerthorpe's words served to have no effect upon Holmes other than to cause him to purse his lips, they sent a small chill up my spine.

"With regard to the ghost," she said, "perhaps I overstated when I said I am being haunted by it. I have not personally experienced any of the various manifestations that might lead one to conclude that a revenant walks the corridors of Fellscar Keep. There have been reports from several of the servants, however, concerning inexplicable noises in the castle's east wing at night. Thuds, bangs and suchlike. Strange breezes, too, that extinguish candle flames like a puff of breath. I do not frequent that part of the building, so cannot attest to any of this first-hand."

"The east wing is where your mother took her own life," said Holmes. "I imagine it holds negative associations for you."

"Exactly. There is little call for me to go there anyway. It is a somewhat remote corner, far from the usually inhabited sections of the castle. Only during the Christmas family get-together, when we are overrun by houseguests, are its rooms occupied. For most of the year it lies, as it were, fallow."

"The question, I suppose, is whose ghost it might be. How long have these manifestations, as you call them, been occurring?"

"For several months now. Since spring at least, if not earlier."

"I am hesitant to suggest this, but might the spectral shade conceivably be that of your late mother?"

Miss Allerthorpe nodded. It was apparent that this unhappy thought had already occurred to her. "Hence it is fair to say that I am being haunted by it, even if I have not seen it with my own eyes. What if it is my mother? What if Mama's restless departed spirit has returned to the very place where she drew her last breath?"

"Strictly speaking, your mother drew her last breath in the lake, not in the east wing."

"Holmes!" I rebuked him.

"I apologise, Miss Allerthorpe," my friend said with a small bow. "I am a stickler for accuracy, but I appreciate that in this instance my comment may have seemed poorly judged."

The young woman tendered a forgiving nod. "In any case, I have no desire to meet the ghost. Would you, in my shoes?"

"What about this 'creature from nightmares', then? Have you had an encounter with that?"

"Yes," Miss Allerthorpe said firmly. "Let me ask you, sirs, has either of you heard of the Black Thurrick?"

I shook my head. Holmes did likewise.

"There is no reason why you should have, I suppose," Miss Allerthorpe said. "London lies many miles from Yorkshire, and what I am talking about is very much a regional thing, confined principally to the East Riding. The Black Thurrick is, one might say, the dark antithesis of Father Christmas. It is an entity that appears only at yuletide, but unlike Father Christmas, the Black Thurrick is evil."

"What has it done to earn such a reputation?" said Holmes.

"According to the tales Mama used to tell, the Black Thurrick punishes children who have behaved badly during the course of the year. It replaces the presents they were due to receive from Father Christmas with clusters of birch twigs."

"That is hardly evil. Mischievous, perhaps, but not evil."

"It is the least of it. Legend also says that the Black Thurrick steals infants from their homes. If parents do not leave out food for it on their front doorstep on Christmas Eve – a loaf of bread, perhaps, or a handful of vegetables – they will wake up to find their children gone the next morning, never to be seen again. The Black Thurrick will have shinned down the chimney and stolen the babes from their beds while they slept. It stuffs them into the sack it carries on its back and scurries off to its underground lair, where it eats them at its leisure."

"I stand corrected. An anthropophagous, child-abducting monster is, indeed, very much the epitome of evil." The hint of facetiousness in Holmes's voice was perceptible to me but not, I thought, to Miss Allerthorpe.

"On many a dark winter's night, Erasmus and I would sit by the hearth while my mother told us about the Black Thurrick," she said. "She was a Yorkshirewoman born and bred and had been raised on a diet of local folklore. The county abounds with it, the East Riding most of all. There is the Gypsey Race river, whose waters are said to flow only when calamity is about to strike the nation. There is the Rudston Monolith, a mysterious ancient standing stone reckoned by some to be a portal to the fairy realm. There are numerous reports of werewolves, dragons and phantom hounds, and once, almost a century ago, a meteorite fell to earth near Wold Newton during a thunderstorm."

"Nothing too preternatural about that last example," said Holmes.

"Yes, but the meteorite's glowing journey through the sky had a queer effect upon the passengers of a stagecoach below, who fell into a swoon and came round afterward with no recollection at all of anything that had happened. The Black Thurrick is yet another of these legends from the area, and is the one that has left the strongest impression upon me. Mama would portray the creature in such vivid terms. Its long, gangling limbs. Its bright white eyes. Its coal-black skin, darkened by chimney soot. Its sinister, loping gait. The sack upon its back, which writhes as its living contents fight vainly to break free."

Miss Allerthorpe's descriptive powers seemed every bit on a par with her mother's. I was easily able to conjure up an image of this horrid demonic being in my mind's eye, and although I was safe in the confines of Baker Street, in the heart of the greatest city in all the world, bulwarked by modern civilisation for ten miles in every direction, I could not suppress a small shiver.

"Whenever Mama told us about the Black Thurrick," she went on, "I would experience a thrill of fear and reaffirm my resolve to be well-behaved. Sometimes, during Advent, as Christmas loomed, I would have nightmares about it. I would dream that the creature was slithering down the chimney to kidnap me, and would awaken in a cold sweat, panic-stricken. I took to placing an offering of food outside the castle for the Thurrick every Christmas Eve, to ward it off. In this endeavour my mother assisted me. I doubt she believed the Black Thurrick was real, but she encouraged my fancies. Mama was all in favour of her children developing their imaginations, and read to us extensively from the classics when she was not filling our heads with folklore. It is to her that I owe my love of literature and in particular of poetry."

"Did they disappear?" I enquired. "The offerings you left for the Black Thurrick?"

"A valid question," remarked Holmes.

"They did indeed, Doctor. At the time, this seemed to

me concrete proof of the Black Thurrick's existence. With hindsight, I am inclined to think that my mother simply retrieved the food and returned it to the kitchen once I had gone to bed."

"A no less valid answer," said Holmes. "I am to take it, then, Miss Allerthorpe, that the Black Thurrick has now incontrovertibly graced Fellscar Keep with its presence."

"One morning a little over a week ago, I went out for a walk. It was a fine, clear day and I felt the urge to stretch my legs. There is a paved causeway some twenty yards long, connecting the castle to the lake shore. It serves as a drive, and at its shore end stands a gateway. As I passed through this, with the intent of taking a stroll through the woods nearby, I noticed an object lying in the snow at the foot of one of the gateposts. It was a small bundle of twigs."

"Birch twigs?"

"I did not identify them as such immediately. At first glance, they were just twigs to me. They were bound with string, and clearly had been left there by someone. Curious, I picked them up to examine them. When I realised which species of tree they came from, that was when I made the connection in my head."

"The Black Thurrick."

"The Black Thurrick," she confirmed. "Well, Mr Holmes, I dropped that bundle as though it were suddenly red hot. My heart started racing. I looked around, feeling both fearful and foolish. I half expected to see the Thurrick, perhaps peering out at me from the woods. At the same time I kept reminding myself the creature was merely a figment of fantasy. 'You are a grown woman, Eve,' I chided myself. 'Such things as the Black Thurrick do not exist.' Suffice to say, there were no eyes upon me. No sinister being lurked close by. There were just the trees, the whisper of the wind through the bare branches, the cawing of rooks – nothing out of the ordinary. I nerved myself to pick up the bundle of twigs again and hurled it as far as I could into the woods."

"Who do you think might have put the twigs there?" I asked.

"I decided it must have been local children," Miss Allerthorpe replied. "There are a number of scallywags in Yardley Cross, semi-feral little tykes born to inattentive parents. Yardley is the nearest town to Fellscar, only three miles distant – I say town, but it is barely more than a village – and I sometimes see those children out by the lakeside, in a gaggle. The castle seems to hold a fascination for them. They are on our land and know they should not be there, and they dare one another to approach as close to the causeway as possible before running away. Their antics are harmless, and all I could think was that the birch twigs were a prank perpetrated by them. They, like me, will have heard of the Black Thurrick. Perhaps they were sending a message. Perhaps they consider us Allerthorpes to be undeserving of Christmas gifts, for some reason."

"Your conclusion strikes me as eminently logical," Holmes said. "A childish prank seems the most plausible explanation. Tell me, were there footprints in the snow around the gatepost?"

"Several sets, as I recall."

"Had snow fallen recently?"

"Not for three or four days."

"And in that time, I presume a number of people must have passed to and fro through the gate."

"Servants make the journey into Yardley Cross at least once a day, to fetch groceries and other supplies. My father and my uncle often go out shooting, too."

"A pity. Footprints in snow can speak volumes, but in this case, in the absence of a single set of distinctive tracks, they would seem to have little to tell us."

"I curtailed my walk anyway, and returned indoors," said Miss Allerthorpe. "I had rather lost my enthusiasm for exercise. Then, the very next morning, Erasmus came down to breakfast with a bundle of birch twigs in his hand. He brandished them irritably and demanded to know who had left them on the window ledge outside his bedroom. My father replied that nobody could have, because Erasmus's bedroom is on the first floor. 'Are you proposing that one of us scaled the wall to deposit a bunch of twigs outside your window?' Papa scoffed. 'Don't be ridiculous, boy!' I, for my part, was dumbfounded."

"Had you told anyone about the twigs you found the previous day?"

"No. I hadn't thought it worth mentioning. I was a little ashamed by my reaction, to be honest, and was rather hoping to forget the whole incident. Moreover, if the culprits were children from Yardley Cross, as I believed, I did not want to get them in trouble. My father would take it greatly amiss, and would probably go out and horsewhip them the next time he saw them. However, the sight of another set of birch twigs in my brother's hand utterly undid me. Even as Raz and Papa exchanged words hotly – one adamant that somebody had placed the twigs outside his window, the other adamant that such a thing was impossible – I found myself in a sort of partial faint, feeling at one remove from all the fuss and vexation around me. I must have said something, because all at once I realised that every pair of eyes at the table was fixed upon me. 'What's that, Eve?' Uncle Shadrach said."

"Uncle Shadrach?" said Holmes. "Would this be the same uncle you mentioned a moment ago? The one who goes shooting with your father?"

"Yes. Papa's younger brother. He is resident at Fellscar, along with his wife Olivia, their daughter Kitty and her husband Fitzhugh."

"Thank you. Proceed."

"Erasmus answered Shadrach's question for me. 'Eve uttered the words "the Black Thurrick",' he said. 'I distinctly heard her. And in truth, that had not occurred to me, but now I see it. Yes. My goodness. These are birch twigs. Who else leaves a bundle of birch twigs outside a house but the Black Thurrick?' There was a discomfited frown on his face. Raz remembered as well as I did Mama's stories and was reliving the eerie dread those tales had engendered in us.

"'The Black Thurrick?' my father ejaculated. 'What preposterousness is this? Everyone knows that's just superstitious claptrap! Give me that.' So saying, he snatched the bundle of twigs from my brother's grasp, strode over to the fire and tossed it onto the flames. Twigs and string burned to cinders in a trice.

"As you may imagine, I was thoroughly discombobulated throughout the rest of that day. No longer could I pretend to myself that this was the handiwork of children. Some other agency was involved, and if not the Black Thurrick, then what?

"The next morning, I went to my study. I am fortunate enough to have a little room of my own where I keep my books and where, when the mood takes me, I write poetry at my desk. It is my refuge. On that day, however, its sanctity was breached, for when I got there I discovered, to my horror, that there was a bundle of twigs perched

on the window ledge, just as there had been outside
Erasmus's bedroom.

"I'm not embarrassed to admit that I screamed. Erasmus
heard and came running. I was beside myself with fear. He
held me until my shudders subsided, uttering soothing
words in my ear, but I could tell that he, too, was alarmed.
Plucking up his courage, he opened the casement and
shoved the bundle of twigs off the ledge with a sweep of his
hand. They tumbled into the snowdrift below the window,
vanishing from view.

"I told Erasmus about the first bundle of twigs I had
found by the gate. 'Three times, now, Raz,' I said. 'Three
times birch twigs have been left at the castle. Who is doing
this to us? Who hates us so much that they would conduct
this sinister campaign?'

"'I do not know, Eve,' replied he. 'But one thing is certain.
It is not the Black Thurrick. There is no Black Thurrick.'
He did not sound any too convinced by his own statement,
however, and I was little comforted.

"I remained in a feverish state all day and, fearing I
would not sleep that night, took chloral hydrate at bedtime.
I dropped off straight away, but then at some point during
the small hours I snapped wide awake. Moonlight was
streaming in through the window, bright enough almost to
read by. I realised I had fallen asleep so swiftly that I had
neglected to close the curtains. I got out of bed to remedy

the oversight. As I began drawing the curtains, movement outside caught my eye.

"My bedroom, Mr Holmes, faces outward from the castle. It has a triple aspect, the main set of windows looking northward over the lake. Currently the lake is frozen over. Did I mention that?"

"You did not," said Holmes. "Now I am the wiser."

"Upon its icy white expanse, I spied a figure. A spindly, dark figure, picking its way across the frozen surface. A figure bent almost double, with a heavy sack upon its back."

Miss Allerthorpe's voice lowered to a hush.

"Mr Holmes," she said. "I knew, in that moment, just what I was looking at. It could surely be none other than the Black Thurrick itself."

Chapter Four

AN ARCHETYPAL
PETRARCHAN SONNET

Miss Allerthorpe paused briefly before resuming her account. I took the opportunity to help myself to some of the brandy, for restorative purposes. Holmes observed the action with a wry smirk. He might not have been unnerved by the events being related to us, but I certainly was.

"Tell me more about this figure, Miss Allerthorpe," he said. "In which direction was it travelling?"

"Away from the castle, towards the north shore of the lake," came the reply.

"So you did not see its face?"

"I did, and I did not."

"Elucidate."

"As I watched, the thing turned round to look back

towards the castle. It was only a brief backward glance, but enough to reveal that its face had no features, save for eyes. The eyes shone bright, seeming almost to glow, but the rest was just empty blackness. It was then that I knew, once and for all, that it could not be any man. It must be the Thurrick.

"Onward it went, while I, trembling, rooted to the spot, could only stare. Then, gathering myself, I flung the curtains shut and scurried back to bed. The effects of the sleeping draught must still have been in my system, for though my blood was racing and my thoughts were a terrified whirl, I fell asleep again soon enough. When I awoke the next morning, it was late, nearly ten o'clock. I came to a hasty decision. I had to leave Fellscar Keep. I could not abide at the castle an hour longer. I packed a bag and ordered the coachman to take me to Bridlington station, where I caught the York train and thence to London. I have been in the capital for three days now, staying with friends in Primrose Hill, and only today have I felt even close to rational again."

"I trust your family know you are here, safe and sound," I said.

"They do. I have wired them to that effect."

"But do they know what precipitated your abrupt departure?" asked Holmes.

"I have mentioned nothing to them about seeing the Black Thurrick. They are under the impression that I have come down for a couple of days to do some Christmas shopping. It wasn't until today, however, that I was able to stir myself to go out and face the crowds in the West End. That is how I chanced upon the two of you, and now here I am. I have told you everything that has befallen me. You know the predicament I am in. The only question that remains is will you help me, Mr Holmes?"

"No," said Holmes.

Miss Allerthorpe was understandably crestfallen, as was I.

"No?" she said.

"No. *We* will help you. That is, Watson and I. Provided, of course, Watson, that you can take time away from your practice."

"My caseload is invariably heavy at this time of year, what with all the seasonal maladies," I said, "but arrangements can be made. How is *your* caseload, Holmes?"

"Comparatively light. There is the problem of the disappearance of the butcher's apprentice at Smithfield Market, but I am confident that that has none of the gruesome connotations the rumours ascribe to it. Indeed the matter should resolve itself within a day or so, regardless of my involvement, and the outcome will be positive for all concerned. As to the perplexing affair of the Conte di Ruspoli and the vanishing hansom, it is a case of mistaken identity, nothing more. I will send my notes to Gregson or, failing that, Athelney Jones. Either of those doughty bloodhounds will be adequate to the task of following the case through to its conclusion. The business of the Bishop of Chichester and his collection of rare Amazonian butterflies is more worrisome, but I strongly doubt there will be a second attempt at a burglary, the first having been so successfully averted by our cleric-cum-lepidopterist's bull terrier. What about your wife?"

"What about her?"

"You will need to square things with Mrs Watson, I am sure. Your absence so close to Christmas will not, I imagine, be welcome."

"I shall talk to Mary. She is usually amenable when it comes to my accompanying you on an investigation. She has family coming over on Christmas Day. Provided I am home by then, to do my part as host, all should be well."

"And I," said Holmes, "have no plans of my own. On the whole I find Christmas fatuous and tawdry. I would rather do something – anything – else."

"Oh, thank you!" Eve Allerthorpe exclaimed. "Thank you, both."

Holmes raised an admonitory forefinger. "I am minded to think, Miss Allerthorpe, that you require the services of a priest more than you do those of a consulting detective. I have still to be convinced that a crime has been committed, or that there is any danger of such. Yet there remain elements to the case that pique my interest. What are your immediate plans?"

"I intend to return to Primrose Hill, to my friends, then journey back up north first thing in the morning."

"Excellent. Watson and I will follow on a later train. That will give you a chance to forewarn your family of our impending arrival and prepare the ground for us."

The young woman gathered up her belongings. I escorted her downstairs to the hallway.

She was on the point of leaving by the front door when, seemingly on a whim, she fetched her notebook out from her pocket. She opened it, rifled through to the page she was looking for, and tore out the sheet.

"For you," she said, folding up the piece of paper and handing it to me. "A poem. I wrote it at the coffee house, while summoning up the courage to approach you and Mr Holmes. When I am in a dilemma, or ill at ease, it often helps to set my thoughts and feelings down in verse form. It gives them an outlet, and crystallises them. I should like you to read the poem, but not until I have departed. I am shy about showing my work to anyone, but more so to a distinguished author such as yourself."

The door opened. The door closed. Miss Eve Allerthorpe was gone.

I unfolded the piece of paper, upon which I found the following handwritten lines of verse:

Ode to a Potential Saviour

When all the world lies cold and empty white
And yet most folk have cause to feel glad,
My poor, drab, winter-matching heart is sad.
My suff'ring soul lacks will to rise and fight.
Evil stalks – a dark-faced, loathsome sprite
Whose presence brings offence to lass and lad.
I am sore-taxed and very nearly mad,
A bird with no safe bough whereon to light.

But here in mazy streets, 'mid giddy throng,
At last it seems that fickle fate turns kind.
There is yet one who might assuage my strife.
With handsome friend, the man sits, gaunt and long,
Renownèd far for agile wits, sharp mind –
Sherlock Holmes. 'Pon him I'll stake my life.

I felt moved to show it to Holmes.

"A touch florid, perhaps," I said, "but a decent stab all the same. It's an archetypal Petrarchan sonnet, by the way."

"If you say so," he replied airily. "As you know, literature is not one of my fortes. Hum! The 'handsome friend', eh?"

"Miss Allerthorpe is no less complimentary about you."

"So I see, although the adjective 'long' appears to have been chosen more for rhyme than descriptive accuracy."

I chuckled in assent. "That notwithstanding, the poem

reveals what a sensitive, intelligent girl its author is, which inclines me to wish to help her all the more."

"You ever were a fool for a pretty face, Watson, especially when it is attached to a damsel in distress. Yet does not Miss Allerthorpe's abundant imaginativeness give you pause?"

"Your implication being that she is the type prone to fantasy, and therefore an unreliable witness."

"It is quite possible that a young woman with high-flown poetical tendencies might have invented some, if not all, of the remarkable events she has regaled us with. I refer in particular to the shadowy, glowing-eyed figure she claims she saw out on the lake ice."

"Do you think she is putting us on? Hysterical, even?"

"Possibly," said Holmes. "You must also bear in mind that she had, by her own admission, taken a dose of chloral hydrate that evening. The drug's hypnotic qualities may have impaired her faculties."

"You mean she was still half asleep when she saw the Black Thurrick. It may have been just part of some waking dream."

"It is a medically plausible scenario, is it not?"

I shrugged my shoulders, as if to acknowledge that it was. Sleeping draughts affected people in different ways, and among the potential side effects of chloral hydrate, as with most sedatives, were bouts of disorientation and even hallucinations.

"Furthermore," Holmes continued, "why has the Thurrick chosen to terrorise her and her brother? Each is an adult and has no offspring, and we are told that the creature has a particular grisly penchant for the very young. What might account for this alteration in its time-honoured habits?"

"You speak as if the Black Thurrick were real."

"Oh no, Watson. It is not. I am merely pointing out an inconsistency which may or may not be pertinent. All in all, there is not yet sufficient data for me to make a definitive determination regarding Miss Allerthorpe's case. Hence I have no alternative but to give the lady the benefit of the doubt, for now."

"In some ways, I am rather surprised that you have agreed to take the case at all. As you say, there is no sign of any crime."

"Yet a large inheritance is involved, and where one finds one of those, and moreover a vulnerable recipient, one is apt also to find malicious intent. Besides, the whole thing has a somewhat outré aspect, and you know the appeal the outré holds for me. Give me the outré over the humdrum any day! Above all else, I am curious to meet the extended Allerthorpe tribe. Large families intrigue me. They are stews of rivalry, jealousy and long-held enmity, and in the wealthy ones those qualities are only amplified." Sherlock Holmes rubbed his hands together. "Yes, old friend, I am rather looking forward to the next few days. You might consider this a little Christmas gift to myself, although it remains to be seen whether, when unwrapped, it proves to be treasure or trifle."

Chapter Five

FELLSCAR KEEP

O ur train rattled out of King's Cross shortly after ten the next day, bearing us northward to York. Overnight, clouds had set in over London and the Midlands and yet again snow had begun to fall heavily. Fat flakes flurried past the carriage windows, mingling with the smoke from the locomotive's funnel to create a flickering, chiaroscuro whirl of white and grey outside.

Some thirty minutes into the journey Holmes remarked that we were making good time, in spite of the conditions. "We are travelling at a mean speed of sixty-eight miles an hour," he said.

"How on earth can you tell?" I asked.

He put away his half hunter, which he had been consulting. "Simple. The standard length of a piece of rail track on the Great Northern Railway is sixty feet precisely. The wheels beneath us make a distinct clack every time they cross the join between one rail and the next. The clacks are occurring at a rate of approximately a hundred per minute. The rest is pure arithmetic. One may make a similar calculation using the trackside telegraph poles, but at night, or on a day like today when visibility is so poor, the rail-length method is more practical."

Having changed at York for the Scarborough line, we pulled in at Bridlington station some three quarters of an hour later. A brougham awaited us out front, along with a taciturn coachman who, in a thick Yorkshire brogue, ventured the following greeting: "Mr 'olmes and Dr Watson? Miss Eve has sent me ter tek thee ter Fellscar. Put thah bags on't back, gentlemen, and 'op in. Thah'll find blankets on the seats ter wrap this'sen in."

The snow had by now stopped falling but lay thick all around. The brougham trundled through white-blanketed countryside, its wheels and the horse's hooves making scarcely a sound on the road. The gently undulating landscape was parcelled up by drystone walls, which were mostly buried under snowdrifts. Here and there a tree strained upward from the ground, seeming to claw the overcast sky with its bare branches. We passed the occasional mean-looking, half-derelict dwelling – a croft, a smallholding – which if not for the skein of smoke rising from its chimney would have appeared uninhabited.

Then the road dipped down through a valley. At a junction, I spied a fingerpost pointing to Yardley Cross, but we took a different, unmarked route along a narrow track, and presently, as the brougham crested the brow of a hill, Holmes and I gained our first glimpse of Fellscar Keep.

I cannot say I was filled with any great joy, for the castle, huge as it was, seemed eminently forbidding. I had had little idea what to expect, but it surely was not this rambling agglomeration of black stone topped by an equally black slate-tiled roof. The edifice, built in the Gothic Revival style, had neither symmetry nor elegance. The windows were small and mean, and the battlements lofty and teeming, topped with toothsome crenellations. Wing abutted against wing, showing, to my mind, no obvious plan – a collision of irregular geometric shapes such as a child might make with wooden building blocks.

In all, the castle looked not to have been constructed so much as to have grown, coral-like, from the lake island upon which it perched and whose surface it fully covered. Ribbons of snow lying atop lintels, eaves, copings and buttresses did something to soften the stark cheerlessness of it all, but not much.

The track wound downward through woodland, emerging from which we had a much better view of the castle. Nearer to, however, Fellscar Keep was only the more oppressive-seeming. It loomed gracelessly against the glowering sky, as though its architect desired any who came before it to feel small. Its overall demeanour was that of a brooding, hulking thug challenging all comers to engage in fisticuffs.

As the brougham approached the gateway that afforded access to the causeway connecting the castle to land, a gunshot resounded from close by. Our horse, startled, bucked within the traces, and the coachman cried out, "Whoa there!" and was obliged to steady the beast with a tug on the reins and a tap of the whip.

A second gunshot followed, louder than the first, and the anxious nag came to a complete halt, whinnying.

As Holmes and I peered out of the cab windows, we saw a pair of men stride out from the woods to the left of us. Each was dressed in tweeds and bore a double-barrelled 12-gauge shotgun – a Purdey, if I did not miss my guess. Neither, I noted, was carrying his weapon broken as he ought.

They walked towards the four-wheeler with a purposeful air, and I, overcome by a growing unease, wished that my service revolver was immediately to hand, rather than outside the brougham, packed in my holdall on the back. Holmes, sensing my agitation, patted my arm.

"We are in no imminent danger," said he. "Do you not recall Miss Allerthorpe telling us that her father and uncle go out shooting together? These two, I am certain, are they, indulging in that very pastime. Their age and dress marks them out as wealthy landowners, while their self-confident bearing announces that they are masters of their domain, with every right to be here."

"Yet they fired their guns, when they must surely have seen us coming," I said. "They knowingly frightened the horse. That bespeaks hostile intent, does it not?"

He shook his head. "A certain casual meanness, perhaps. I believe that you and I are being greeted in a manner meant to intimidate. Let us not give these fellows the satisfaction of thinking they have succeeded."

With that, Holmes stepped out of the brougham, putting on a broad grin and lofting a hand in salutation. I followed, somewhat more circumspectly, darting a glance up at the coachman as I did so. His face showed resigned stoicism, as though this wasn't the first time his employer had subjected him and his passengers to such a stunt. I fancied I saw a similar expression on the face of the horse and heard disgust in the little snort it gave.

"Do I have the pleasure of addressing a Mr Allerthorpe, or even two such?" Holmes said.

"I am Thaddeus Allerthorpe," growled one of the men, whose luxuriant muttonchop whiskers hid fully half of his face.

"My name is Sherlock Holmes." My friend extended a

hand towards Thaddeus Allerthorpe, who took it only after evincing the greatest reluctance. "And you," he added, turning to the other man, "must be Shadrach Allerthorpe, unless I am much mistaken."

The second man was clean-shaven but shared certain distinctive features in common with his brother, in particular a prodigious nose and a pair of cold, piercing blue eyes. They were both the same height, but Shadrach was not quite as sturdy as Thaddeus, being leaner of frame, with a slight hunch to his shoulders.

Holmes shook Shadrach's gloved hand. "I surmise that you wished to acknowledge our arrival in a suitably demonstrative manner by firing into the air," he said. "A two-gun salute, as it were."

The Allerthorpes exchanged wry glances.

"If you choose to put such a construction on it," said Thaddeus, deadpan, "then indeed, Mr Holmes, that was our intent."

"Then Watson and I consider ourselves welcomed. Don't we, Watson?"

I, for my part, was never fond of gunfire, especially when it was aimed my way. I had experienced all too much of that in Afghanistan, at personal cost. Even if the Allerthorpes had only shot at us in jest, their goal not to harm but only to alarm, I did not find this in any way amusing; nor did I wish to pardon it any time soon.

In emulation of Holmes's example, however, I forced a smile and made polite noises.

"My daughter Eve has only lately returned from the capital," said Thaddeus Allerthorpe. "She warned us to expect an additional pair of houseguests in the form of Sherlock Holmes, the famed London sleuth, and his colleague. I may as well let you know now, sirs, that your presence is not appreciated in my home. If Eve had not been so insistent that you stay with us, I would order Winslow here" – he gestured at the coachman – "to turn around and take you straight back to the station. For one thing, the Allerthorpe Christmas gathering is a private affair. Relatives and in-laws only. For another thing, it would seem that Eve has invited you on the flimsiest of pretexts. This nonsense about birch twigs! The lass is fretting needlessly over what is, to my way of thinking, a foolish practical joke. Yet she has extended hospitality to you, and, seeing as she is my flesh and blood, I cannot deny her that invitation, even if I cannot endorse it."

"Trust me, Mr Allerthorpe," Holmes said, "Watson and I will make ourselves as unobtrusive as mice. You shall hardly know we are here."

"I hope so," came the dubious reply.

"I am confident, too, that whatever misdemeanours we uncover, if any, will be dealt with in a swift and discreet fashion. I cannot foresee that we will darken your threshold for any more than a day or two."

"See that you don't." Thaddeus turned to his brother. "Well, Shadrach, we have an hour or so's daylight remaining to us. I spied grouse prints in the snow back in the woods, heading towards Poacher's Hollow. What say we follow them and bag ourselves a brace or two before dusk?"

"Why not?" As Thaddeus stalked off towards the trees without so much as a fare-thee-well, Shadrach Allerthorpe nodded wryly at us and touched finger to forehead. "Gentlemen."

"Well," Holmes said as he and I climbed back into the brougham, "at least we now know which of those brothers is the more reasonable, if only by a small margin."

"Shadrach Allerthorpe does appear to have the better manners of the two."

"And it wasn't he who shot at us. Both the hammers on his shotgun were cocked, whereas the ones on Thaddeus Allerthorpe's were in the closed position. All the same, Shadrach seemed infected by his elder sibling's antipathy towards us."

"He lives in his brother's shadow."

"And in his brother's house by his brother's good graces. I daresay, were he to offend Thaddeus, he might find himself thrown out on his ear. Therefore whatever his personal feelings, he must curry his brother's favour and be ever in agreement with him. Not an enviable position."

Winslow the coachman lashed the reins, and the horse,

still somewhat skittish, proceeded through the gateway. The brougham trundled between the causeway's two low parapets with a scant eighteen inches of clearance on either side. Ahead, an arched entrance in the castle's outer walls rose like some vast, yawning black maw. A pair of stout oak doors stood wide open, with a wicket gate inset into one of them. Beyond lay a cobbled courtyard some twenty yards in width and a little greater in length. Here the four-wheeler halted once more, and Holmes and I again disembarked.

Having retrieved our bags from the back of the brougham, we were instructed to wait. Winslow led horse and carriage off through a smaller arched aperture, presumably to a stable. We anticipated his swift return, but in the event we stood there in the bitter cold, stamping our feet for warmth, for a good ten minutes. Dozens of windows peered down at us in the courtyard, and in none did there appear the face of someone curious to learn whom the brougham had brought. Nor, for that matter, did Winslow grace us with his presence again.

Eventually Holmes snatched up his suitcase and mounted the broad flight of steps, which led to what appeared to be the castle's front door. In the absence of any bell pull, he grasped an iron knocker that must have weighed in the region of six or seven pounds and gave a firm rat-a-tat-tat on the wood. The knocks echoed vastly within, like peals of thunder.

In time we heard footfalls indoors, and at last the door was opened by a young liveried footman, who eyed us with a certain wary bafflement.

"Are you expected?" he enquired.

"Sherlock Holmes. Dr John Watson. We are guests of Miss Allerthorpe. Eve Allerthorpe, that is, in order to avoid possible confusion."

Without ushering us in, the footman closed the door and disappeared.

"They really are an unfriendly lot," I observed.

"On current showing, yes. Great riches are a boon but they can also be isolating. The majority of those around you regard you merely as a resource to be plundered, and it erodes your trust in your fellow men."

"So you build a castle like this and hide away in it, cut off from the very world that has provided you with your wealth."

"And, thus self-segregated, you begin to lose sight of how to behave amongst other people. A quality which, it would seem, extends to your servants as well." Holmes saw that I was starting to shiver. "We have been left to freeze out here long enough," he declared, raising a hand to the door knocker once more. "I have a good mind to—"

The door reopened, and the footman bade us enter.

"I am to show you to your rooms," he said, not offering to carry our bags, as he ought. "This way."

An enormous hallway vaulted around us, the floor flagstoned, every wall panelled to the ceiling in dark hardwood. In a fireplace that could have accommodated an entire roasting pig on a spit, and may well have been built for that purpose, a large log fire blazed, radiating just enough heat to mitigate the gelidity of the air. Oil paintings gazed down at us on all sides, their sombre subjects clad in clothes ranging from ruffs, capes and cross-garters to more modern attire – these were portraits of ancestors, no doubt – while above the fireplace's mantel hung a shield adorned with three gold stripes angled down to the right on a scarlet background, this design surmounted by a rearing, gape-mouthed lion. The Allerthorpe family coat of arms, I presumed.

Ahead, a curving staircase swept upward, and at the footman's invitation, Holmes and I ascended to a balustraded gallery at its apex and followed him thence along a labyrinth of winding corridors, past door after door and up and down countless other flights of stairs, some short, some long. It was a good five minutes, by my estimate, before we arrived at what were to be our quarters, by which point I had thoroughly lost my bearings. Even though I had done my best to keep track of landmarks along the way – a suit of armour, for instance, or a stuffed and mounted stag's head – I did not think I could make it back to the central hallway without the aid of map and compass, or better yet a guide.

Holmes and I had been given bedrooms on opposite sides of the corridor, mine facing out towards the lake, his overlooking a small quadrangle, with both of us sharing the use of a bathroom several doors down. The accommodations were well-appointed but cold. "Central heating is not, it appears, a feature of Fellscar Keep," Holmes averred, while I was unpacking my holdall. Wisps of vapour curled from his mouth as he spoke.

"Can you imagine how many miles of pipe and how much hot water would be required to keep a place this big warm?" I said. "Let alone the size of the boiler, which would be something akin to that on an ocean liner. At least we have fireplaces and may hope that someone lights fires for us before we retire to bed."

We re-entered the corridor outside, anticipating that the footman would be waiting to escort us wherever we might require to go. We should have known better. The man was gone, and so we wended our way rather trepidatiously through that vast building, I trusting that Holmes's sense of direction and powers of recall were greater than mine. This faith was borne out when, presently, we found ourselves back in the gallery overlooking the hall.

Below I saw, to my relief and delight, Eve Allerthorpe. She was with a younger man whom I judged, by his age and the clear familial intimacy between them, to be her brother Erasmus.

"And you're sure there was no recurrence of the twigs while I was away, Raz?" Miss Allerthorpe was saying.

"Not a one," replied he. "I'm sure, had there been, someone would have reported it. If not a family member, one of the staff."

"That is something, I suppose."

"Is that what compelled you to leave? The twigs?"

"I'm afraid so. I could not bear the suspense of waiting for the next bundle to turn up. It was driving me to distraction."

"But your departure was so unexpected, sis. Until we received your telegram, I was worried. We all were."

"You make sudden, unannounced trips to London. Why cannot I?"

"We didn't even know London was your destination. When Winslow returned from Bridlington, all he could tell us was that you had boarded a train. He had no idea to where. Papa was furious at him for not being more inquisitive."

"Papa needs little excuse to be furious these days."

Miss Allerthorpe couched these words in a wistful tone, which Erasmus Allerthorpe matched as he said, "To be honest, he was short-tempered even when Mama was alive."

"But it was never this bad."

At that moment, Holmes decorously cleared his throat.

"Ah, there you are!" Eve Allerthorpe cried out, with a little clap of the hands. "I was beginning to wonder whether I should send out a search party. Jennings was supposed to bring you to the drawing room once you had settled into your rooms. Clearly that instruction slipped his mind. I shall have words with him."

"It is of no great consequence," Holmes said, descending the stairs.

"He is new and inexperienced, but that is no excuse. What good is a forgetful footman? Still, you are here, and I am glad to see you. Both of you."

"Us likewise to see you," I said, thinking that Miss Allerthorpe appeared marginally more relaxed than she had in London. Was it because she was back on home turf, or was it the arrival of Sherlock Holmes, with its implied promise of a solution to her conundrum? The latter, I reasoned. From what she had told us, Fellscar Keep was not a place of sanctuary for her at present.

"Allow me to introduce my brother," she said. "Erasmus, this is none other than Sherlock Holmes, whom I spoke of to you, and of course Dr Watson."

"Yes," said the young man with a small bow. "An honour."

I must say Erasmus Allerthorpe was making a mixed impression upon me. His speech was a louche drawl, as though the effort of proper diction was too much for him, and now that I was close to him I discerned the strong whiff of alcohol on his breath, which may or may not have had some influence upon his speech patterns. I recalled his sister referring to him as "boisterous" and saying that he was an habitué of the gossip columns, which further inclined me towards disfavouring him.

For all that, he had a handsome, personable face, and his smile was charming and his handshake firm. He also seemed to genuinely care for his sister.

In terms of physical resemblance between the two of them, whereas Eve Allerthorpe had the blue eyes of her father and uncle, Erasmus's were hazel. His hair, though brown like hers, was several shades lighter, and overall his features were that little bit finer. He was as slimly built as she was, but whereas it could be said that Eve's slenderness was attributable to her recent, marked loss of appetite, in his case I ascribed it to dissipation. There was, indeed, scarcely a spare ounce of flesh on his frame, suggestive of someone who preferred to take his nourishment in liquid form rather than solid.

"This business with the birch bundles," Erasmus continued. "It's a rum do, and no mistake. When I found those twigs outside my own window... well, I couldn't make head or tail of it. Not till Eve mentioned the Black Thurrick, and then it all came rushing back. The fairytales Mama used to tell. The legend of the Thurrick. I was taken aback, for certain. It crossed my mind that maybe the beast was real after all. Only for a few moments, though."

"You are not of that opinion now?" Holmes said.

"Oh no, Mr Holmes. I mean to say, how ridiculous! No, now I reckon it's all just a bit of a hoot. Somebody's playing games. Those ragamuffins from Yardley Cross, isn't that what you think, sis?"

Eve Allerthorpe nodded noncommittally.

"Such little rapscallions, they are," her brother continued. "Wouldn't put it past them. The nerve of them, trespassing on our property. They often stray onto Allerthorpe land, but onto the island itself? That's unheard of. Yet it can be the only logical explanation."

"It is one logical explanation, of that there is no question," said Holmes. "There may yet be others. I wonder if I might prevail upon you, Miss Allerthorpe, to show me the three locations where the birch twigs were discovered. I see no reason not to begin my enquiries as soon as possible."

"Of course, Mr Holmes."

"I shall come too," said Erasmus Allerthorpe. "I cannot pass up the opportunity to watch the great Sherlock Holmes at work. And you will need access to my bedroom."

Eve Allerthorpe led us first to her study, the little room she had described to us, where she composed her poetry. It was on the ground floor and was pleasantly snug, its walls lined with bookshelves whose contents formed a small but enviably well-chosen library. A writing desk faced the diamond-leaded window, which in turn faced the lake.

Holmes opened the window's sole casement, letting in a thin breeze, and peered out. The ledge was thick with snow, and below it the outer wall of the castle dropped sheer to the rocky fringe of the island. It was, I estimated, a distance of some twenty feet from the window to the lake's frozen surface.

"Where, precisely, did you find the twigs, Miss Allerthorpe?" Holmes asked.

"Just there, if memory serves." She pointed to a section of the ledge immediately to the right of the open casement.

"And your presumption is that somebody went out onto the lake, walked round to this corner of the castle, scaled the wall, deposited the twigs, then retraced his steps?"

"It is possible, is it not?"

"Is the lake ice thick enough to support the weight of a person?"

Eve Allerthorpe turned to her brother. "So far this winter I have not gone skating on it. Have you, Raz?"

"No. If the cold spell persists then perhaps I shall, but I do not believe the lake is so consistently frozen as yet that there is no risk of falling through thin ice. For a grown man, at any rate. A child, on the other hand…"

"The Thurrick could manage it, of course," Miss Allerthorpe added. "After all, when I saw him…" She faltered, casting a look at her brother.

He frowned. "What's that, sis? You actually saw the Black Thurrick? This is news to me."

"I did," Eve Allerthorpe allowed, somewhat shamefaced. "That is the real reason why I left for London in such haste."

Briefly she outlined to Erasmus her nocturnal encounter with the Black Thurrick – how she had watched it cross the lake, and how the sinister creature had turned and looked up at her with glowing eyes before resuming its journey.

"Why did you not see fit to mention it at the time?"

"I was confused and upset, Raz. I was not thinking clearly. You know what everyone here thinks about me. 'That Eve, always going around with her head in the clouds. So erratic. So *imaginative*.' At best, I would have been disbelieved. At worst, it would have confirmed people's darkest opinions."

"You could perhaps have confided in me." Erasmus Allerthorpe sounded hurt.

"And should perhaps have." She laid a hand on his arm. "I am sorry. Absenting myself from home for a while seemed the simplest solution. Would you be so good as not to share what you have just learned with the rest of the family? Can you do that for me?"

"I suppose so. For your sake."

"Let me get this straight," said Holmes. "No human would dare venture out upon the ice, but a supernatural entity might safely walk upon it?"

"And also scale the wall below this room to put the birch twigs on the ledge," said Miss Allerthorpe with a nod.

"A twenty-foot climb. It is quite some athlete, this Black Thurrick of yours."

"If it can clamber onto a roof and wriggle down a

chimney and back up again, Mr Holmes," said Erasmus, "why should a wall present much difficulty?"

"A good point, well made," said Holmes, with just a suggestion of sarcasm. "May we now take a look at the window ledge of your bedroom, Mr Allerthorpe?"

"Certainly. This way."

We followed Erasmus Allerthorpe to a first-floor bedchamber of sizeable proportions, furnished with a four-poster, a large mahogany wardrobe and a comfortable-looking armchair. Like his sister's study it had outward-facing windows, with a commanding view across the lake to the shore. Here the drop to the lake's surface was a good thirty-five feet or more, and just as sheer.

"Where exactly on the ledge was the bundle of twigs?" Holmes asked. "Show me."

"Here, I think." Erasmus indicated a spot just outside one of the casements.

"You think or you are sure?"

"I'm sure."

Holmes opened the left-hand casement and, as before, leaned out. His face was inscrutable. He looked down, up and to either side, then scraped the snow off the ledge and inspected the surface of the stonework closely. Finally he pronounced himself satisfied.

"It would take a man with the wall-adhering capabilities of a fly to pick his way over masonry such as I see here," he said. "The gaps between the runs of blocks are exceedingly narrow, affording little in the way of handhold and toehold. There are no scratches or other marks on the ledge to suggest that a grappling hook or similar contrivance has been employed."

"That does not rule out the possibility that the culprit is a child," Erasmus said. "A very agile child might conceivably be able to make the ascent."

"Or the Black Thurrick," Eve Allerthorpe added.

"No, we must not forget the Black Thurrick," said Holmes. "The last location for the twigs is the gateway at the end of the causeway, is it not? Let us examine that, while there remains sufficient daylight."

The Allerthorpe siblings fetched their overcoats, and outside we went, tramping across the courtyard, through the entrance and along the slender land bridge. Eve showed Holmes exactly where she had discovered the first bundle of twigs, and he subjected the gatepost and the surrounding area to careful scrutiny.

"No," he concluded, "I doubted there would be any clues here, and I was right. Too much time has passed, and too much snow has fallen. I included this spot in my survey purely for the sake of completeness."

As we were preparing to head back to the castle, Thaddeus and Shadrach Allerthorpe reappeared from the woods, their boots crunching through the snow. Each brother had a couple of dead game birds dangling from his belt. I remembered that I had heard a smattering of distant gunshots while we were indoors.

"Ah, the mighty hunters return," said Erasmus. "And not empty-handed, either."

"None of your cheek, Raz," snapped his father.

"I thought I was being complimentary."

"There is ever a note of sardonic insinuation in your voice, my boy. Your headmasters, both at the Priory School and at Harrow, remarked upon insolence as being your most noteworthy characteristic."

"I was merely—"

Thaddeus cut him off. "You were merely flapping your lips uselessly, as usual. Never a word comes out of your mouth that does not remind me how feckless an heir I sired. And your sister, with her faddlesome ways, is scarcely any better."

Erasmus scowled but, if he had some retort ready, he did not give vent to it. Eve, for her part, chewed disconcertedly on a fingernail.

"And you, Mr Holmes," Thaddeus Allerthorpe said, rounding on my companion. "You are conducting detective work? Or dare I to hope that you are at the gate because you are leaving us sooner than predicted?" He uttered a mirthless chuckle, which his younger brother echoed.

"You are not rid of me so easily," Holmes replied with an affable smile.

"Can't blame a fellow for wishing. Come along, Shad. Let's get these birds to Mrs Trebend, so that she can pluck, gut and hang them. They should be good to eat by New Year. I rather fancy one of her succulent game pies. In fact, I shall demand she cook one for us."

The two older Allerthorpes swept past us and traversed the causeway back to the castle. With the light swiftly ebbing from the sky, we four followed suit.

As we went, I noticed Erasmus glaring at his father's back. His eyes were filled with resentment, and at that moment I felt a surge of sympathy for the lad. I had misjudged him. It could not have been easy, growing up the son of so brusque and callous a man. If Erasmus affected an insouciant, devil-may-care attitude, and liked a drink, I could well understand why. These things were armour to him, inuring him against his father's jibes.

Just as we re-entered the courtyard, a manservant came out to close the pair of great bolt-studded doors that hung in the archway. They thudded shut, and a heavy iron bar was lowered to secure them. Fellscar Keep was now well and truly closed off from the outside world, to all intents and purposes impregnable; but I could not help feeling, rather than secure, confined.

Chapter Six

DINNERTIME PURDAH

At dinner that evening, my already dim view of the Allerthorpe family as a whole was in no way improved. For that was when Holmes and I met the remaining resident members of the clan.

We sat at a table roughly the size of a cricket pitch, in a room not much smaller than the dining hall at a Camford college. Aside from the four Allerthorpes whose acquaintance I had by then made, there were three others. These were Shadrach Allerthorpe's wife Olivia, a prim, pinched-looking female whose eyes were rather too large and chin rather too small; their daughter Kitty, who had her mother's looks and appeared to take scarcely any more pleasure in life than she did; and Kitty's husband Fitzhugh Danningbury Boyd, who was quite the rakish devil, with his mane of wavy, dark hair, array of bright teeth and firm, jutting jaw.

With regard to the food, I could have no complaints. A rich oxtail soup was followed by a nicely suety steak and kidney pudding, with blackberry and apple crumble for afters. All of it was fine, tasty fare. The wines were excellent, too, and were poured by a butler whose name, I quickly gathered, was Trebend. This man, solemn-faced and slight of stature, was the husband of the Mrs Trebend whom Thaddeus had mentioned earlier in the day, the cook.

With regard to the company at table, however, that was another thing altogether. The Allerthorpes did very little to make Holmes and me feel at home. For most of the meal their conversation revolved around the many relatives who were due to turn up at Fellscar the following day, as well as other family matters, subjects to which my friend and I could offer no useful contribution. I do not know whether we were being deliberately excluded, but it certainly seemed so. Only Eve, and to a lesser extent Erasmus, made any effort to engage with those poor souls not blessed with Allerthorpe blood or married into the clan. By the rest we were consigned to dinnertime purdah.

While I was disgruntled at this treatment, Holmes appeared to find it entertaining, if his wry expression was any indicator. He observed the family much as though their antics were a play staged for his amusement.

What struck me as notable was the undue amount of attention Fitzhugh Danningbury Boyd paid to Eve. Seated next to her, he monopolised her for the first two courses. Whenever her interest strayed elsewhere – to speak to me, for example, about a novel she had recently read, Mrs Radcliffe's *The Mysteries of Udolpho*, with a view to garnering my thoughts on Gothic fiction – Danningbury Boyd would tap her arm and practically demand that she occupy herself with him instead. He leaned towards her in a manner one might almost call impertinent, from time to time resting an elbow upon the back of her chair, and his eyes were alive with fascination. It was clear to me that Eve did not reciprocate this fascination but was too timid to rebuff him as perhaps she ought.

The effect Danningbury Boyd's behaviour had upon his wife was all too obvious. The looks she shot him across the table were venomous, and on more than one occasion she addressed him peremptorily, in an effort to divert his focus away from Eve and towards a more appropriate recipient, namely herself. Each time, her husband responded with a complacent smile and an uxorious compliment or two, which just about mollified her.

Only when the ladies withdrew did the talk around the table broaden in scope and encompass Holmes and myself. Over port and cigars, Thaddeus Allerthorpe challenged Holmes to reveal what insights he had gained into "this twigs foolishness", if any, during the day.

"On the face of it," my friend said, "one must at least give some credence to the idea that the culprit is none other than the Black Thurrick."

"Oh, bosh!"

"Please, Mr Allerthorpe, hear me out." Holmes began counting off on his fingers. "Point one. It is Christmas time, when the Thurrick traditionally makes its rounds. Point two. Twice has a bundle of birch twigs manifested in a place to which nobody could obtain easy access by climbing – no ordinary human, that is. Point three. What does anyone who is not the Black Thurrick have to gain by leaving the twigs around the castle?"

"Why can it not be a hoax?"

"I did not say that it was not. I was simply enumerating all the reasons why this Christmas demon might be regarded as a likely suspect."

"Then there's the fact that Eve saw the Thurrick with her own eyes," said Erasmus.

I fixed the young fellow with a hard stare. Had he not, just a couple of hours earlier, assured his sister that he would tell no one about her sighting of the creature upon the lake? Yet here he was, blurting it out to his father and uncle. Erasmus had been drinking heavily throughout dinner, and eating little of the food in front of him which might have mitigated the effects of the alcohol, with the result that his inhibitions were lowered. Still, that was no justification for betraying Eve's confidence.

He remained oblivious to my baleful look as, in a tone somewhere between jest and deadly earnest, he regaled Thaddeus and Shadrach Allerthorpe and Fitzhugh Danningbury Boyd with a potted version of everything Eve had told him.

His father was quick with a repudiation. "Pshaw! The girl is either making it up or confusing fancy with fact. Knowing Eve, the one is as probable as the other. Desperate for attention, she is. All the more so since her mother passed away. She's not been in her right mind for months. Hit her hard, Perdita's death did. Hit us all hard."

For the briefest of moments Thaddeus's face darkened, and I caught a glimpse, or so I thought, of something beneath the man's irascible exterior, something wounded and tragic. It did not linger long. Swiftly enough the bluff and bluster reasserted themselves.

"Doubtless she wishes to have seen the Black Thurrick," he continued, "because it affords a link to her late mama. It was Perdita, after all, who would tell those stories about the Thurrick and all the rest. With this fabrication Eve, in a roundabout way, is trying to demonstrate that she has not forgotten her mother and still mourns her."

"That," said Holmes, "is an astute piece of psychological insight, if I may say so, Mr Allerthorpe."

"You are too kind, sir," came the droll reply.

"Interesting thing about the Thurrick..." Shadrach Allerthorpe began.

"Here we go," said Thaddeus, rolling his eyes. "Shad is about to share with us the benefits of his book-learning. My brother, Mr Holmes, in case you didn't know, is the brainy one. Did far better at school than I, and now styles himself an amateur historian."

"There is a little more to it than that," Shadrach interjected.

"If you insist. Out of the pair of us, you see, Mr Holmes, Shad got the intellect. Whereas all I got was the property, the title deeds, the money..." Thaddeus chortled at his joke.

Shadrach Allerthorpe sighed. "All I was going to say was that the Black Thurrick is a Yorkshire variant on other, similar Christmas-related figures which may be found all over Europe. There is Zwarte Piet, or Black Peter, in the Low Countries – a fire-singed devil who was enslaved by Saint Nicholas and is now forced to accompany him on his rounds. If children misbehave or disobey their parents, Zwarte Piet is permitted to thrash them soundly. Then there is the Germans' Knecht Ruprecht, likewise an indentured helper of Father Christmas. He carries a staff and a bag of ashes, and invites children to pray. If they pray well, he rewards them with sweetmeats. If they do not, he belabours them about the head with the sack of ashes. There is the shaggy, horned Krampus, who is found in the

Christmas iconography of not only the Germanic countries but their eastern neighbours. He uses birch branches to swat wayward children. In Francophone nations you will find Père Fouettard. He is usually depicted with a bundle of sticks on his back, with which he, too, is wont to beat children. His name, after all, translates as 'Father Flogger'. Sometimes he carries a wicker basket as well, into which the bad children are thrown so that he can bear them away."

"Much like the Thurrick and his sack," said Erasmus.

"There are countless other similar folkloric beings," said Shadrach. "The same characteristics recur: twigs or branches and a violent disposition at odds with Father Christmas's benevolence, as if you cannot have the one without the other. A necessary counterweight, perhaps. No light without shadow. It isn't too much of a stretch to suppose that, in the dim and distant past, travellers from abroad visited the north of England and shared anecdotes about their own Christmas demons, and so was born a regional equivalent, the Black Thurrick."

"Alternatively," opined Fitzhugh Danningbury Boyd, "the Black Thurrick might be the original, the progenitor of his European counterparts."

"Alternatively still," said Erasmus, "the Black Thurrick is real." There was a glint in his glassy, crapulous eye, and I discerned that his purpose now was mischief-making. "If Eve saw it, it must be."

"For heaven's sake, Raz!" Thaddeus barked. "I've had about as much as I can take of this. Bad enough that you live under my roof, on the allowance I give you, and have not yet shown any inclination to learn about running the estate. Must I put up with listening to your inane jabber as well?"

Erasmus Allerthorpe flinched, as did I to a lesser extent. His father's outburst was even more vitriolic than it had been this afternoon and, in my view, just as unwarranted. I anticipated a ferocious rejoinder from the young man, and might even have applauded it; but, as before, Erasmus simply bit his lip. Then, abruptly, he thrust back his chair and stalked out of the room, snatching a decanter of whisky off the sideboard as he went and slamming the door behind him.

"Don't think me too harsh on the lad," Thaddeus said to Holmes and me, as if in answer to our unvoiced question. "I am simply losing patience with him. He is coming to the age when he should at least be giving thought to his duties as a prospective heir. I won't be around forever, and keeping things going at Fellscar is a full-time job. So is managing the family's finances. We have sold off our businesses but somebody has to keep an eye on the money; it can't be left entirely in the hands of stockbrokers. I try to get the lad interested in these things, but he would rather fritter his life away, either here or with his ne'er-do-well friends down in London. I drive him hard because much is expected of him and he is signally failing to live up to his responsibilities. One day I hope the pressure I put on him will yield results."

I refrained from saying what I wanted to – that the results might not be ones that Thaddeus Allerthorpe would like. My own brother, as the firstborn son, had had onerous expectations imposed upon him by our father, and the consequences had been a life of anxiety and dissolution and a premature death.

"Anyway," Thaddeus said, rising from the table, "the ladies have had plenty of time to themselves. Shall we join them?"

We made our way to the drawing room, where, it transpired, a loud argument was taking place. Shrill feminine voices were raised, and I recognised them as Eve's and Kitty's, although the sound was muffled and I could not make out any words.

Just as we arrived at the door, it was flung open and out came Eve, in floods of tears. She brushed past us and hurried down the corridor.

I looked at Thaddeus, Shadrach and Fitzhugh Danningbury Boyd. None of them seemed perturbed, or indeed greatly sympathetic, not even Eve's own father. I turned to Holmes. He, intuiting from my expression that I desired to go after the girl, gave me the merest of nods.

I hastened along the corridor, catching up with Eve just as she reached the central hallway.

"Miss Allerthorpe," I said, "whatever is the matter? What has upset you so?"

Her face was red, her eyes swollen. "It is nothing."

"It is abundantly not nothing. I am happy to listen, if there is something you would like to get off your chest."

"I have had a few sharp words with Kitty, that is all. She… She accused me of flirting with Fitzhugh at table."

"But that is absurd! I was watching. You did nothing to encourage him. If there was flirting, it came from only one direction."

"Fitzhugh is an incorrigible lecher," Eve Allerthorpe said. "He always has been. It is his practice with every halfway presentable woman he meets. Kitty is well aware of this, and it isn't as if he has never acted like that towards me before. She has borne his roving eye patiently during the three years they have been married. Perhaps this evening it just proved too much for her, and she snapped."

"You must in no way shoulder any of the blame. Your cousin has been unfair. You should seek an apology from her."

Eve sniffed hard in an effort to compose herself. "Maybe tomorrow I shall. Tonight, I am just too distressed. I am going to bed. Goodnight, Doctor. Thank you for being so kind and understanding."

"You are more than welcome, Miss Allerthorpe. Goodnight."

I returned to the drawing room, where Olivia Allerthorpe was consoling her daughter. Thaddeus, Shadrach and Fitzhugh, meanwhile, stood around in various attitudes of embarrassment and unconcern. Holmes, for his part, affected an amused detachment.

My dander was up, and I did not trust myself to speak temperately to our host or any of the assembled company. Rather, I excused myself and said I was going to bed.

"A capital notion, Watson," said Holmes. "I shall do so too. Allerthorpes, Danningbury Boyds, I bid you all good evening."

At Thaddeus's instruction, Trebend the butler fetched an oil lamp for us, which Holmes carried as he and I navigated through the illuminated sections of the castle to the unilluminated area where our rooms lay.

Along the way, my friend said, "What did I tell you, Watson? Families! They never know contentment. Some of them will present a united front to the world, all smiles and ease, while the undercurrents of disharmony reveal themselves only in private. With others, the turbulence shows all too readily upon the surface, even before strangers."

I was relieved to discover that the fire had been lit in my room and the air was not quite as frigid as it had been that afternoon. The bed, however, was old and extraordinarily uncomfortable. I say this as someone who has endured the meagre padding of a boarding-school pallet and, moreover, slept on the bare, rocky ground of the Hindu Kush with insidiously bitter winds whipping down from the Himalayas and only a thin blanket to cover him, and still in both instances managed a decent slumber. My bed at Fellscar Keep was an abomination of poking-out springs and mattress ticking so threadbare I could feel the coarse fibres of the horsehair through it. The bedstead rocked and groaned at the slightest movement of my body. It was a fitful night, and I rose at five o'clock feeling hardly at all rested.

As I dressed, I opened the curtains to look out at the lake and the countryside beyond. The moon had set, but the starlight scintillated, giving the scene of snow and ice an eerily beautiful lustre.

My eye fell to the window ledge, where sat a small, dark object, nestling in the layer of snow.

I let out an involuntary gasp.

It was a bundle of twigs, fastened with string.

Chapter Seven

A MARVELLOUS MEDIUM

"Evidence!" declared a jubilant Sherlock Holmes who, clad in a dressing gown, had just joined me in my bedroom. "And on our very doorstep, as it were. Most fortuitous."

"I am pleased for you," I said. "For myself, all I can say is that it gave me a dashed fright, seeing those twigs out there."

"Come, come, Watson. A big, bluff bravo like you, scared of a few small scraps of wood and a length of string?"

"It isn't the bundle of twigs itself, but what it represents."

"The Black Thurrick?"

"Well, yes. We are on the second floor. The item appeared on the window ledge overnight."

"How do you know it wasn't placed there while we were at dinner?"

"Because when we came up, I noticed that one of the window casements was rattling. The latch was undone, and I secured it. The twigs were not there then. I would have seen them. Therefore it must have happened after I got into bed, sometime during the night, and I heard nothing. It isn't even as if I slept soundly. I would have been aware of the smallest disturbance, I am sure, and yet silently, someone – something – crept up the wall outside and singled me out for its sinister attentions. *Me*, Holmes."

"And have you been a wayward boy this year, Watson?" my companion enquired with a smirk. "Do you merit punishment?"

"Please do not belittle my feelings," I said hotly. "I am quite aware how ludicrous it is to be as flustered as I am. On the other hand, it was not *your* window that received this visitation."

"Which is, in itself, suggestive. You did right by coming to me first, by the way, rather than opening the window and fetching the bundle."

"I thought it best to leave it *in situ*," I said. "I know how you like your crime scenes undisturbed." To be honest, I had no great desire to touch the object.

"Crime scene? Yes, I suppose it is one, after a fashion. Now then…" Holmes lit a lamp, for it was still dark outside, and passed it to me to hold. Then he eased one of the casements open. The bottom of the casement skimmed the top of the layer of snow that had accumulated on the ledge. Poking his head out, he peered to either side and upward. Then he bent to examine the ledge itself minutely.

"Look here," he said, motioning me to bring the lamp a little closer. "Do you see these tiny marks in the snow, just beyond where the twigs lie?"

He was pointing to three small grooves on the outer edge of the snow layer. Two were thin and straight, like incisions, while the third was curved, more like a scrape. Each was separated from its neighbour by a distance of no more than quarter of an inch.

"I see them."

"What do you make of them?"

"Could they have been left there by a bird?" I wondered.

"Or maybe by the talons of the Black Thurrick. I'm joking, Watson! Don't grimace like that. The Black Thurrick's talons would leave much larger marks. Again, joking! Really, old fellow, even if you think the creature is real, you must learn to be cooler-headed about it. Are you an infant whose parents have not left out a food offering? No? Then you are safe from the Thurrick's worst depredations. Do you have a pen?"

I produced one from my jacket pocket.

Holmes inserted one end of the pen into one of the loops of the knot with which the string was tied, then lifted the bundle of twigs very carefully, carried it inside and deposited it on the dressing table. While I closed the window, he sat and studied the bundle from every possible angle by the light of the lamp.

"The twigs have been gathered to order," he said eventually. "The majority appear to have fallen from the tree through natural processes, and are of a more or less uniform length. Those that were longer have had one end broken off, so as to shorten them appropriately."

"I see."

"Obviously our Thurrick is that rare type of marauding fiend who likes things neat and tidy. As for the string, it is standard triple-strand sisal twine, the sort one might purchase from any stationers or newsagents. The trimmed ends show a slight compression. That tells us much, of course."

"It does?"

"It tells us that the Thurrick uses scissors, rather than that less sophisticated utensil, a knife."

"How can you be sure?"

"The compression I spoke of is the kind that scissors cause, whereas a knife leaves a more frayed result, thanks to the sawing action required, with the shorn ends of the fibres exhibiting a definite trend in one direction. So, we may infer that the Black Thurrick has access to items of stationery such as one might find in any moderately well-supplied household. Yet the creature is reputed to dwell in an underground lair, which is hardly indicative of domesticity."

"This is all very well, Holmes, but the twigs were placed on a window ledge, high up, just as they were in the case of Eve Allerthorpe's study and Erasmus's bedroom."

"And in each instance the room concerned faces outward from the castle, implying that the depositor of the bundles is from without the premises, rather than from within. That is why I remarked how suggestive it was that your room was chosen and not mine. Mine faces inward."

"I do not follow."

"Doesn't it look, Watson, as though somebody is making a point? Rather clumsily, at that. This somebody wishes us to assume that the bundles are the work of an external agency, by dint of the fact that they only ever appear on outward-facing window ledges. I deem it clumsy because, according to legend, the Black Thurrick can come down chimneys. Why, then, would the creature restrict itself to the outward-facing window ledges of Fellscar Keep when it has the ability to scale roofs? When its agility is such that surely no part of a building is off-limits? When any window ledge in the castle is theoretically accessible to it? No, the locations of the bundles of twigs is pure misdirection. It is an attempt to reinforce the notion that the twigs are the Black Thurrick's doing – an attempt, moreover, made by someone who is not as cunning as he thinks he is."

"Unless it is the Yardley Cross children who are

responsible. They could not get to any window ledges that are not outward-facing."

"Children! Bah!" Holmes snorted. "I concede that it is just feasible a child might have gained access to the window of Eve's study, but climbing to the window of Erasmus's bedroom on the first floor, not to mention your window here which is something close to fifty feet up, would surely be beyond the capabilities of even the nimblest and most determined adult, never mind a youngster. No, this whole business, my friend, is what the criminal fraternity call an inside job. It has been, right from the very start. Consider this. The first bundle of twigs appeared by the gatepost. Anyone from the castle could walk along the causeway and place it there. The person might just surreptitiously drop it as he was passing. The second bundle was outside Eve's study. It sat to the side of the casement, of which the window has just a single one. If it had sat directly in front of the casement, then there would be more of a mystery. Because it did not, it is easy to deduce that someone opened the casement from within to place the bundle on the ledge. He or she could not have shut the window again if the bundle had been in the way of the casement, for the twigs would impede the closing of it. It stands to reason."

"What about Erasmus's window ledge? He said the bundle was in front of one of the casements."

"That's just it. *One* of the casements. There is more than one, as here. A person need only open the left-hand casement to plant the bundle in front of the right-hand one, and vice versa."

"All well and fine," I said, "but nobody came into *this* room during the night and opened the window. I would swear to it."

"No, nobody did," Holmes agreed. "In this instance, a different method was employed. Note that while we may be on the second floor, we are not on the uppermost storey in this wing of the castle. There is another floor above us. I put it to you that the bundle was lowered onto the window ledge by someone at the window above."

"Good gracious! And what leads you to that conclusion?"

"Here is where snow proves itself to be a marvellous medium for the detective's purposes. Under certain circumstances it offers an abundance of clues, for it preserves the imprint of anything that rests upon it, however insubstantial. You will recall the three distinctive marks in the snow on the ledge. What is the simplest and likeliest method someone would use to lower a small, light object a distance of four or five yards and leave it behind? A fishhook and fishing line, surely. This castle is built upon a lake. It is hardly improbable that there will be fishing tackle on the premises. Now, picture our culprit leaning out from the window above and paying out a length of fishing line with the bundle of twigs suspended from the fishhook by one of the loops in the string. The bundle lands safely upon the window ledge here. Now the fellow has to extricate the hook from the loop. He pays out a tiny bit more of his line. It is not enough. He pays out a tiny bit more. This at last creates sufficient slack for the hook to slip free from the loop, and he reels the line back in. Does this seem a plausible sequence of events?"

"Eminently so," I said. "But how are you able to state with such certainty that that is what happened?"

"The marks tell the story in every detail. The leftmost straight mark denotes where the slack in the fishing line first touched the snow. The middle mark, ever so slightly longer, denotes where the greater length of slack did so. The third mark, just to the right of that one, was left by the fishhook as it slid out from the loop of the knot. Can you gainsay this interpretation of the data?"

"It is hard to."

"It is all but impossible to. If you'll allow me, I will make my way upstairs to verify one last element of my postulation."

"I shall come with you."

"No, I would prefer you to remain here. I shan't be long."

Holmes was absent for ten minutes, and when he returned, all he said was, "Well?"

"Well, what?"

"That is all the answer I need."

"I am glad, for your sake," I said. "But perhaps you would care to enlighten me as to how I have managed to satisfy your curiosity."

"I daresay you would have told me, when I prompted you with that 'Well?', if you had heard anything from the room upstairs. A creak, say, or a footfall."

"I heard none."

"Just so. Treading slowly and softly, I crossed the room and stood at the window. I even took the precaution of removing my shoes and going on stockinged feet, as our fellow with the fishing line may well have done. The floorboards did not give away my presence, as you have confirmed. I opened and closed the window. That, too, was an all but silent procedure. Likewise the opening and closing of the door as I came and went. The room is another bedroom, by the way, and is currently unoccupied but looks as though it will be shortly, which is a pity."

"Why?"

"Because it has recently been made ready for occupation by, doubtless, one of the coming houseguests. That means, unhappily for our purposes, that the floor has been freshly swept. If only the room had been used for something else, as a storeroom, for instance. Then the floor would have borne a convenient coating of dust in which one might have found tell-tale footprints. Still, I have proved that a stealthy person could avail himself of the use of the window without alerting his intended victim below, and so my fishing line theory is corroborated. Or, at any rate, it is not undermined."

"So you have disproved once and for all the possibility that the Black Thurrick is the one leaving bundles of birch twigs everywhere," I said.

"You still believe there even is such a creature?"

"Until you can account for what Eve Allerthorpe saw from her bedroom window, I am reserving judgement."

"That is your prerogative."

"But who, then, is conducting this campaign of harassment against the residents of Fellscar Keep?"

"One of those self-same residents, obviously," said Holmes. "Perhaps even Miss Allerthorpe herself."

"Really?"

"You were there when we overheard her talking to her brother in the hallway. He said there had been no mysterious twig bundles while she was in London."

"Why would she, of all people, be behind it all? It makes no sense."

"An unstable, fragile young woman pretending she is the target of inimical supernatural forces? It is as probable as it is pathetic. A plea for attention, maybe, or a cry for help."

"If it were either of those, why did Eve beg Erasmus not to tell anyone she had seen the Thurrick on the lake? Surely, for the purposes of drawing notice to herself, she would wish everyone to know."

"Unless she realised in that moment she had gone a step too far. It is one thing to place a few bundles of twigs around the castle, quite another to claim to have clapped eyes upon a mythical beast. The line between plausibility and absurdity is, in this instance, a fine one, and Eve felt that she had crossed it."

"But then why drag Erasmus into it in the first place, by leaving the third set of twigs outside his window?"

"To deflect the very accusation I have just made. How could Eve be the guilty party if her brother is also a victim?"

"I do not like it. The kind of terror she exhibited to us at Baker Street, that cannot easily be falsified."

"I merely air a possibility," Holmes said. "Her father might equally be responsible. He exhibits a strong dislike for both of his children. Or it could be Kitty Danningbury Boyd, angered by the attention her husband pays to her cousin and keen to render Eve a less enticing proposition by driving her half mad. If Eve is to be believed, Fitzhugh Danningbury Boyd tries to seduce practically every woman he meets, but since he lives at Fellscar, Eve herself is the one likely to suffer his flirtatious behaviour the most consistently. Therefore his wife would be at some pains to spike his guns, would she not?"

"I suppose so."

"It all seems so petty, in its way," Holmes said, "and none of it would matter in the slightest if not for that singular codicil in Lady Jocasta's will. That is the reason I think these apparently inconsequential goings-on may mask something more insidious, and that is the reason you and I, Watson, must remain at Fellscar at least until Eve's birthday. For her sake, too, it would be wise to keep this latest incidence of Thurrick activity just between us – us and whoever perpetrated it."

"You are worried that, as far as her mental health is concerned, it could be the straw that broke the camel's back."

"You have a way with a proverb, old friend, as befits a wordsmith of your calibre."

Compliment? Or not? With Sherlock Holmes, it was sometimes hard to tell.

Chapter Eight

THE MONOLITH IN THE GLADE

The prospect of spending another three days and nights in that cold, inhospitable Yorkshire castle with that cold, inhospitable Yorkshire family was not one I relished. My reluctance was, however, somewhat mitigated by the breakfast I ate that morning. The dining-room sideboard groaned with edible delights. There was kedgeree, kippers, venison pie, cold ham, black pudding, fried bread, and eggs prepared in several different ways. There was toast with a range of curds and jams to spread on it. There was a local delicacy known as Easter-Ledge pudding, a cake of nettles, sorrel, onion and barley fried in bacon grease. There was coffee and tea aplenty. If I were to single out any item on the menu for praise, however, it would be the marmalade, which was remarkably good – so much so that

I felt moved to convey my compliments to the cook.

To that end, I made my way to the kitchen. There was no one there, but I heard noises in the adjacent scullery, where I found a scullery maid, hard at work scrubbing dishes. I enquired of her whether the cook was around.

"Mrs Trebend, sir? She's just this moment stepped out. Gone to the larder. Would thah like me to fetch her for thee?"

"I would, very much."

The maid scurried off and returned shortly with Mrs Trebend in tow. The latter proved to be a plump, not unattractive woman in cap and apron, who greeted me with an obliging smile. She was carrying two hefty legs of mutton which, I presumed, were for lunch.

"Forgive the imposition, madam," I said. "I simply wished to tell you how much I enjoy your cooking, especially that marmalade of yours."

"You are too kind, sir," Mrs Trebend said, laying the mutton down on the kitchen table and folding her meaty arms in a gratified manner. "My marmalade *is* good, even if I do say so myself. The secret lies in choosing only the best oranges – Seville, of course – and throwing in a little grapefruit as well, for added tanginess. Also, I shred the peel extra finely. It brings out the flavour better and is more pleasant on the palate. Mr Trebend – that is, my husband – allus says he could never find another woman who can make marmalade the way I do. Such a romantic he is, my Robert. Goforth! What were that?"

This last remark was directed through the doorway to the scullery, from where there had come a loud clatter.

"It were nowt, Cook."

"Didn't sound like nowt."

"A plate slipped from my hand. It's fine. Not broken."

"Clumsy minx!" Mrs Trebend scolded. "You need to be more careful. Any piece of china in this house is worth more than you make in a month, and if you break summat, it will be coming out of your pay."

"Yes, Cook. Sorry, Cook. Won't happen again, Cook."

"See that it doesn't." Mrs Trebend turned back to me, her scowl easing. "Will there be owt else, sir? Only, I am rather busy."

"No, madam. I simply wished you to know that your efforts are much appreciated."

"And your appreciation is, likewise, much appreciated," said the Allerthorpes' cook, bobbing a curtsey.

I returned to the dining room for one last fortifying cup of coffee. Up until then, it had been only Holmes and I at the table. Now, however, Shadrach Allerthorpe joined us, to make it three. His cheeks were ruddy and he was rubbing his hands together and blowing into them to warm them up. I did not need the analytical prowess of my friend to determine that he had just come in from outdoors.

"Been for a stroll?" I said.

"Yes, Doctor. Yes, that is just what I have been doing. Nothing gets the blood pumping quite like a brisk walk on a cold morning. Makes you feel like you've earned your breakfast."

"Sounds like a fine recommendation," said Holmes. "How about it, eh, Watson? Fancy some exercise?"

I would have demurred. However, something in Holmes's tone suggested I was not being presented with a choice but, rather, an edict.

Thus several minutes later, suitably bundled up against the weather, he and I sallied forth from the castle. We had not gone more than a dozen paces from the landward end of the causeway when my companion paused and began inspecting the snowy ground.

"What are you looking for?"

"Tracks, old fellow. What else?"

"What sort of tracks?"

"Footprints. The human kind, I hasten to add, in case you were wondering whether I am seeking any left by some loathsome child-stealing beast."

"I see a fair few sets of human footprints." There were a dozen at least, angling this way and that across the open countryside, alongside the neatly dotted tracks left by animals – fox, rabbit, perhaps badger. In combination these criss-crossing stippled lines reminded me of sutures on a severely lacerated patient; and then I chided myself for likening an innocent winter's day scene to something so unpleasant. Perhaps more than a decade as a medical man had so accustomed me to injury and illness that I saw those things everywhere. I wondered, though, whether the castle's darkly gloomy atmosphere was somehow contaminating my thoughts, and this and the lack of a decent night's sleep were making me inclined towards morbid fancies.

"The ones I am interested in are the freshest," Holmes said. "Older footprints, even from yesterday, will not have the same crisp edges as any that have been made during the past hour or so. There will always be some small amount of erosion, either through wind or the melting effect of sunshine or a combination of both, which will make them appear, for want of a better word, blurry."

I put two and two together. "You are trying to work out where Shadrach Allerthorpe went on his walk."

"Really, Watson, I can well see you abandoning general practice one of these days, in preference for the role of consulting detective. Your skills are coming along nicely. Tell me, did you notice the tiny appendage Shadrach bore in his trouser cuff?"

"I did not."

"Then you still have a little way to go, alas."

"What was it?"

"The appendage? A fragment of twig had become lodged in the cuff. Birch twig," he added, with dry emphasis.

"My goodness," I said. "You mean to say Shadrach was out this morning on a foraging expedition? Gathering material for yet another Black Thurrick bundle?"

"I might not necessarily leap to that conclusion myself, but it certainly bears following up on, wouldn't you agree? A-ha! There!" Holmes pointed to a line of footprints that stretched all the way to the woods and to another that ran practically parallel with it. He made a wild gesticulation which, under the circumstances, I thought unwarranted. "Yes. Yes. These must be his. I have observed that Shadrach Allerthorpe takes a size nine shoe, and these prints are size nine. Furthermore, the tread pattern of the sole matches that of a pair of size nine walking boots I spied on the mat by the front door, caked with snow and awaiting the ministrations of the boot boy. One of them was lying on its side. You saw this too? No? Ah well. Your progress towards setting up your own detective agency lengthens a tad further. Now, if we consider the position of heel and toe, in tandem with the slight 'drag' at the rear of each print, it tells us that *these* tracks are heading towards the castle, while *these* are heading away. All we have to do is follow this dual spoor and it will lead us along the route Shadrach took."

Accordingly, we started retracing Shadrach Allerthorpe's journey. For the first few minutes Holmes was in such a transport of delight, flailing his arms and cavorting, that I began to wonder if there was some deeper significance to the discovery of the tracks than appeared.

He calmed down once we were deep in the woods and trudging through snow that sometimes came up to our shins. It was a bright, breezeless morning and the hush around us was profound. All we heard was our crunching footfalls and the occasional soft patter of loose snow tumbling from a tree branch. I was put in mind of the wintry march my regiment had undertaken through the Shivaliks, the Himalayan foothills, amid forest just as dense as this and just as breathlessly still. I felt, again, the tingle of fear that had come with the knowledge that the enemy might be lurking behind any tree; that hostile eyes could be upon me, and gunsights too. I doubt I shall ever be free of my memories of the war. They will haunt me to my grave.

Holmes kept his gaze fixed downward, keen not to lose the trail. On occasion, however, he would dart a glance over his shoulder. This did little to assuage my feelings of unease. Was he merely being cautious, or was somebody following us? If the latter, I myself saw no indication of it, but then my friend's senses were far keener than mine. I began to wish I had had the foresight to bring my service revolver with me. Holmes had given no hint that a weapon might be needed, however, and generally speaking, when it came to making provision for danger, I took my cue from him.

After we had gone perhaps two miles, I said, "We have passed countless birch trees, each with an ample sufficiency of fallen twigs around it. If Shadrach's remit was collecting such twigs, he need not have travelled quite so far, surely."

"Indeed," Holmes replied. "His morning walk must have had some ulterior motive."

"Or else none at all, save that which he claimed for it."

For the most part Shadrach had followed pre-existing paths through the woods, but then, abruptly, his tracks veered off across rougher terrain, showing that he had ascended a steep, root-riddled slope and subsequently descended it along much the same course. Holmes and I toiled uphill, now and then losing our footing and sliding back, until eventually we came to a ridge.

Just beyond, we found a natural glade that occupied a shallow, bowl-like depression. At its centre stood a single, upright stone, some two and a half yards tall and roughly conical. The ground around the stone, for a radius of approximately ten feet, had been cleared of most of its snow, revealing leaf mould and glimpses of bare soil. The removed snow lay banked up around the perimeter of this circle.

"Well now," said Holmes, "this is a curio indeed. You will recall the standing stone mentioned by Miss Allerthorpe, the Rudston Monolith. Here we appear to have another such monument." He walked around the stone, studying it by eye and even running a hand over its lichen-speckled surface. "There are carvings which, from their weather-worn faintness, can only be several centuries old. The patterns are not all of them familiar to me. However, I detect a distinct Celtic influence. Here, for example, we find the particular kind of ornamentation known as a Celtic knot, and here the triple spiral, also of Celtic origin, which I believe is known as a triskele. This is not my field of expertise at all, but one may safely assert that the stone was erected in accordance with some ancient pagan tradition, as a locus of worship, perhaps, or as a place of ritual sacrifice."

I affected a nonchalance I did not feel. All at once the glade seemed less innocent, the grey, rough-hewn monolith pregnant with foreboding. Had dark, heathen ceremonies been held at this spot, long, long ago? Had blood been spilled here on that standing stone? Perhaps even human blood?

Next Holmes began to examine the patch of ground that was more or less free of snow.

"This has been swept," he concluded. "A consistent circular motion has been used. You see the grooves in what little snow remains? They rotate around the stone in a clockwise direction, concentrically. The utensil employed, however, was no common-or-garden broom. The width of the stroke is too broad, while the grooves are too irregular to have been left by evenly-spaced bristles. Something more natural was involved. Something such as…"

He cast an eye around him, and suddenly let out a little chuckle.

"Yes, there you are, my beauty," said he, skipping to the edge of the glade. He picked up a large branch, which had been leaning propped up against the trunk of a tree. It was a slender birch bough, with a fan of smaller stems spreading from one end like a river delta. In a spirit of experimentation, Holmes raked the fan-shaped end across the ground, following the course of the circular grooves already there. "A perfect match. This is the 'broom'. I would wager good money on it. The only question is why Shadrach Allerthorpe has been out here this morning, engaged in this peculiar piece of forest husbandry."

"It does seem a dashed odd thing to do," I observed.

"I concur. Perhaps the man himself would be willing to explain his reasons."

I made sceptical noises.

"As it happens, we can ask him right now," Holmes said. "Can't we, Mr Allerthorpe?"

My friend was looking off into the forest, and I, following the line of his gaze, perceived someone skulking behind a tree, half-hidden. The hackles rose on the back of my neck. How long had this person been loitering there, secretly spying on us?

The skulking figure, as if acknowledging that the jig was up, stepped out into the open. It was, as Holmes had conveyed, Shadrach Allerthorpe. He looked chagrined and also somewhat sheepish.

"You knew I was following you?" said he to Holmes.

"Knew? I lured you out, sir! My sudden decision to go for a walk would have aroused your curiosity, and so I was unsurprised when I caught sight of you watching furtively from a window as Watson and I were leaving the castle. I made quite a song and dance about locating the tracks you had left earlier. All that arm-waving and gambolling when I found them – I was practically begging for your attention. And I am most grateful that you have obliged by shadowing us all this way. It has saved us a great deal of trouble. You visited this glade not an hour ago and performed some kind of formal sweeping with a birch branch. What, pray, was the purpose of that?"

Shadrach pondered, then said gravely, "I shall tell you. But before I do, be so good as to promise me one thing."

"What?"

"Once I have explained my actions, you will not mock me and you will not breathe a word about it to anyone."

"Very well."

"You too, Doctor."

Taking my lead from Holmes, I gave my word.

"Thank you."

And so Shadrach Allerthorpe embarked upon a brief but most curious narrative.

Chapter Nine

SHADRACH ALLERTHORPE'S BRIEF BUT MOST CURIOUS NARRATIVE

"I am, as my brother told you, an historian," Shadrach Allerthorpe began, "although I suppose you might more correctly call me an antiquary. My knowledge of history is fairly wide-ranging but, if I were to be said to have a speciality, it is pre-Christian culture and society. I am fascinated by the ancient world in all its forms, whether it is the might and majesty of imperial Rome, the Hellenes, with their wit and sophistication, or the Egyptians, as brilliant as they were cruel.

"However, what interests me as much as any of those civilisations, if not more, is the civilisation that existed in our own country prior to the Norman Conquest, prior even to the Roman invasion. Britain in the Bronze Age and the Iron Age, and earlier still. It is an era shrouded in a fog of mystery through which we obtain occasional, tantalising peeks at the truth. Contemporary documentation is sparse, and so we must rely upon rare archaeological finds – a burial barrow here, a collection of potsherds there – and extrapolate from these.

"It is the opacity of our nation's distant past that is so intriguing to me. The challenge is to make the most of the few clues one has. In that respect, I suppose you could liken it to detective work, eh, Mr Holmes? Sifting through the data, examining the minutiae, eliminating the impossible, and so forth."

Holmes inclined his head to one side, as though he did not wholly agree with the comparison but did not disagree with it either.

"At any rate," Shadrach continued, "I have devoted many hours to the study of ancient Britain, and during the course of my researches I have developed a fascination for the customs and conventions of the Celtic druids.

"A druid was not just a tribal religious leader. He was a diviner of auguries and a healer, and served as arbiter in judicial matters as well. He could start a war against an enemy tribe, and stop it. His word, in every sphere of life, was final.

"The druids left no written record of their lore, which was communicated from one to another orally alone, doubtless in order to preserve secrecy. According to the writings of Caesar and Pliny the Elder, among others, they conducted certain barbaric rites in which the immolation, drowning or decapitation of sacrificial victims was not unheard of."

"Human victims?" I said, casting an uneasy look at the standing stone.

Shadrach nodded. "The purpose of the death was not only to appease the gods. The very manner in which the victim perished, from the way the blood flowed out to the convulsions of his limbs, could be used to prophesy the future."

"Ghastly."

"By our lights, yes, but to the Celts it was just how things were. Above all else the druid had a close connection with nature. The world around him was pregnant with meaning. He understood the cycles of the moon, the sun and the seasons, and observed these religiously. Plant life was, to him, particularly important. Every tree, every shrub, every flower was sacred in some way or other and had a power that he could harness."

"Would that by any chance include the birch?" said Holmes.

"It would. The birch symbolised rebirth, renewal, fresh beginnings. It was a tree admired for its resilience, since it thrives in conditions where other trees might not. Its wood was used to build maypoles and also to ignite fires at Beltane, the festival held on May Day to usher in summertime. In addition there was the practice of using a broom made of birch to drive out evil spirits and invoke divine protection for a person or property."

"And that last is a practice that you yourself have seen fit to uphold here?"

Shadrach Allerthorpe shifted his feet, his eyes downcast. "You will probably think me something of a fool, but my interest in druidical lore has not remained purely academic. Perhaps two or three years ago I began to adopt various of its elements into my own personal philosophy. I am a good Christian, please do not misunderstand. I attend church. Indeed, today being Sunday, I will shortly be accompanying the rest of the family to the mid-morning service at Yardley Cross. I have not become some godless heathen.

"At the same time, the ancient mystical ways hold considerable appeal. I accept that that may seem contradictory, but I find it is perfectly possible to hold both beliefs at once, druidical and Christian. When you are in woodland like this, surrounded by all these stately trees, can you not sense a kind of numinous godhead suffusing things? Do you not feel awed, as though you are in the presence of something greater than yourself, some divinity? The more so in this very spot, where a long-dead Celtic sage commissioned the erection of a sandstone menhir and oversaw – perhaps even executed himself – the inscribing of occult motifs onto its surface.

"This glade, gentlemen, is a place of power. It is a nexus where the natural lines of force that run like veins through the earth converge; where there is an almost palpable thrum of energies, which the menhir channels and radiates. No? Your faces suggest you are unconvinced – yours, Mr Holmes, markedly more than Dr Watson's. Well, we live in an empirical age. You are entitled to your doubts.

"I myself often come here simply to bask in the ambiance and contemplate. I find it calming. I have even been known to talk to the menhir, expressing my inmost thoughts to it. Nobody else knows that I do this. If any of my family were to find out, I would be a laughing stock. Thaddeus especially would never let me hear the end of it. That is why I vowed you both to secrecy, and I entreat you, once again, to reiterate that guarantee."

Holmes and I did as bidden.

"As soon as I saw you singling out my tracks in the snow," Shadrach said, "I realised you would inevitably ascertain where I had gone. My only option was to follow you, explain myself, and throw myself on your mercy. This I have now done, and I hope that there will be an end to the matter."

"Not quite," said Holmes. "You still not have told us why you have so assiduously swept the area around the menhir."

"Ah well, you see, life at Fellscar Keep is troubled at present. You do not need me to tell you that. It was never the most tranquil of homes, but Perdita's death seems to have brought its inner divisions into sharp relief. My sister-in-law may not have been a balanced individual, but when she was in her right mind, she was a delight. She was the glue that held the household together, and without her, we seem gradually to be falling apart. This queer business with the bundles of birch twigs appearing around the castle is just a symptom of the malaise that oppresses us. You have heard, too, about the ghost in the east wing? No doubt someone must have mentioned it."

I myself had more or less forgotten about the phantom reputed to haunt the castle. It had rather been overshadowed in my imagination by the Black Thurrick.

"Your niece did," said Holmes. "She seems to think it may be the unquiet spirit of her mother."

"Given that the ghost started manifesting a matter of months after Perdita died, chances are that it is," Shadrach said. "Whether it be her or not, though, *something* is undoubtedly roaming the corridors in that section of the castle, some unearthly presence. Several of the servants have spoken of eerie noises there at night – groans, scrapes, footsteps and such. A scullery maid who was carrying a candle saw the flame blow itself out and heard a terrible, insinuating whisper. She fled in abject terror. Then there was Mrs Trebend."

"The cook," I said.

"A more pragmatic, level-headed woman it would be hard to find."

In light of my recent, albeit brief meeting with the culinary miracle worker, I could not argue with this description.

"It is Mrs Trebend who actually saw the ghost in the flesh, so to speak," said Shadrach. "She decided to follow up on the scullery maid's account, in order to prove it to be just so much nonsense. This was back in the summer, as I recall. Mid-July. Well, that good lady returned from the expedition looking white as a sheet and shaking so badly she needed a tot or two of whisky to calm down.

"When at last she recovered her wits, she told us that she had been walking along the main corridor on the ground floor and felt something brush past her, something invisible. Its touch was like ice, she said, bringing her out in gooseflesh. She managed to pluck up the courage to speak, addressing this unseen presence. There was no reply, but then from the corner of her eye she saw a flicker of white, a pale figure flitting around the corner. It resembled a woman in a dress, Mrs Trebend said, and at that point her nerve broke and she ran.

"Now, a single report of ghostly happenings one might dismiss, even two, but half a dozen? And amongst them, moreover, an eyewitness account from such an unimpeachable source? Something must be up. Hence, the following evening I took it upon myself to investigate."

"Brave man," I said.

Shadrach shrugged off the compliment. "You are aware, now, that I am in thrall to mysteries. Here was another one, in my own home. I could not help but enquire into it."

"And did you too encounter the ghost?" Holmes asked.

"No. I don't know whether that is to be regretted or not. I felt distinctly uneasy in the east wing, I can tell you that. I had the strongest inkling that something was amiss there. But no ghost sighting, no."

"Nevertheless, in an attempt to rectify the situation, you have swept around this menhir with a birch broom, since such an action is, as you say, supposed to drive out evil spirits and invoke divine protection. Fellscar is poisoned by some sort of malign influence, and here, in what you term a 'place of power', lies what you regard as the antidote."

"It sounds absurd when you put it like that, but I believe it. I feel it was worth trying, at least."

Holmes mused for a moment, then said, "It is quite some coincidence, is it not, that your magical, evil-cleansing broom is composed of the same stuff as the bundles the Black Thurrick has been leaving about the castle."

"I beg to differ," said Shadrach. "We have established that the birch tree is regarded as an emblem of renewal and rebirth. What else is this particular time of year concerned with but those very things? Christmas has its roots in traditions that antedate modern religion. It is a Christian celebration bolted onto a far older pagan one. Today marks the winter solstice. The days are shortening, but soon will begin to draw out once more. It is cold and dark, so we bring greenery indoors to brighten our homes and remind us that spring will, eventually, return. We ring out the old year and ring in the new. Renewal. Rebirth. That is why those Christmas characters we discussed last night – Zwarte Piet, Krampus, Père Fouettard, and yes, the Black Thurrick – are all associated with birch branches. It harks back to the past, a tacit acknowledgement of the true origins of the season's festivities."

He consulted his watch.

"But I must be getting back," he said. "The coach leaves for Yardley Cross in an hour, and it wouldn't do to miss church. We should return to the castle separately. If I am seen coming back with you, it might prompt awkward questions."

"Very well," said Holmes. "But before we part company, Mr Allerthorpe, might I prevail upon you to answer me this. Are you the one behind the parcels of birch twigs?"

"No. Absolutely not. I can see why you might think it is me, but I swear to you, sir, upon my life, it isn't. The birch twigs would seem to be exacerbating the unrest at Fellscar, something that I, by contrast, am desirous of quelling. I can only hope that, through my efforts here today at the menhir, I will have accomplished that goal."

As Shadrach tramped off, I said to Holmes, "That was forward of you, asking him outright if he is the Thurrick."

"I seldom pose a query to which I do not already know the answer," said Holmes, "and I received nothing from him but confirmation of my supposition. Shadrach Allerthorpe is an eccentric fellow, perhaps a little weak-willed, but what does he stand to gain from tormenting Eve and Erasmus? Or you, for that matter? You have seen how he is with Thaddeus, ever kowtowing to him, ever obeisant. His position within the family hierarchy is too precarious for him to imperil it by misbehaving. Were he the culprit and his offences exposed, there is every likelihood his older brother would cast him out, and his wife, daughter and son-in-law with him. Don't think Thaddeus Allerthorpe would not do it. He is nothing if not petulant. No, we must needs look elsewhere for our Black Thurrick, Watson. Somebody at Fellscar is hell-bent on sabotaging the status quo, but I am sure now – even surer than I already was – that it is not Shadrach. That means we have one fewer suspect and are consequently one step closer to success."

Chapter Ten

ICE AND SOIL

By the time we neared Fellscar Keep again, I was chilled to the bone and very much looking forward to being back indoors. The castle seemed no less stern and gloomy than before, but at least it held out the prospect of relative warmth.

Holmes, it transpired, had other ideas.

"Shall we circumnavigate the lake?" he proposed.

"Do I have a choice in the matter?"

"I am not your master. You are fully at liberty to go your own way."

"But if I do, there is a chance I may miss out on some clue-gathering."

"Could it be that I have simply been seized by a whim?"

"I know you, Holmes. You rarely do anything on a whim. In fact, you are the least whimsical soul I have ever met."

"Oh dear. I fear I am no longer an enigma to you, am I?"

"On the contrary. You remain damnably enigmatic. But I have learned to identify certain of your more obvious idiosyncrasies."

Our lakeside promenade was hard going. The banks of that body of water were uncultivated and unkempt. The grass grew rank and full of tussocks, treacherous underfoot even without the additional hazard of snow, and there were dense thickets of hawthorn, bramble and willow further impeding progress.

The lake itself spanned some half a mile across at its widest and was roughly oval, with finger-like bays protruding here and there. I thought that in summer it might present a very pleasing prospect, its surface dappled with sunlight, reeds and bulrushes along its shoreline whispering in the breeze, perhaps the delicate *plop* of a fish rising to gulp down some unwary insect; but on that day its bare, frozen-over stillness struck me as profoundly intimidating. There was no telling the lake's depth, no knowing what lay beneath the sheet of ice it had drawn over itself like a glaucous shroud. I thought of an eye paled by a cataract, revealing nothing with its blind stare.

Holmes scanned the ground intently as we went, although what he was looking for, he did not vouchsafe. The further we travelled, the more his pace slowed, until by the time we had completed nearly a half circuit of the lake, he was walking toe to heel like an aerialist on a tightrope, his gaze seldom straying more than a yard ahead.

Presently he came to a stop. We were now practically opposite Fellscar. The northernmost tip of the island on which the castle sat was projecting towards us, with the beetling flanks of the building rising from it, silhouetted against the low morning sun and casting a long shadow over the lake.

Going down on his haunches, Holmes spent several minutes keenly surveying a section of the bank.

"There are signs of disturbance," he said at last. "Grass stems broken and flattened. Not recent, hence the traces are indistinct, but it would appear as though somebody climbed up and down the bank several times in close succession. This would have been about a week ago."

He looked at me expectantly. It took me a moment to parse the import of his statement.

"That is the castle's north wing," I said, pointing across the lake. "Eve Allerthorpe's bedroom is situated in the north wing, its windows overlooking the lake." I felt a small inward thrill that was a mixture of disquiet and comprehension. "Are you telling me that there *is* a Black Thurrick after all?"

"I am telling you no such thing. What I am putting forward as a possibility is that Eve truly did see a dark figure crossing the lake after all. If not the actual Black

Thurrick, then someone either deliberately impersonating the creature or else someone whom she mistook for it. Now, I need your help."

He extended a hand to me, which I took.

"Hold tight," he said.

"What are you going to do?"

"Test the ice, of course, to see if it can bear a man's weight."

"I really would advise against—"

Ignoring me, Holmes lowered himself carefully down the bank. I planted my feet and kept a firm grip on his hand.

Keeping one foot on the bank, he placed the other onto the ice. In slow increments he shifted his weight onto the forward foot.

"So far, so good," he said.

Now he brought the rear foot to join its counterpart on the ice.

Immediately there came an ominous cracking sound from below. Holmes winced. I winced too. I trusted that the water was shallow this close to shore, but I did not know that for certain. Even if it were a comparatively safe depth of, say, three feet, Holmes would still be immersed to the waist were he to fall through the ice, which would put him at risk of contracting a severe chill and possibly pneumonia.

Experimentally, he shuffled forward. I leaned out as far as I could until I was in danger of toppling.

"I cannot reach any further," I said.

"Then let go."

"No, you come back to shore."

With a forceful twist of the wrist, Holmes extricated his hand from mine. Now all I could do was watch, with bated breath, as my friend eased himself inch by inch across the ice. Every so often there came another of those cracking sounds from under him, or else a long, low creak which, although softer, was somehow just as menacing. I was fully prepared to launch myself onto the ice to rescue him if need be, although I cannot say I relished the notion.

Some ten yards out, he halted and, to my considerable relief, commenced the return journey. I assisted him up onto the bank again.

"There we have it," he said. "I tip the scales at nine stone twelve, slightly below average for a man of my height, but then my frame is spare. The ice supported me. It could support an individual of a similar or lesser weight."

"Assuming the person was foolhardy enough to do as you just did."

"Or brave, or compelled by necessity. Let us presume that our Thurrick traversed the lake not just once on the night Eve saw him but a number of times."

"How do we know that?"

"We do not with complete certainty. However, he climbed up and down the bank more than once. Would he do that if he had conducted just a single journey over the ice? Why? It is more likely he went back and forth multiple times, following the exact same route and stepping off and back onto the ice at this same spot on the bank."

"Was this to fetch birch twigs?" I hazarded.

"But no bundles of twigs were deposited outside the castle on the night in question, that we know of. Besides, there is a plentiful supply of birch twigs in the woods on the other side of the castle. That spot is far easier to reach and, moreover, obviates the need for crossing the ice and potentially falling through. No, the Thurrick was on some other errand."

"Eve reported that the Thurrick was carrying a sack upon his back. Could it be he had a child inside it and was looking for a nice secluded spot to consume the infant?"

I tendered this ghoulish suggestion in jest, although the laugh with which I framed it was not a comfortable-sounding one, even to my own ears.

Holmes's corresponding laugh was far more jovial, and not a little self-deprecatory.

"Ha, Watson! Sometimes you astound me."

"I do?"

"Here am I, wracking my brains to reconcile all these perplexing data, and you have come along and with just a casual, offhand comment cut straight to the heart of the matter."

"I have?"

"Unquestionably you have. The sack. The Black Thurrick's sack. Remind me, how did Eve depict the figure of the Thurrick to us at Baker Street?"

"I am not sure. Dark, did she say? And I think she used the adjective spindly as well. Those glowing eyes, of course."

"Very good. But with regard to the creature's posture, what do you recall? Her precise words."

"You are asking me to quote verbatim from a conversation held almost two days ago."

"Well, if you cannot, I can," said Holmes. "She said, 'A figure bent almost double, with a heavy sack upon its back.' Bent double. A heavy sack. Our Black Thurrick was indeed carrying something as he crossed the lake. He was ferrying said burden from the castle to here. Eve happened to catch sight of him in the throes of just one such trip, but one may safely assume he repeated the process several times that night."

"But what was in the sack?" I said. "And where was he taking it to?"

"Excellent questions, both. Was there a rendezvous with some accomplice here on the bank?"

"Does the snow not reveal anything?"

Holmes gave a hapless shrug of the shoulders. "About activities conducted a week ago? No. As at the castle gatepost, too much time has passed and too much new snow has fallen in the interim. The grass stems on the bank retain the imprint of the Thurrick's passage, but I found that particular piece of evidence because I was looking for it explicitly and had a fairly good idea where it might lie." He wafted a hand towards the expanse of open ground that lay beyond, dotted with shrubbery and hillocks. "To search for similar traces across the good hectare of land we see before us would be a fool's errand. It would be like looking for…"

"…a needle in a haystack," I finished for him.

"Again, the right proverb for any occasion," Holmes said, eyebrow arching. "You are a veritable *Brewer's*, Watson. All is not lost, though. If for the moment we leave aside the possibility of an accomplice being involved, where might our Thurrick have travelled onward with his burdensome load? If the sack was as heavy as his stooped posture implies, he would surely not have cared to go very far. It is also likely, now that I think of it, that he is of slim build."

"What makes you say that?"

"Were the Thurrick as heavy as, say, me, then his weight, combined with that of the sack, would put him at undue risk on this ice. If that is the case, then he is exceptionally courageous."

"Or exceptionally rash," I said.

"Well, quite. The more so in the event that he was performing multiple journeys back and forth across the lake. But back to my previous avenue of enquiry. Where did he go from here? He would have deposited the sack, or at least its contents, somewhere not too far from here, somewhere conveniently situated…"

Holmes started scanning the vicinity, his gaze sweeping in an arc from left to right like the beam from a lighthouse.

Then, with a sudden start, he cried, "Needle in a haystack! Watson, you have done it again! In your chronicles of my exploits you often paint yourself as something of a dunderhead, but that does you a disservice. You are little short of a genius!"

Flattered though I was to be thus acclaimed, I was utterly in the dark regarding the nature of the inspiration I had sparked in Holmes. I opened my mouth to beg for clarification, but my friend was already off, bounding across the snow with rapid strides. We had been standing still for some while, and it took me a moment or two to stir my numb limbs and chase after him. I am sure Holmes was feeling the biting cold as keenly as I, but he seemed immune to its effects. I could only assume the excitement of following clues acted as an extra layer of insulation.

Our destination was a copse of conifers that stood some three hundred yards from the lake, their snow-weighted branches hanging almost to the ground. As Holmes parted the pendulous fronds, dislodged snow tumbled down upon him from above in glittering, iridescent spicules. He plunged into the copse, and I saw nothing of him for a full minute, instead only hearing him as he trod around and let out the occasional murmur or muted cry.

Eventually he said, "Watson, would you care to join me?"

I thrust my way into the copse, where I found Holmes on hands and knees, inspecting the soil. The trees provided a thick canopy that snow could not penetrate. There was just bare earth around the bases of their trunks.

"What do you see?" Holmes asked.

"A man ruining his trousers."

"Aside from that."

"Soil."

"Precisely."

"What of it?"

"What does one normally find lying beneath conifers? Needles and pinecones, of course. A thick bed of needles and pinecones, which the trees have shed."

"Ah, so when I mentioned a needle in a haystack…"

"My mind alighted upon the idea of the needles of coniferous trees, such as the ones in this copse which happened to lie within my field of vision. But back to my point. Here on the ground, in place of needles and pinecones, there is a layer of soil. We have to dig through it to find what we would otherwise expect to." Holmes demonstrated by clawing away handfuls of the loose earth to reveal the matted brown needles and occasional pinecone beneath. "Now, why would that be? What makes this copse so exceptional?"

My face must have registered blankness, for he tutted and said, "The soil has been transported hither and distributed evenly over the ground."

"Transported and distributed by... the Black Thurrick."

"I would have thought it the most elementary of deductions," Holmes said with some asperity.

"His sack contained soil, then?"

"That is what I am saying, Watson. Soil removed from elsewhere and disposed of in this copse, out of sight, where it is highly unlikely to be stumbled upon by another party. Several sacks' worth of the stuff, I would say."

"I cannot for the life of me fathom the purpose of that."

"I am entertaining one or two hypotheses, but none that I can affirm with any great certitude as yet." Holmes straightened up, brushing down his trouser legs. "Well, this has been a useful exercise, but I think you and I have communed with Mother Nature long enough for one morning. What say we repair to the castle and find ourselves a roaring fire to get the circulation going again, eh?"

"I doubt I have ever heard a more agreeable proposal," said I.

Chapter Eleven

AN ADDITIONAL BENEFIT
OF DOMESTIC RETAINERS

The hearth in the main hall at Fellscar was blessedly ablaze, and Holmes and I luxuriated in its radiance until the chill was banished from our bodies. Throughout, I noticed Holmes's gaze wandering time and again to the shield that hung above the mantel. At one point I caught him tapping a forefinger against the cleft in his chin, a mannerism I had come to associate in my friend with a state of deep concentration.

Whatever it was that he found so absorbing about the shield eluded me. It was a rather plain escutcheon, as these things go, with only the prancing lion on top lending it any great visual interest. I had seen many a family coat of arms with more to commend it to the eye.

Thanks to our excursion around the lake, we had arrived

back at the castle after the coachload of Allerthorpes had departed for Yardley Cross. It is an odd sensation to be a guest in someone's house when the hosts are absent, even if only temporarily. It feels almost as though one is an intruder, and one is loath to make oneself seem too much at home, lest it be construed as impolite.

I voiced this sentiment to Holmes, who replied to the contrary.

"For our purposes, Watson, the position could not be more advantageous."

"I do not see how, but I imagine you are about to tell me."

"Who is at Fellscar now but us and the servants?" said he. "And one must never underestimate the usefulness of servants when it comes to criminal detection. You will recall our involvement some four years ago in the matter of Lady Eva Brackwell and the blackmailer Charles Augustus Milverton."

"All too well," I said with a shudder of revulsion. "You dubbed the latter 'the worst man in London', and you were not far wrong."

"You will also recall how I, in the course of my investigation, adopted the guise of a rather roguish plumber, Escott by name, and wormed my way into the affections of Milverton's housemaid Agatha."

"You did somewhat more than that. You became engaged to the girl."

Holmes acknowledged this with an unabashed bow. "For as long as was necessary. When I broke it off…"

"At my insistence. You would have been happy simply to disappear from her life, never to be seen again. That would not have been fair."

"When, at the insistence of the most scrupled man I know, I broke it off," Holmes resumed, "Agatha soon got over her heartache and found consolation in the arms of my love rival. As I understand it, they are married now and have a child, with another on the way, so all is well. No harm done. But what was the aim of my deception?"

"You learned from the maid the exact layout of her master's house, so that we might burgle it."

"The point of this little reminiscence being simply to remind you that domestic retainers can be a mine of useful information, which the diligent prospector may extract by means of painstaking, methodical digging. A servant sees more, hears more, knows more about his employer's doings than even the employer's dearest friends. Likewise he or she possesses an intimate understanding of the day-to-day workings of the household, which may prove invaluable. If one can crack the shell of the individual's discretion, one can bring to light all manner of facts one might otherwise never have learned. And hark! I hear just such a person approaching now." He lowered his voice to a level only I could hear. "Why, I do believe it is Trebend. What luck. The very member of staff I was most hoping to talk to, for who is a greater authority on life both below stairs and above than a butler? Quick, Watson. Look casual. No, not like that. Not so stiff. More natural. That's better."

Trebend glided into the hallway, pausing to direct a courteous nod towards Holmes and me.

"Good day to you, Mr Trebend," said Holmes.

"Good day, sir."

"I gather Dr Watson and I have been abandoned. The family have gone to church."

"That is so. They should be back around noon. Is there anything I may help you with?"

"Not at present, thank you. This excellent fire is providing all we could ask for. Unless, that is, you would be willing to satisfy my curiosity on a few small matters."

"I shall endeavour to do so, sir," said the slenderly built servant, "although I must point out that I have a great many demands on my time just at present. Mr Allerthorpe has tasked me with overseeing personally the erection and decoration of the Christmas tree. The gardener and two of the footmen are even now bringing said tree in from outside. Furthermore, sundry Allerthorpe kin are due to arrive today for the celebrations, and I am to arrange the distribution of them amongst the guest bedrooms."

"Of course, of course," said Holmes sympathetically. "And how are the Allerthorpes to work for?"

"I've no cause for complaint, sir. None whatsoever."

"I imagine Thaddeus Allerthorpe keeps you on your toes."

"I have been in service my entire adult life. I have suffered worse masters."

"Does he pay well?"

"My salary is perfectly adequate, commensurate with my station."

"And you feel well treated by him and the rest of the family?"

"Why should I not?"

Trebend was becoming pained and even a touch testy. He was impatient to get on with his duties, but more than this, I could tell that Holmes's probing was discomfiting him. He was loath to be drawn on the subject of his employers, doubtless through ingrained professional discretion.

My friend seemed to sense the same thing, for he changed tack. "I note that your accent is not a local one."

"It is not, sir."

"Other staff, those whom I have heard speak, speak uniformly in a Yorkshire brogue. You are clearly a Londoner."

"Born and bred, sir."

"Yet the surname Trebend betrays Cornish roots, does it not? Many a name in Cornwall, whether place or person, begins with the 'Tre-' prefix."

"Well, that's as maybe. I am not one who has been bothered overmuch about his genealogy. Although, come to think of it, I do recall my father once mentioning something about ancestors in Cornwall. Bodmin, I think he said."

"Nevertheless, you are a fair way from London."

"A man may travel where he likes, sir, and take work where he finds himself," said Trebend with a complaisant smile. "As it happens, I consider the neck of the woods where I have fetched up to be very congenial. Some consider the landscape rather too rugged and bare, but I, having grown up amid the hurly-burly of a city, find its wildness and emptiness bracing. The locals are friendly, too, more so than in London. I have been made to feel quite at home."

"Then there is your wife's marmalade," I interposed good-humouredly.

"You are correct about that, Doctor. Margery's marmalade is a significant regional attraction."

"She cited it as the reason you will never sue for divorce."

"Said that, did she?" Briefly, Trebend's lugubrious expression softened into something close to amusement. "Well, she may not be wrong. But she, above all else, accounts for why this Londoner has found a contented berth in the East Riding. She is a fine woman, as anyone with eyes can see. I knew, from the day I took up my post at the castle, that she would become my wife."

"Mrs Trebend was here at Fellscar before you?" Holmes said.

"She was, sir. She has been the family cook for nigh on a decade."

"And how long have you yourself been in the Allerthorpes' employ?"

"A little over two years. And now really, gentlemen, if you will excuse me. There is much to be done."

"Of course," said Holmes, with a gesture that craved pardon. "We have detained you long enough."

After Trebend was gone, Holmes tugged my sleeve and said, "To the kitchen. You have already made the acquaintance of Mrs Trebend. I should like to do so myself. She sounds a redoubtable woman, and moreover she is among those select few who can lay claim to having seen an actual ghost. I am keen to interrogate her on the topic."

"Please be circumspect, Holmes," I said. "Mrs Trebend is such a marvellous cook. I should hate for you to aggrieve her and thus possibly impair the quality of her fare. Mealtimes are about the only thing that makes staying at Fellscar Keep bearable."

"Ever mindful of your gastric welfare, Watson," said Holmes, "I shall, I assure you, be the soul of tact."

Chapter Twelve

THE SMELL OF MELANCHOLY

The kitchen was full of steam and scurrying bodies. At the centre of it all, the calm hub amid the frenzy, was Mrs Trebend, labouring over the stove and occasionally doling out commands. The two legs of mutton I had seen her with earlier were being transformed into a casserole, and the smell which emanated from the bubbling pot in front of her was so appetising that my stomach started to growl.

"Can you come back later?" the lady said to Holmes plaintively. "I have two dozen extra people to prepare lunch for, and after that, supper for the same number plus a further dozen."

"I beg just five minutes of your time, my good woman. You can surely spare me that."

"What is it concerning?"

"Oh, this and that," Holmes said airily.

Mrs Trebend pondered, then made up her mind. "Five minutes, and not a second more." She beckoned to a kitchen maid. "Keep pouring in the lamb stock and the carrot juice, a little at a time, and stir. Do not let it boil over. It must simmer. Do you hear, girl? Simmer not boil."

"Yes, Cook."

"And, Goforth!"

The scullery maid sidled in from her workplace. "Cook?"

"I see half a dozen saucepans all in need of washing up. Hop to it!"

"Yes, Cook."

"Why can't you be more attentive to your duties, you dozy creature? It isn't as if they are that arduous."

Goforth bit her lip, looking as though she had much to say to Mrs Trebend but was prohibited from doing so by her lowly station. "Sorry, Cook. I shall try harder, Cook."

"See that you do." Wiping her hands on a cloth, Mrs Trebend ushered Holmes and me out of the kitchen.

"Well?" she said.

"I am interested to learn about the ghost you saw not so long ago," said Holmes.

"Oh. That."

"Would you be so kind as to rehearse the details of the incident, and also show us where you saw this apparition. It was in the east wing, was it not?"

She shook her head warily. "I'm not sure as I'd be willing, Mr Holmes. It was the most frightening thing, and I don't much care even to think about the incident, let alone relive it. Besides, it happened in the east wing, as you say, and the journey there and back will by itself use up the best part of your five minutes."

"It would help a great deal with our enquiries. I would, moreover, regard it as a personal favour." Although Holmes had no particular fondness for the opposite sex and had developed none of the finer feelings for them which motivate most men, he was perfectly capable, when required, of affecting the kind of urbane masculine charm that was known to win women over. Nor, with his aquiline profile and high widow's peak, was he unhandsome, and when he softened his usually piercing gaze a certain way, it lent his eyes a captivating twinkle. In most cases the results were favourable to him, and Mrs Trebend proved no exception.

"Very well then," said she with a mild sigh. "I know enough about you to know you are a persistent fellow and rarely take no for an answer."

"Watson's writings do perhaps exaggerate my tenacity when I am on a case, but not much. If it makes any difference, we are both formidable fellows, he and I. I seriously doubt any spectre, even the most ill-intentioned, would dare show its face while you are in our company."

While Mrs Trebend escorted us to the east wing, Holmes sought corroboration of the facts that we already knew about her ghostly encounter, although he did not reveal that Shadrach Allerthorpe was their source. "From what we have been told, reports about strange sounds in the east wing started not long after Perdita Allerthorpe's unfortunate demise."

"I discounted them myself, at first," said Mrs Trebend. "I mean, in a building like this, as large as this, there's bound to be the odd creak and moan, isn't there? Floorboards warping as the weather changes. Window casements straining in their frames when a gale blows in off the moors. Then there's the mice scuttling around behind the wainscoting; we lay down traps for them, of course, but you can never catch them all. Yet time and again I was hearing tales about noises that allegedly were not... normal."

"From whom? Was it just fellow members of staff? No one else?"

"Oh no, none of the family goes into the east wing, Mr Holmes. Especially not after dear Mrs Allerthorpe..." She faltered. "Well, you know. These days they avoid it like the plague, and who can blame them? Terrible associations it has for them. Staff, on the other hand, are required to polish and dust there, once a month on average. If we didn't keep on top of things and only cleaned the wing the one time a year it is actually used – at Christmas – the job would be far harder."

"So you yourself did not hear any of these noises," said Holmes, "and rejected the idea that they might have some unnatural origin?"

"Absolutely. I hate to say it, but some of the employees at Fellscar are not what you'd call sophisticated. The East Riding is an area steeped in superstition, and folk around here from a certain background seem to thrive on stories of witches and strange beasts and meteorites and the like."

"But not you."

"Not me, sir. I've always thought of myself as a sensible lass. Still do, which makes it all the more difficult for me to reconcile myself with what went on that July night."

"You went to the east wing to investigate something a scullery maid claimed happened to her."

"Becky Goforth," Mrs Trebend confirmed. "The girl you saw me addressing a moment ago. And by the by, if you thought I was being hard on her, really she is the stupidest creature. A pretty face but precious little going on behind it. You have to explain even the simplest task twice or even three times in order for her to grasp it. And she is truculent, as though she thinks her position beneath her. It is a poor combination in a scullery maid and fair tries the patience.

"Yes, Goforth came back from the east wing all of a dither and trembling like a leaf, and spun a yarn about this unseen being who blew out a candle. She said she'd heard muttering, too, as though somebody was speaking right by her ear, and yet when she looked round, there was nobody there. 'I could not make out the words,' she said, 'but it were a horrid-sounding voice, Mrs Trebend, it were. Low and hoarse and full of hatred and wickedness, like. Whoever it was that were talking, they did not want me there, and that decided me that I did not want to be there either; and so I ran. I ran like the wind.'

"Now, I thought this just so much blether, and I made no bones about it. 'You are quite the giddy simpleton, Goforth,' said I. 'You have let your imagination run away with you.'

"'No, Cook,' replied she, 'I swear to you, on my mother's life, it's true!' And she was so adamant, and so het up, I was halfway to believing her."

"Might I ask what Goforth was doing in the east wing so late in the day?" said Holmes. "That she was carrying a candle indicates she was there after nightfall."

"Cleaning, I should imagine. Although her duties are largely restricted to the kitchen, she is expected to carry out more general household tasks as well, and her hours are long. The time, as I recall, was around ten o'clock, and my own working day was coming to an end, but I felt I ought at least to follow up on her claims, if only to show her how foolish she was being. I invited her to come with me and point me to the spot where her candle had been extinguished and where she'd heard the voice, but she refused point-blank.

"'I shan't ever go back to the east wing after dark, Mrs Trebend,' she said, 'not for all the money in the world.' I saw no alternative, then, but to go on my own."

"Very intrepid of you."

Mrs Trebend shrugged her shoulders. "I like to think I am not without mettle."

"You did not ask someone else – your husband, perhaps – to accompany you?"

"Robert was just then going over the wine cellar inventory with Mr Allerthorpe, and besides, why should I trouble anyone to join me on what I fully expected to be a fruitless exercise? I fetched a lamp and performed the very journey we three are now undertaking. Goforth had identified the location of her strange occurrence as being midway along the main ground-floor corridor. This corridor, indeed, that we are just coming to."

After a trek through the castle that included a fair few twists and turns and ups and downs, we had arrived at a long, broad passage with windows positioned at ten-yard intervals along one side and a row of doors, similarly distributed, along the other. The windows faced north, so the daylight was muted. Perhaps for that reason, the air felt chillier and damper than elsewhere on the premises. Added to that was the impression that this was obviously an unfrequented place. Even if I had not known it already, I would have been able to tell. Unfrequented places have their own unique atmosphere, and also their own faint yet distinct odour, one that is hard to describe but still readily identifiable. If melancholy can be said to have a smell, that is what it smells of.

Down the gloomy corridor we traipsed, and with every step, the tingle of apprehension that had started up in my belly deepened. I did not anticipate us running into a ghost, not in the middle of the day. Ghosts were nocturnal creatures, were they not? Yet the mere possibility that this part of Fellscar was haunted had me entertaining uneasy thoughts, the kind I might normally have given short shrift. My senses were alert for any anomaly – a shift in the light, an incongruous sound. Within me warred two paradoxical desires: a burning curiosity to witness something truly inexplicable, and a pusillanimous reluctance to. Increasingly the latter was gaining the upper hand.

Mrs Trebend halted. "It was just here," she said. I discerned the slightest of quavers in her voice, and my admiration for her grew. She was grappling with her fears and mastering them, perhaps better than I was – and she had more justification for being afraid than I did, since she was the one who had run into a ghost here before, not I.

"Now, be precise please, Mrs Trebend," said Holmes. "Relate the sequence of events exactly as they unfurled."

"Well, to begin with there was nowt untoward, as best I could tell. I shone the lamp around, and its light revealed only that which you yourselves can see right now. The moon was the merest sliver that night, so there was scant other illumination. I waited a minute or two, not clear what I was waiting for but almost completely certain that no weird manifestation would occur. I was all prepared to give it up as a waste of time, but then I… I felt it."

"It?"

Her voice dropped almost to a whisper. "It is hard to put into words, Mr Holmes. You know that uncanny sensation one has, that tickle at the back of the neck, when one thinks one is being watched? Not just thinks but *knows*. I had that. It was as though another person had joined me in the corridor and was creeping up on me from behind. I looked back and saw nobody, but the feeling – no, the *certainty* – would not go away."

Almost on a reflex, I glanced over my shoulder. There was no one in that corridor save the three of us. Of course there wasn't.

"Then came the touch," Mrs Trebend continued. "This ice-cold sensation on the bare skin of my forearm, as though someone were drawing their fingers across it, not in any comforting way, but meanly, insinuatingly. At the same time, the lamp flame guttered, and if not for the chimney surrounding it, I daresay it might have gone out.

"I summoned up the courage to speak. Frankly, I'm not sure how I managed it, and I can tell you now, the sound that came out of my throat was a reedy croak, hardly my usual voice at all.

"'Who's that?' I said. 'Is someone there? Who are you? State your name.'

"Well, answer came there none, and in a sense I was glad, for I had precious little desire to hear the 'horrid-sounding voice' Goforth had described. Frankly, if it had accosted me, I might have fainted on the spot.

"'Is that you, Mrs Allerthorpe?' said I. 'If it is, please know that we miss you and grieve for you. You were a kind mistress, and Fellscar Keep is not the same without you.' I meant it. As you must be aware, Mrs Allerthorpe had her troubles, but between bouts of madness she was as good-hearted and gentle a soul as one could hope to meet. 'I'm sorry if you are unsettled in your eternal rest,' I went on. 'But for your own sake and the sake of those you have left behind, you must move on. You shouldn't remain here when a much better life awaits you in the great beyond.' I believe that quite sincerely, sirs. If anyone deserves the solace of heaven, it is Mrs Allerthorpe.

"More time passed, and I was beginning to think that my mind had been playing tricks on me. Then... It was just over there."

She raised a forefinger to point. At the same time her eyes grew wide, as though she was seeing right now the same macabre sight she had beheld two months previously.

"I shan't go any closer," she said, her voice even more hushed, "but you see where I mean. Where the corridor turns the corner. To this day I cannot say quite what I saw, but it was a figure – a figure in motion. A pale, fleeting shape, clad in a long flowing garment. And it was – what is the word? Diaphanous. Like tulle or cheesecloth. I could see through it to the wall behind. All I had was the merest glimpse, there then gone in an instant, but that was all I needed to see. I could not quit that spot quickly enough, gentlemen. I ran so fast, in such a mad panic, that I stumbled and fell several times. You should have seen the bruises on my shins. In my mad dash I collided headlong with Mr Allerthorpe – Shadrach, that is – who was good enough to escort me to the drawing room and ply me with whisky in order to calm my nerves."

"Spirits to banish a spirit," Holmes remarked.

I shot him a look. This was no time for glibness. Mrs Trebend was panting, her body reacting to the memory of the traumatic stimulus much as it must have reacted to the traumatic stimulus itself.

"Take slow, deep breaths," I advised her, in my most soothing tones. "You are safe. It is in the past. Sherlock Holmes and I are here, and we can protect you." Could we? From a discarnate entity? Possibly not, but it seemed the right thing to say.

Before too long, Mrs Trebend's fit abated. Her stare

became less wild and her breathing returned to normal.

"I can't stay a moment longer," she declared. "I *shan't*." And, suiting the action to the word, she spun on her heel and hastened away.

Holmes watched her go with a detached, faintly ironical look on his face.

"Poor woman," I said. "She is scared half to death even just remembering the incident."

"It certainly would seem that way. Yet what did she feel? Frigid fingers? Or was it a gust of cold air, much like a draught? Say what you like about Fellscar Keep but it is definitely draughty, and even in July the air outside at night would not have been warm. And what did she see? A 'pale, fleeting shape'. It could have been anything. The shadow of a cloud passing across the moon. An afterimage in her vision, perhaps, left there by the lamp's flame. She styles herself sensible, but what if, in fact, she is no less suggestible than the scullery maid? I contend that Goforth's account of extinguished candles and strange voices primed Mrs Trebend for some sort of unearthly shenanigans, and lo and behold, unearthly shenanigans was the interpretation the good woman put on otherwise perfectly explicable phenomena. So often do we bend reality to conform to our expectations, rather than the other way round. Say I told you that the front door at Baker Street is dark blue."

"It is not. It is black."

"But say I was quite strident about it, even to the point of becoming angered at your obtuseness. A blue so dark, it could be mistaken for black."

"I would think you quite deluded. I might also suggest you lay off the cocaine for a while." This was a constant refrain of mine at the time. The drug's deleterious effect upon my friend's constitution were marked, and I was keen for him to wean himself off it.

"But," said Holmes, "the next time you entered the house, might you not look askance at the door's paintwork? Might you even think that, viewed in a certain light, possibly it *was* dark blue?"

Grudgingly, I allowed that I might.

"Mankind is inherently inclined towards co-operation," Holmes said. "It is how we create societies and moral consensus. We want to agree with one another, on the whole. Thus, if one of us insists a certain thing is true, and maintains his standpoint in the face of all opposition, others will eventually come around to his way of thinking."

"If it is somebody who commands respect," I said, "then I grant you it may happen. I hold you in high esteem, for instance, and therefore I would be more likely to see your dark blue front door than if it were, say, Lestrade making the allegation – or Wiggins. And that is where your premise falls down."

"How so?"

"Because Mrs Trebend does not respect Goforth. You have seen the contempt in which she holds the girl. She bullies her. If the roles were reversed and Mrs Trebend were Goforth's subordinate, then it is conceivable that Goforth could have an influence on her thinking. As things stand, Mrs Trebend would have been more likely *not* to see a ghost, simply because Goforth is of so little consequence to her and she would rather spite her than support her. She said herself that she went to the east wing with the express purpose of proving Goforth wrong. The fact that she *did* see a ghost therefore surely lends weight to her testimony. Instead of refuting Goforth's claims, she ended up reinforcing them. You stand contradicted."

I was quite pleased with this counterargument of mine. I thought it a model of deductive reasoning, one that would have done Holmes himself proud.

He, for his part, simply said, "Or else I stand vindicated, if what I am beginning to suspect is borne out later on."

"And what are you beginning to suspect?"

"At present, I am but dimly grasping the outline of something. But then it may be that I am guilty of the very crime I just deplored – bending reality to conform to expectations – and that I perceive a coherent image where there is none. We shall see."

He would not be drawn to clarify this rather enigmatic statement, but instead embarked upon one of those energetic flurries of activity that so often attend his investigations. For a while he stalked back and forth along the corridor, pausing every now and again to study some piece of minutiae that caught his notice. More than once he went down on all fours, crouching with his nose so close to the floor that he looked like a Mussulman at prayer. He opened each of the doors in turn, revealing a succession of bedrooms and in one instance a bathroom. By way of conversation, nothing escaped his lips apart from an occasional wordless grunt, to which I did not feel duty-bound to respond.

Leaning back against the wall with my arms folded, I waited. I have to confess that my eyelids drooped, my chin sank to my chest, and I may even have dozed off. My night of poor sleep was taking its toll.

Holmes startled me out of my drowse by clapping his hands.

"Done, Watson!" he declared.

"And?"

"My examination has been instructive, up to a point."

"What have you found?"

"Very little, but then even the absence of evidence can be useful, in that it eliminates certain possibilities, leaving the field clear for others. I will, however, draw your attention to this window, and in particular to the frame here adjacent to the stone mullion that divides the two casements."

The frame in question was made of iron. A small section at the base was warped out of true. It bent outwards, leaving a narrow gap between frame and casement that was roughly the size of a throat lozenge.

"In this, I propose, lies a reasonable explanation for Goforth's blown-out candle and the eerie touch Mrs Trebend felt. On a windy night, a gust of air forcing itself through this tiny aperture would have some considerable impetus, sufficient to snuff a candle flame and to mimic the sensation of cold fingers on flesh. This same gust might, moreover, generate a sound resembling a guttural, inarticulate voice, by making the casement vibrate within its frame somewhat like a clarinet reed. Do you not agree?"

"It is plausible."

"And yet... When was the section of frame bent? And how?"

"Does it matter?"

"Possibly not. Nor does it matter that the bent section is at the bottom of the frame and that the mullion is a sturdy stone pillar. Or does it?"

"You are talking in riddles."

"It must sound that way to you. It does even to me. But sometimes it helps to air my thoughts aloud, disjointed though they may seem. I can weigh their value with my own ears, and also judge them according to your reaction. Now then, this way." He marched to the corner where Mrs

Trebend had glimpsed her darting ghost. "What lies along here, I wonder?"

A short second corridor, running perpendicular to the one we were on, terminated at a small, arched door. Holmes twisted the ring-shaped handle and the door swung outward.

Before us lay a black emptiness. We leaned in through the doorway, and as my eyes adjusted I gathered that we were looking at a cellar. The dim light filtering in from the corridor behind us picked out rough stone walls that were hung with ragged strands of cobweb. A dank, clammy smell rose to greet my nostrils.

Just visible was the cellar's earthen floor, which lay some ten feet below and could be reached by a flight of steep wooden steps.

Or so I thought, for no sooner had I set foot on the top step than Holmes arrested my progress with an arm across my chest.

"Steady, old friend," he said. "Look down. You will see it is not as straightforward as you think."

I looked down, as instructed. Beyond the first step there was a second, but beyond the second there was nothing. I had thought that the rest of the wooden staircase was lost in darkness, but actually it had rotted away. Only the topmost portion still clung in place, anchored just beneath the door's threshold by rusty iron bolts.

"Bless me!" I said. "If not for you, I would have fallen

and broken my leg, maybe even my neck. That staircase is a liability. You would have thought someone would put a warning sign on the door; better yet, ensure it was locked."

"I wonder if anybody realises that the staircase is gone," Holmes said. "By the looks of it, it collapsed some time ago. One can just make out the remnants down there in a heap on the floor. The cellar itself, perhaps a cold store once, is clearly long disused. Who is to say the family even know it exists? Especially since it is in the east wing, where few go."

"We should mention the staircase to someone. Have something done about it."

Holmes shrugged indifferently. "If you like, but I doubt it will be a high priority to the Allerthorpes."

I retreated from the doorway, and Holmes closed the door. Then, with a frown, he reopened it.

"Why did you do that?" I enquired.

"I have my reasons," said he, eyeing the hinges. "And yet – at the risk of being accused of talking in riddles again – those reasons may be inconsequential."

He turned the handle a couple of times, raising and lowering the latch. Then, closing the door once more, he strode off down the corridor. I, for one, was glad to put the east wing behind us. I sincerely hoped that, during the remainder of our stay at Fellscar, we would never have cause to go back there.

In that respect, alas, I was doomed to be disappointed.

Chapter Thirteen

THE GATHERING OF THE CLAN

Following our visits to the kitchen and the east wing, Holmes located a gunroom filled not only with shotguns and ammunition but with various other items of sporting equipment. He quickly established the presence of fishing tackle, including several reels of line and a whole host of hooks and flies.

"Plenty of material here for our Black Thurrick to have availed himself of," he said. "So much so that the absence of a single hook and a reel would hardly be missed."

"You remain convinced that the bundles of birch twigs are, as you put it, an 'inside job'?"

"It could hardly be otherwise, Watson."

Around midday, the Allerthorpes and Danningbury Boyds returned from Yardley Cross, and shortly thereafter their Christmas guests started arriving. Some came in their own coaches and were met in the main courtyard by the castle's ostler, who led the horses away for stabling. Some were ferried from Bridlington by Winslow in the brougham. Some made their own way from the railway station by hired dog-cart.

In all, this first wave of invitees comprised some twenty or so persons, ranging in age from infants to octogenarians, and as they streamed in, Fellscar Keep grew incrementally busier and noisier. Servants bustled hither and yon, carrying luggage and other belongings. Whereas before it had been easy to find solitude and silence in the castle, those commodities became rarer, and the place felt all the better for it.

To add to the general sense of excitement, a twenty-foot-tall, freshly felled fir now stood in the central hallway. It was supported by a purpose-built structure made of cross-braced planks, nailed about the base of its trunk. True to his word, Trebend had supervised the tree's installation, and various lesser servants had been assigned the job of decorating it. Shinning up and down stepladders, they had adorned the boughs with gilded walnut shells, painted stars, angels, overflowing cornucopias and other such baubles. Candleholders had been attached to the tips of branches and paper chains draped around the tree in gay, colourful patterns.

Further festive opulence could be seen everywhere one

looked. A gigantic ribbon-strewn holly wreath had been affixed to the exterior of the main door, while, all over the castle, bannisters were entwined with sprigs of evergreen, doorways festooned with velvet swags, and fireplaces garnished with tinsel. Mantels now displayed Christmas cards, many of which depicted the traditional scenes of snow, joy and harmony but a few of which showed perverse and even bizarre images. One, for instance, boasted a lovingly detailed watercolour of a dead robin, while on another a row of comical frogs paraded beneath umbrellas and, on another still, insects danced in a circle, wielding musical instruments and seemingly drunk.

For the first time since Holmes and I had got there, I was finding Fellscar no longer quite so depressing. The decorations brought life to its gloomy, austere hollows, while the influx of Allerthorpe relatives had a similar rejuvenating effect.

My mood improved further at lunchtime, for once the members of the extended family learned that Sherlock Holmes was a houseguest, he – and I too, to a lesser extent – was lionised. Holmes's celebrity was not yet what it would latterly become. By 1890 I had published only two volumes of his exploits, *A Study in Scarlet* and *The Sign of Four*, each of which, while having met with a respectable critical reception, had so far sold only in modest quantities. Yet in certain circles, their subject's fame was spreading and his analytical methods were much discussed.

As the meal progressed, the Allerthorpes – for simplicity's sake I shall refer to the extended family collectively as such, even though a good quarter of them were related by marriage and did not share the surname – prevailed on Holmes to demonstrate his powers of observation and inference. He obliged, if with a certain reticence. He correctly identified a man's preferred brand of cigarette, the significance of each of the various adornments on a woman's charm bracelet, and the name of a small boy's teddy bear, based upon the scantest of clues. It irked him to be pressed to perform these feats, I could tell. He thought them frivolous and beneath his dignity. Politeness, however, constrained him from refusing. "It would be a poor guest indeed," he told me afterward, "who declines to give his hosts what they ask for. So what if it entails prancing around like the organ-grinder's monkey? As long as one ingratiates oneself."

Next, the Allerthorpes looked to me to entertain them, and I spent an hour relating a number of Holmes's more notable cases. The role of raconteur comes naturally to me, I have found, and it was no hardship to tell them about Neville St Clair and his impersonation of a disfigured beggar, or about Holmes's accomplishments at the racing stables at King's Pyland, or about the notorious bank robber John Clay and his so-called Red-Headed League. Our pursuit of the Countess of Morcar's missing blue carbuncle, which had taken place the previous December, provided my audience with great amusement, while an account of Dr Grimesby Roylott's ghastly crimes elicited shocked gasps and even at one point, to my regret, caused a young girl to squeal in terror and bury her face in her mother's skirts. I had already begun preparing some of these narratives for publication. The chance to hone and refine the telling of them was not one I could sensibly pass up.

Lunch ended around three-thirty. There was barely time to pause for breath, however, for now the remainder of the houseguests turned up, and in fairly short order everyone was dressing for supper and we found ourselves once more in the dining hall. This time the children ate separately, in another room, but there were still so many people seated around the table – over forty – that, huge as it was, it felt crowded.

The wine had flowed freely at lunch, and it flowed even more freely now. My feelings towards Thaddeus Allerthorpe were becoming that bit more charitable. Say what you like about the man, but he kept a good cellar.

After the main course was cleared away, there were toasts. Thaddeus stood and invited us to stand and raise a glass, first of all, to the Queen.

"The Queen!" we chorused.

"And to the Prince Consort, without whom the Great British Christmas would be a far drabber affair than it is now."

This was certainly true, for it was the late, lamented

Albert who had introduced many of his homeland's yuletide customs to this country and who had thus made Christmas an altogether more extravagant and memorable celebration than it once was.

"The Prince Consort!"

"God rest his soul," someone added.

"And finally," said Thaddeus, "to all of you, my kith and kin, for once again gracing Fellscar with your presence."

"Hear, hear!" said Shadrach.

"And not forgetting our esteemed friends from London," Thaddeus said with a courteous nod towards Holmes and me.

"To us!" everyone cried.

That he had referred to Holmes and me as "esteemed friends" suggested Thaddeus's initial coolness towards us was at last thawing, or at any rate he was becoming accustomed to us. Or was it that, in front of all these other Allerthorpes, etiquette demanded he act cordially towards everyone under his roof, even those for whom he harboured feelings of hostility?

"It has," he continued, "been a difficult year. You all know that."

There were murmurs of sympathy around the table.

"I swore to myself that I would not mention Perdita, but I find myself incapable of not doing so. Perdita loved Christmas. She, more than anyone, looked forward to this annual gathering of the Allerthorpe clan. She would be planning it for months ahead. She…"

His voice cracked and his eyes glistened. The gruff façade he usually presented to the world began to crumble, and for a moment he became lost in sombre contemplation. Then, steeling himself, he resumed his speech.

"She would have wanted to be here, I know. It is through no fault of hers, or anyone's, that she has not been able to make it. She was an angel, but her inner demons were strong, and in the end they got the better of her. What we must do, to honour her memory, is be of good cheer. When last you were all here, it was for her funeral and wake. Then, sorrow ruled. Now, over the coming week, we shall be the opposite of sorrowful. Perdita would want it. I want it, too. And in that spirit, I enjoin you all to make this final toast to Perdita, and to joy."

"To Perdita," we said, "and to joy."

I felt rather moved, and my opinion of the Allerthorpe patriarch rose a further few notches.

In accordance with the dinnertime custom, before the arrival of the pudding course every woman moved two places clockwise around the table. This meant that I was no longer hemmed in between a rather crusty dowager and the peevish Olivia Allerthorpe, but instead, as luck would have it, I had the pleasure of Eve's company to my left and, on the other side, that of a distant cousin of hers.

The latter was of a similar age to Eve and a delightful girl, although I'm afraid I do not recall her name. Together, the two of them were attentive and charming. They quizzed me about life with Holmes, of course, but also about my experiences as a doctor and my sojourn in Afghanistan. More than once a humorous anecdote of mine brought them out in peals of laughter, to the point where Holmes himself shot me an arch look across the table and waggled the fourth finger of his left hand, as if to remind me of my wedding vows. But was there any harm, I thought, in a happily married man engaging in genial badinage with a pair of bright, vivacious young things? Before now I had seen handsome men paying court to my Mary at parties and she reciprocating with smiles and attentiveness, and I had felt not so much as a flicker of jealousy, so assured was I of her fidelity.

"Might I just say, Miss Allerthorpe," I told Eve during a lull in the conversation, when her cousin had turned to speak to the fellow on her right, "you seem considerably more at ease with yourself. Even yesterday afternoon I noted tension in you still; and then, of course, there was your contretemps with Mrs Danningbury Boyd last night. Today, however, you are quite transformed."

"It is good of you to remark upon it," replied she, "and I am glad to report that I do feel more myself than I have in a good while."

"Your father's speech just now must have been difficult to listen to."

"But it was heartfelt, and Papa is so rarely that. It helps to have all these people with us, too. Conviviality has a way of taking one's mind off one's own problems."

"And your extended family is nothing if not convivial," I said, casting an eye around at the flushed, happy faces, the glasses being raised to lips, the spoons lifting sherry trifle and apple charlotte to eager mouths.

"A cynic might suggest that they are enjoying themselves so much because none of them is having to spend a penny on board and lodging," said Eve. "They come every year expecting to be entertained lavishly, and they know Papa has deep pockets and will not disappoint them."

"No question – on present showing your father gives the lie to the stereotype of the tight-fisted Yorkshireman."

She leaned a little closer to me and said, with a confiding air, "Not everyone is as rich as the Fellscar Allerthorpes."

"Few are."

"What I mean is that there are branches of the family, represented in this very room, that do not share our good fortune at all. And you watch. Over the coming days you will see that there are those who eat and drink more than the rest, and otherwise take advantage of Papa's largesse. They are the ones of more modest means. I would hesitate to call them spongers, but they seem to feel that the

Allerthorpe money is shared inequitably and so every year they must do their utmost to redistribute it."

I chuckled. "A thought that does you little credit, my girl."

"Oh, it isn't just me who thinks it. Raz does too."

"Which reminds me," I said. "Where is Erasmus? I did not see him at lunch, and I do not see him now. Is he unwell? Has he taken to his room? If so, I would be more than happy to pay him a call, in a professional capacity."

"You are kind, Doctor, but Raz is fine. As far as I know, that is. After church, he elected to stay in Yardley Cross."

"For what reason?"

"With my brother, one never can tell. He simply said he was meeting someone and would be home later. In fact, I expected him to be back by now."

"Who is this someone he was meeting? Did he say?"

"He didn't. A friend, I presume."

I resolved to convey this piece of intelligence to Holmes at the earliest opportunity. I was sure that he too had noted Erasmus's absence, and I could now tell him the reason for it, in the event that he himself did not already know.

"You are close, you and he," I said.

"You might say Raz and I have formed a stronger bond than most siblings share. It has been tempered by adversity."

"Your mother? Her condition must have been trying for you two more than anyone, as her children. You grew up, as it were, under a cloud."

She nodded. "And now we find ourselves united in the face of our father's own aberrant behaviour."

"He does seem to treat you with a certain abrasiveness. Your brother in particular."

"I fear it is because each of us in some way reminds him of Mama. Raz has her bone structure and complexion. He is practically the spitting image of her. And I am told that I hold myself much as Mama used to and have a similar vocal intonation. Every day we serve as constant reminders to Papa of what he has lost. It must be hard for him to bear. He did love her, you know."

"One would think that might make him cherish you two all the more."

"Perhaps, in time, things will improve," said Eve. "Speaking of which… Dare I enquire how Mr Holmes is faring with his investigation?"

"Well now, Miss Allerthorpe—"

"You can start calling me Eve, Doctor. I feel we are sufficiently well acquainted by now."

"Of course. Eve." I took a sip of wine. I must have been on my sixth or seventh glass by then. "Well now, Eve, Sherlock Holmes often plays his cards close to his chest. There are times when he is happy to include me in his thought processes, and times when he seems to feel my input might muddy those limpid waters. I am convinced, though, that he is making good progress. He has caught the scent of something, and his nostrils are twitching. I would not be surprised if he were to bring everything to a head before too long and treat us to one of his theatrical dénouements where he whips back the curtain and reveals the machinations going on behind."

"So he can account for my sighting of the Black Thurrick?"

"I strongly suspect it."

"And for the bundles of birch twigs?"

"All four of them," I replied confidently.

Eve frowned. "Four?"

"Yes, four. The one at the gatepost. The one outside your study. The one outside Erasmus's bedroom. The one this morning outside…"

My voice trailed off. All at once I realised I had blundered. Blundered badly.

"Go on, Doctor." Eve appraised me with a speculative eye. "'The one this morning outside…'?"

"I misspoke," said I, hastily backtracking. "I meant three. There have been only three bundles of twigs. Not four."

"No, you were quite specific. There has been a fourth one, hasn't there? Where? Whom did the Thurrick visit?"

Her voice was rising, and with it the clear sense of panic which, until then, she had been successfully keeping tamped down.

"Miss Allerthorpe – Eve – if I tell you all, you must not let it disturb you. Promise me that."

"I can promise no such thing."

"Then bear this in mind. It was I whom the Black Thurrick left twigs for. Not you, nor any member of your family. I, an outsider. The Thurrick would appear to be aiming his sights not at the Allerthorpes exclusively but at any resident of the castle. That, surely, must allay your concerns. You are not being singled out. You are merely one amongst many."

"But I am still one!" she said indignantly. "Still a victim of the creature's attentions, and I do not know why!"

"Please, keep your voice down," I said, glancing over at Holmes.

"No, Doctor, you do not tell me to keep my voice down," Eve said, louder than ever. "You do not have that right. The Thurrick has struck again, and you were keeping it from me?"

"To be fair, it was Holmes's idea. He thought the news might upset you." And, I added to myself, he was not wrong.

"Then perhaps Mr Holmes is the one I should be censuring. Mr Holmes!" she called across the table. "Dr Watson informs me the Black Thurrick has returned and is up to his vicious tricks again."

Other conversations in the dining hall dwindled. Heads turned. A couple of people echoed the words "the Black Thurrick" in a puzzled manner.

"Can you confirm it?" Eve went on.

Holmes skewered me with a look, then said to Eve, "It is true, and I regret that you have found out in this way. I would rather you had not known about it until after I had got to the bottom of the matter and been able to unmask the wrongdoer."

Eve shoved back her chair, tottering to her feet. Her thighs bumped the table, making silverware and stemware jump.

"It is never going to end, is it?" she said fretfully. "I thought I was safe. I thought the mighty Sherlock Holmes would be my bulwark against this nightmare. I thought... I thought..."

She sagged to the floor, dissolving into tears. I moved to help her. Her shoulders heaved.

"Dr Watson," said Thaddeus Allerthorpe in a voice like a rumble of thunder, "what in heaven's name is going on? What have you done to my daughter?"

"Nothing. I – I have made a miscalculation, that is all. We must get Eve to her room, and I will tend to her there." Embarrassed as I was, my only instinct was to look after the young woman. "Will someone help me with her?"

The assembled Allerthorpes were agog. Had Erasmus been present, I imagine he would have rushed to his sister's side. As it was, nobody stirred in response to my entreaty.

"Very well." I hoisted Eve upright, whereupon she practically swooned in my arms. I caught her, supporting her weight.

This second, even more dramatic collapse provoked uproar. Now, at last, someone came to my aid – the distant cousin whose name escapes me. Together, she and I sat Eve in her chair, and smelling salts were fetched. Eve was roused from her stupor, and the two of us escorted her upstairs. I did not look back as I exited the dining hall. I did not want to see Holmes's expression, for I knew it would be full of recrimination.

Chapter Fourteen

MY LONG NIGHT OF PENANCE

An hour later, I had reassured myself that Eve was not in any danger. The cousin had settled her in bed and I had administered a dose of Eve's own chloral hydrate. The young woman was now sound asleep, and her face, in repose, was no longer etched with lines of torment.

I found myself a chair, positioned it outside her bedroom door and sat. I was feeling all kinds of fool. I was resolved to keep a waking vigil, in case Eve should come to during the night and require my services. It was my fault she had had this fainting fit; my fault she had relapsed into the fraught condition from which she had previously shown a marked recovery. The least I could do, then, was look after her.

I could blame my slip of the tongue on the wine. I had drunk plenty of it, and it had lowered my inhibitions. Still, that did not excuse what I had done. Given my brother's predilections and the abyss into which they had sunk him, I try to be temperate when it comes to alcohol. On this occasion I had failed. I had let myself down, and in the process let down Holmes's fragile-souled client – and, for that matter, Holmes himself.

Assorted family members stopped by to enquire after Eve's welfare. Some were sincere, some prying and some scathing. On a couple of occasions I was asked to account for Eve's mention of the Black Thurrick. The subject of Lady Jocasta's legacy was also raised. I refused to give a specific answer regarding either line of enquiry. I told my interlocutors that it was none of my business, by which I wished them to understand that it was none of theirs.

Then Thaddeus Allerthorpe arrived and subjected me to a ten-minute tirade, which I withstood with forbearance. I offered nothing in return except contrite apologies and a promise to ensure that Eve received the very best care I could offer.

"I should think so too, Doctor," he said. "But only until tomorrow morning. We have a family physician, Dr Greaves, whom I shall summon then."

"I will attend to your daughter for as long as is necessary. There really is no need for another doctor."

"There is every need, because as of tomorrow morning you are *persona non grata* in this household. So is Sherlock

Holmes. I will see to it that the pair of you are on your way to Bridlington station at the earliest opportunity."

I put up a protest, but he was having none of it.

"You have brought no benefit and caused only trouble," he said, glowering. "You are done here."

It would seem that any of the approval Thaddeus had bestowed upon us that afternoon was now rescinded. Holmes and I were back to being in his bad books, our names inscribed more indelibly in its pages than before.

Last but not least, Holmes himself came.

"Dear me, Watson," he lamented. "What a shambles."

"Please, Holmes. Not you as well. I have just had Thaddeus Allerthorpe tear a strip off me, and I am still smarting. I made a mistake. I know it."

"The error, arguably, was mine. I should not have sworn you to secrecy about the twigs. You are too honest a fellow. Dissembling is not your forte."

"I know you are only trying to make me feel better, and it won't wash. I have ruined everything. The case is over. We are to be thrown out of the castle first thing tomorrow. Thaddeus made that clear to me in no uncertain terms."

"To me, too. Before he came to you he spent a while ranting at me in his private study. The words 'charlatan' and 'swindler' were bandied about, and towards the end of this ad hominem attack I believe the possibility of legal action was even aired. By that point, I had rather stopped listening; and besides, I know an empty threat when I hear one. He also gave me to understand that he is calling in the family physician."

"Yes. Dr Greaves. I hope the fellow is competent."

"Did he mention to you that he wishes this Dr Greaves to interrogate Eve, with a view to establishing the soundness or otherwise of her mental state?"

"That did not come up in the conversation. What if Greaves finds her mentally defective?"

"Then he will certify her as such, and she will not receive her inheritance."

I bristled. "Dash it all! It just gets worse. And when you were starting to make some headway with the case, too."

"Well, it is to be regretted," said Holmes philosophically, "but if we are no longer welcome, we are no longer welcome. The Allerthorpes will just have to handle their problems without us."

"It is Eve I feel the most pity for."

"As do I. However, if Dr Greaves does not deem her insane and she can last out the next three days, then at least her legacy is secured. You are not coming to bed, I take it. Your position on that chair is very much one of a sentry at his post."

"Until tomorrow morning and our unceremonious eviction, I remain Eve Allerthorpe's physician."

"Then I shall bid you goodnight."

"Goodnight. And, Holmes? I am sorry."

"Don't be," said he with a dismissive wave. "Comestibles aside, there is little I shall miss about Fellscar Keep."

And so began my, as I thought of it, long night of penance. Slowly the general hubbub in the castle settled down as the Allerthorpes, in dribs and drabs, turned in for the night. By around ten o'clock a hush had descended over the place, and by eleven I reckoned myself the only one on the premises who was still awake. Silence filled the stairwells and the long, winding corridors, a silence broken now and then by the lonely sigh of the wind outside and the odd tick, creak and groan such as any building makes, however small or large, at night – as though nothing, not even a manmade structure anchored to the earth by its mass and its foundations, is ever truly at rest.

For the most part I just sat. Once in a while I would get up and walk around in order to ease a cramp in my leg or restore feeling to my numbed backside. I leafed idly through a novel, which I picked out from a bookcase nearby. It was a historical romance whose content struggled to hold my interest – my literary tastes erring more towards the contemporary and the sensational – and eventually I abandoned it. I then busied myself reciting the bones of the hand, starting with the distal phalanges, the intermediate, the proximal, and progressing from there through the metacarpals and the carpals and onward into the arm. I did the same with the feet. This was a technique I had developed while attending my surgical course at Netley, to help keep me awake when on call at night. It had also served to cement knowledge of human anatomy in my memory.

Midnight struck, a number of timepieces chiming the hour near and far within the castle. By one o'clock, I was struggling to keep my eyes open. Though I knew I should stay alert in case Eve needed me, I also knew that, were I to nod off, I would doubtless hear if she called out in distress from her bed and would be up and running in seconds. Surely, I thought, I was permitted to snooze, if only for a few minutes. No one could begrudge me that, especially after the night I had had before.

Once the decision was made, my body succumbed to sleep almost instantly. I jerked awake some while later, thinking I had just had the briefest of naps, only to discover that it was gone four. I peeked in on Eve, who was still sound asleep, then went to fetch myself a glass of water.

Just as I was returning to my chair, I heard the scream.

Chapter Fifteen

LEAPING TO A CONCLUSION

It was a female scream, and my first instinct was that it had come from Eve's room. I flung open the door, but the girl remained exactly as she had been when I had looked in a few minutes earlier: snoring softly, her eyes closed. My sudden, precipitate intrusion did not disturb her.

I shut the door and stood in the corridor for several moments, ears pricked. The scream, though brief, had been full of panic and terror, and had come as such a shock that the hairs on my body had stood erect and were only just now wilting again. I waited for it to be repeated, but that did not happen.

Where had it come from? Close by, I thought, but not too close. This narrowed down my options somewhat, but in a place as vast and maze-like as Fellscar Keep, pinpointing the origin of the sound was still going to be a challenge.

"Think, Watson," I said to myself out loud. "Apply Holmes's methods, if you can."

Concentrating, I replayed the scream in my head. What had been my immediate thought upon hearing it? That it had emanated from Eve. Eve, however, was patently not its source.

Then, if it had not come from her room, but had seemed to, might the scream have come from *beyond* the room?

Now I was getting somewhere. Yes. The scream had been outdoors.

Eve's bedroom was situated at the tip of the north wing, occupying the entirety of the far end of its third floor, with windows on three sides looking out to the east and west as well as to the north. The scream could have come from any of those three directions.

I re-entered the room, more circumspectly this time. I padded across the rug and peered out between the curtains of each set of windows in turn.

Moonlight shone down upon the lake. A part of me was loath to gaze out over that frozen expanse of water in case, as Eve had done, I should spy a hunched, sack-carrying figure loping across the ice. Absurd though I knew this notion to be, the trepidation I felt was real enough. It was a genuine relief to see nothing out there but blank, empty whiteness.

From the west-facing window, I could make out the portion of the castle on that side. From the east-facing window, the view was much the same. There was the east wing, looming like some craggy cliff against the star-strewn sky. Of the two wings, the east was the wilder looking, its architecture somehow more disorderly, replete with more excrescences than the west, as though its design had been inspired by nightmares. Or was my imagination imbuing it with such a phantasmagorical aspect simply because I knew that Perdita Allerthorpe had committed suicide there and that a ghost, possibly hers, was reputed to walk its halls? Was I, as Holmes had said, bending reality to conform to expectation? No, I did not think so. Regardless of its notoriety, Fellscar's east wing outdid the rest of the castle in presenting a crazed, menacing aspect to the world.

I was all set to back away from the window and attempt some other means of fathoming where the scream had come from, when my eye fell upon a shape on the lake. It lay a few yards out from the foot of the castle, humped upon the ice; small, angular, odd, a thing of dappled black and white.

I squinted in order to sharpen my focus, and I noted that there was something awfully familiar about the shape's outline. The irregularity of it. The jumble of it.

My mind harked back to the Battle of Maiwand. To

fallen soldiers littering arid ground. The haphazard splay of their limbs. The sprawled, uncaring dead.

My breath caught in my throat. In that moment I knew, beyond a shadow of a doubt, that I was looking at a corpse.

Minutes later I was pounding on Holmes's bedroom door. He emerged in nightshirt and dressing gown, smoothing his sleep-mussed hair down.

"What is it, Watson? Why are you knocking me up at this ungodly hour?"

Urgently I explained, and in no time my friend was dressed and accompanying me to the east wing. We arrived in the self-same corridor we had visited during the day, and there we encountered a little girl in nightclothes. The child was wandering up and down, dragging a ragdoll behind her and looking sleepy and confused. She could not have been more than five or six years old. I recognised her as the little girl whom I had terrified at lunchtime when describing how Grimesby Roylott fell foul of his own deadly swamp adder.

"I heard a strange noise," she said to us. "It woke me up."

"Which is your room?" I asked her in gentle tones.

The girl pointed.

"Why not go back to bed?" I encouraged. "There is nothing to worry about."

"Why are *you* here?" she challenged. "Did you hear it too? It sounded like a lady screaming."

"It was a fox," I said. "Do you know the high-pitched bark a fox makes at night? It can resemble a human scream."

"Really?"

I nodded reassuringly. "Are your parents in one of these rooms?"

The girl pointed to another door. "I went in and woke them up. Daddy was cross, and Mummy told me I must have dreamed it."

"You didn't, but it was a fox, that is all."

"You're not lying?"

"Heavens, no. Why would you say such a thing, my girl?"

"Because Mummy said you made it up about the snake."

"The snake?" I presumed the girl's mother had told her that the swamp adder was fictitious, in order to quell her fears. "Well, yes, that was a story. But the fox is real."

The child finally accepted my explanation and traipsed off to her room.

In the interim, Holmes had taken up position at one of the corridor's windows and was gazing out. Now he said, "If it were in any doubt that your scream occurred, that little lady was the final proof. Her sharp young ears detected it, even if those of everyone else in the east wing, slumbering more soundly than she, did not. And look."

His lips were grimly pursed. Going to his side, I gazed out too.

It was somehow gratifying to see the corpse, lying on the

ice nearby, just where I had espied it from Eve's bedroom. So, after all, this had not been a trick of the mind, my tired eyes construing something innocent as something sinister. At the same time the sight was, of course, dreadful.

"Who is it?" I asked. "Can you tell?"

"Not with any degree of certainty, but whoever it is, she is wearing a maid's outfit."

There was no question about that. I was able to descry a black dress, a white apron and a white mob cap.

"We must get down there," I said. "There is a chance she may be alive."

"Lying so still? The head bent at an unnatural angle like that? I doubt it very much. Nonetheless, you are right. This is a death in suspicious circumstances, and the sooner I am able to examine the body, the sooner I may determine whether or not foul play is involved."

"Perhaps we should rouse the rest of the household first."

"And cause a hullabaloo? Everyone tearing around like headless chickens, getting in the way? No, thank you."

"Just Thaddeus Allerthorpe, then. He deserves to know what has happened."

"Not yet. Not until after I have done my bit. Now, I don't much fancy the idea of climbing out of this window and slithering down the wall to the lake. There are rocks projecting from the base of the island and one might sprain an ankle when landing upon those, or worse, if one is not careful. I could use a rope, I suppose, fastened to the window mullion, but I wouldn't know where to find one in the castle. No, without a tether the descent is altogether too risky an enterprise. But I have an alternative plan."

Said plan involved first obtaining a dark-lantern, one of which was habitually left beside the front door in case of need. Then we headed outside via the main gate, traversed the causeway, and walked around the perimeter of the lake to the point nearest the east wing. From there we stepped onto the ice and crossed until we reached the spot where the corpse rested. I will not pretend that the last part of the journey was easy or pleasant. My feet kept slipping, and every time the ice creaked and crackled beneath us, my heart was in my mouth.

Soon enough we made it, but Holmes warned me not to get too close to the body.

"She has fallen," he said, shining the dark-lantern upon the poor wretch in front of us. "From some considerable height, it would seem. The impact was severe enough to crack the ice, although not enough that she broke through. The ice must be thicker here than elsewhere, but we should tread carefully all the same. Its integrity has been compromised."

So saying, my friend passed me the lantern. He then went down on all fours and, from this position, eased himself fully prone.

"I am increasing my surface area," he said, "and thus spreading my weight out over the ice and lessening the pressure I place upon it."

"I realise. Just please be careful."

"When have you ever known me to do otherwise?"

I could have cited several past instances when Holmes had acted rashly or with impetuosity, but I chose not to. Instead, I watched, full of misgiving, as he slid forward on his belly until he was within touching distance of the corpse.

Slowly he performed a circuit around the body, staying prone as much as possible, Meanwhile I kept the lantern's beam trained upon a point just in front of him, taking care not to shine it in his eyes.

"Come here," he told me, beckoning. "Now aim the light at her face. Do you see who it is?"

"Why, it is the scullery maid. Goforth."

The girl's face bore that queer look of shock which I have beheld all too often on the just-deceased. It always makes me think that dying, one thing we all have in common, still comes as a surprise to some.

"Indeed. And hullo! What is this? Alter the angle of the beam slightly downward, would you. Just so. See that?"

I glimpsed something sparkling at Goforth's neck, just above her collar.

Holmes reached out a hand and undid the top button of the collar to reveal that, beneath her blouse, she was wearing a pendant necklace. Jewels glittered brightly in the lantern light.

"Bless me," I said. "Are those… diamonds?"

"They appear to be."

"Fake, surely."

"I do not think so, not with that lustre. And the chain they are strung upon appears to be sterling silver. I am no jewellery expert, but I think we are looking at a very expensive piece of feminine adornment."

"But no scullery maid could afford such an item, not on the pittance her sort earns. She must have stolen it."

"Let us not leap to a conclusion," Holmes said, straightening up. "Speaking of which…" His gaze travelled upward, taking in a finial-capped turret which perched atop the east wing, directly above us. A window casement stood ajar there, and I had no difficulty extrapolating the trajectory of Goforth's fall hither from that aperture. It was a straight downward plummet.

"Is that the window from which…?" I began.

"From which Perdita Allerthorpe threw herself? I would wager good money on it. We know that she was in the east wing when she died, and did Eve not tell us that she plunged from the castle's highest tower? We are looking at the castle's highest tower. Goforth seems, for whatever reason, to have emulated Mrs Allerthorpe's example."

"But why?"

"That is something we must establish, along with the reason the girl is wearing a diamond necklace which, for one such as her, is hopelessly unaffordable."

Holmes's eyes narrowed. His expression became grave.

"Watson, the game grows more complicated," said he. "I was already convinced that this case is about more than Lady Jocasta's money, or a sinister figure from folklore, or ghosts. Now I am surer than ever that dark forces are at work in Fellscar Keep. They may not be of supernatural origin but they are no less dangerous for that. Notwithstanding Thaddeus Allerthorpe's demand, you and I are honour-bound to remain here and see this thing through. Do you not concur?"

What else could I say to that but yes?

Chapter Sixteen

NO ACCIDENT

"I ... I don't believe it," stammered Shadrach Allerthorpe, staring down at Goforth's body.

His brother beside him was even more lost for words. The sight of the dead scullery maid had left him utterly dumbfounded.

It was Holmes who had proposed we get Shadrach out of bed first, rather than go straight to Thaddeus. He had thought Thaddeus would take the news of Goforth's death better if he heard it from his brother, rather than from two people towards whom he currently bore a deep resentment. Not only that but, given the manner in which the girl had died, Thaddeus might need the kind of moral support that a close relative could provide.

"Was it – can it have been – an accident?" Shadrach was

not so much asking a question as expressing a wish.

"There is a remote possibility that it might have been," said Holmes. "Perhaps Goforth was cleaning the window. She leaned out in order to polish the outside of the panes, overreached herself, and lost her balance. Until I inspect the room, which I mean to do shortly, I cannot discount this scenario. It would seem, however, on the face of it, somewhat improbable. At four in the morning? I know a scullery maid works long hours, but isn't her first task of the day relighting the stove and otherwise setting up the kitchen in readiness for preparing breakfast? And who cleans windows in the dark? It is a daylight job, surely."

"What's worse is that it is that window, of all the windows in the castle," said Shadrach. "I take it you are aware of its significance."

"Yes. Not to put too fine a point on it, it is the window from which Mrs Allerthorpe also fell to her death. For another person to meet their end not just in a similar manner but by plunging from the exact same spot… Well, suffice it to say that, where suspicious deaths are concerned, I do not believe in coincidence."

The widower spoke up. "Nobody goes there now."

"I beg your pardon, Mr Allerthorpe? Would you care to elaborate?"

"The room." Thaddeus's voice was choked with emotion. "I have made it plain that nobody should go there any more. It is to be left alone."

"I see," said Holmes. "Then that, I'm afraid, lends weight to the notion that this death was no accident. If Goforth was not supposed to be in the room, she was disobeying your edict for a specific purpose, and that purpose in one way or another may well have contributed to her demise."

"She was there to meet someone, who pushed her out of the window?" Shadrach said. "Is that what you are telling us?"

"Or, driven by some unbearable inner torment, Goforth decided to follow in her late mistress's footsteps. Again, until I have gathered more data, I cannot assert or reject anything with any definitiveness. I trust that in this one instance you will make an exception to your embargo, Mr Allerthorpe, and permit me to enter the room?" My friend addressed this last remark to the senior of the two brothers.

Thaddeus's gaze went from Goforth to the window and back again. He could only have been thinking of his wife and reliving the moment of her suicide. Were it not for the lake's thick skin of ice, servants would now be dragging its waters to look for a body, just as they had done a little over a year ago.

"I could call the police, I suppose," said he.

"And I would recommend it," said Holmes. "But not yet. Before the officials become involved, give me a chance to establish first whether we have a murderer in our midst or there has simply been an unfortunate recurrence of a tragedy. You must know that there is no one more capable in this regard than me. You should also bear in mind that the local police may find themselves out of their depth and an inspector will have to be summoned from London to handle the case. I know for a fact that Scotland Yard is currently snowed under with work, no pun intended. You would be lucky if the fellow arrived by this evening. It is far more likely you would have to wait till tomorrow. Do you really want this hanging over you in the meantime, with all your houseguests present?"

"Do you honestly think you can clear the matter up quickly, Mr Holmes?" asked Shadrach.

"I promise to give it my best try."

Shadrach turned to his brother. "Thad, I say we should take Mr Holmes up on his offer."

Thaddeus gave a noncommittal grunt, but Shadrach persisted, and now I understood that there was an additional reason why Holmes had insisted on waking up the latter and bringing him in on this. He had foreseen that Thaddeus might need cajoling, and Shadrach stood a far better chance of succeeding on that front than we.

At last Thaddeus gave in. "Very well, Mr Holmes," he said, with a nod of assent so tiny it was scarcely a twitch of the head. "You get your wish."

"Thank you," said Holmes. "Just for clarity's sake, Watson and I are no longer to be summarily ejected from Fellscar?"

"You are not."

"And what about Dr Greaves, your family physician?"

"What about him?"

"Do you still wish to call him in to attend to Eve?"

"I don't see why not."

"Might I suggest instead that Watson remain her doctor for the time being?"

Thaddeus eyed my friend warily. "Is this because I told you of my plan to have Greaves evaluate her mental condition?"

"In part, yes."

"You do not think that I should."

"I think that it is your prerogative as a father to do whatever you feel is best for your daughter," Holmes said. "It is not my place to tell you what is and is not appropriate where she is concerned."

"Too right, sir. What you have perhaps failed to grasp is that I am motivated by nothing but concern for Eve's wellbeing. I am not seeking, through Greaves's auspices, to prove that she is in some way mentally deficient. On the contrary. I would be less than diligent if I did not have him assess her, in the hope that he will give her a clean bill of health, in spite of her present affliction. Then it will be official, with no room for doubt, and all can proceed with the execution of the will as planned. I have no desire for her to lose out on her legacy from Jocasta. I did not much care for the woman myself. Far too bossy and strident for my tastes. But she was my wife's sister, and if it was her wish for Eve to receive her money, then I must respect it and do all I can to see that it is fulfilled."

From the way Thaddeus spoke, I believed him to be in earnest. I realised I had misjudged his intentions regarding Eve. The error was pardonable, though, in so far as Thaddeus had hitherto given precious little indication that he cared about his daughter, or his son for that matter.

"All the same," said Holmes, "it might be better to delay bringing Dr Greaves in. This nasty business…" He motioned at the body in front of us. "It will hardly improve your daughter's condition when she finds out what has happened, as she inevitably will. It may indeed cause a further setback, meaning that Dr Greaves will be more, not less, likely to deliver a negative appraisal."

Thaddeus Allerthorpe let that sink in for a moment, before giving another of those barely perceptible nods. "I take your point. I shall leave Greaves out of it, for now."

"Good man. Incidentally, can either you or your brother tell me anything about the necklace Goforth is wearing?"

Holmes pointed to the item of jewellery where it hung around the girl's throat.

Both brothers peered. Both frowned.

"What on earth is she doing with such a thing?" Shadrach said.

"You have not seen it on her before?"

"Never. I would remember if I had. It is quite remarkable. What about you, Thad?"

"Same. Is it the genuine article, Mr Holmes?"

"To the best of my knowledge, yes. I would say there is in the region of a hundred pounds' worth of diamonds strung together there. Unless you are exceptionally generous towards your servants, Mr Allerthorpe, that is equivalent to twenty years' salary for someone such as Goforth."

"An heirloom?" offered Shadrach.

"Hardly," said Thaddeus. "The girl hails from a local family of negligible means."

"And if you were poor in every respect save that you owned a valuable diamond necklace," said Holmes, "would you still choose a life of drudgery? Or would you not sell the necklace in order to further yourself in the world?"

"Then the only assumption one can make is that she stole it," Shadrach said. "Do you think that is so, Mr Holmes? The girl is a thief? She has purloined the necklace from one of our houseguests? In which case," he continued, warming to his theme, "is it beyond the realms of possibility that the necklace proved her undoing? Hear me out. Goforth had an accomplice with whom she was supposed to share the proceeds of her crime. They arranged a meeting in the tower, perhaps to discuss the division of the spoils. There was a quarrel. The accomplice, in anger, pitched her out of the window."

"Far-fetched but not wholly inconceivable," Holmes said. "My principal objection to the idea you have outlined is simply this: the accomplice would not have defenestrated Goforth without first wresting the necklace from her possession. It is too valuable for him not to have secured it for himself before killing her."

"But what if the accomplice was a man, much stronger than her, and the pair argued so strenuously that they came to blows? It stands to reason, then, that Goforth, knowing she would be overpowered and the necklace taken from her by force, might throw herself from the window rather than let him have it. She chose death over being done out of her share of the criminal proceeds."

"It would account for the fact that she is still wearing the necklace. A desperate measure, but one that afforded vengeance against him who double-crossed her. All of this remains speculation, however, until I have examined the room concerned. Would you, sir, be so good as to show Watson and me the way there?"

Shadrach consented.

"And I will muster up some servants," said his brother, "and have them bring a blanket to cover the girl with, and boards upon which to carry her off."

"Where will you put her?" I asked.

"There is a lean-to shed close by the stables. I do not want her in the castle proper."

"Sensible."

"You realise I cannot keep this a secret from my family," Thaddeus said to Holmes. "The servants will talk. Word will get around the castle in no time."

"You must deal with it as you see fit, Mr Allerthorpe. I would advise making an announcement to your family at breakfast. Perhaps, however, you should refer to the death in terms of a regrettable mishap, nothing more. It will cause less fuss and, so far as any of us yet knows, it is the truth."

Chapter Seventeen

A DEADLY *PAS DE DEUX*

From the top floor of the east wing a winding staircase led up to the tower. We arrived at a narrow door, which Shadrach Allerthorpe opened, not without a certain hesitance.

"My brother spent the days between Perdita's death and her funeral sitting in this room, mourning," he said. "Thereafter, he insisted that it be left untouched. I suppose he wanted it to be a shrine to her memory."

"Untouched but not locked?" Holmes queried.

"He is not a sentimental man and it is rare he makes requests of that nature. All the more reason for us to respect his wishes, without them having to be enforced by means of a key. To which end, I shan't myself go in, if you don't mind."

"I do not mind at all. Indeed, I would crave Watson's

indulgence and ask that he likewise remain outside, at least for the moment. What I am hoping is that the territory within, having remained virgin for several months until this morning, will yield clues more readily than well-trodden ground would."

Holmes, lantern in hand, disappeared through the doorway. Shadrach went back downstairs, and I was left standing on the staircase in the dark, twiddling my thumbs.

Fifteen minutes passed, and then Holmes emerged and beckoned me inside.

"Halt just there," he said as I crossed the threshold. "Not a step further."

The room was large and cylindrical, occupying the entirety of the topmost section of the tower. Chilly air sighed in through the wide-open window. There was little in the way of furniture, just a pair of mouldering leather-upholstered armchairs, a rocking chair and a couple of occasional tables, one of them upturned. Even before Perdita Allerthorpe's death, I doubted anyone would have had much cause to come here. The windows dotted all around the room's circumference would, given the tower's height, doubtless command panoramic views during the daytime, but aside from that there seemed little incentive to visit.

Holmes was looking pleased with himself. "This has been as profitable an exercise as I could hope for," said he.

"Let me take you through my discoveries. The floorboards, as you can see, are covered with a goodly layer of dust. In that dust you will perceive a number of footprints. Some are mine, but I have been at pains to keep those to a minimum. Remember how I rued the fact that the floor of the room above yours had been newly swept, so that the Black Thurrick had left no tangible trace of his presence there? Here, by contrast, we find a veritable cornucopia of dust-divulged evidence. To begin with, we can tell that a man entered the room first. Observe the line of larger footprints leading away from where you stand."

"How do you know he entered first?"

"I will come to that in due course. The man crosses to the middle of the room." Holmes illustrated by walking alongside the set of footprints, picking them out with the lantern's beam. "He stops here and waits. Note how the footprints cluster together, overlapping one another? They are somewhat like the petals of a tulip, angling out in different directions from a common centre. Our man remains in place but he is ill at ease. Nervous or impatient, possibly both, he shuffles his feet. At last a second person arrives."

Holmes returned to the door and picked out a second set of footprints.

"These prints are smaller than the others. The heel is narrower. They are unquestionably a woman's."

"Goforth's."

"They must be." Again, as with the man's footprints, Holmes traced their path. "She walks up to our unknown fellow. Notice how her prints are overlaid on his here, and here, partly obliterating them. That is how I know she came in second. Now the two stand facing each other. Presumably there is a dialogue of some sort. Then the man moves off to the window at a fast lick. The outline of his footprints is less well-defined than when he was walking at a more measured pace. The woman goes after him. She is up on her toes, running. As her footprints arrive alongside his, all at once they become scuff marks. He has seized hold of her, do you see?"

Holmes imitated a man grabbing another person by the scruff of the neck.

"But what happens next? As ever, the footprints tell the tale. There is a struggle beside the window. Both sets of footprints slither from side to side. It is now, during this sudden outbreak of violence, that the occasional table lying on its side here gets knocked over. It can only have been then. Goforth fights valiantly but our man prevails and manhandles her through the window."

So vigorously and convincingly did Holmes perform the mime that I had no difficulty conjuring up the sequence of events in my mind's eye. I now had a vivid image of Goforth's final moments as she was propelled from the tower to her death, emitting that last terrible scream. I felt, as if it were mine, her horror, her sense of helplessness.

"All that remains is for our murderer to quit the room," said Holmes, "which he does with understandable haste. His footprints leading back to the door are spaced further apart than any of the others. His stride is longer, therefore quicker. The grisly deed done, he wishes to leave the scene of the crime in a hurry, for fear that his victim's scream should draw attention. Yes, Watson, every single step of this deadly *pas de deux* is delineated on the floor. I defy you to gainsay my interpretation."

"It would be foolish even to try. The obvious question is who is this killer?"

"Ah, there you have me. We may eliminate Shadrach Allerthorpe from the list of suspects by simple virtue of the fact that the prints here belong to someone with size eight feet, and Shadrach, as we know from yesterday, is a size nine. However, that leaves plenty of other candidates. There are, by my estimate, some thirty adult males on the premises, counting both family members and servants. Since eight is the average shoe size for a man, the field remains wide open."

"The fellow was known to Goforth, though. That much is clear."

"Indeed. This has all the hallmarks of an assignation. He summoned her to this room. Were it the other way round, Goforth would have been waiting for him. The initiator of a rendezvous is invariably the first to arrive. Whether he meant to kill her all along, or it was a spur-of-the-moment decision, remains to be determined. I incline towards the latter view because he attacked her only after they had had a conversation. If he had wished Goforth dead from the outset, he would have lain in wait out of sight, perhaps behind the door, and sprung an ambush. I rather fancy that there was an attempt at negotiation here, which went awry."

"Nothing you have said so far invalidates the theory that the diamond necklace was the bone of contention between them."

"No," said Holmes, "and I am glad you mentioned the necklace. I will let you in on a little secret. I have seen its like before at Fellscar."

"You mean you know to whom it properly belongs? Then we know whom Goforth stole it from."

"Pay attention. I said 'seen its like'. By that I refer not to the necklace itself but to another item of matching jewellery. The diamonds on the necklace are of the particular cut known as a radiant cut, square in shape, trimmed at the corners. It is not a common style. Their setting is also distinctive, consisting of eight prongs per stone rather than the more customary four. At supper last night, one diner was wearing a bracelet made of radiant-cut diamonds in eight-prong settings."

"Who?"

"She was seated next to me for most of the meal, as it happens. Kitty Danningbury Boyd. Now, I realise that Mrs Danningbury Boyd is not a man, nor does she take a size eight shoe, so she cannot be our murderer. I realise, too, that just because she owns a bracelet that would seem to be a partner to Goforth's necklace, it does not automatically follow that the necklace is her property. Nevertheless it is she who I am most interested in talking to next."

Chapter Eighteen

DIAMONDS BEFORE SWINE

N ews of Goforth's fatal fall brought a resurgence of the febrile atmosphere that had previously gripped the castle, and it is perhaps no surprise that this time the mood was more intense. Wherever one went, the scullery maid was all anybody was talking about. I could not help but note, with irony, that a girl about whom none of the Allerthorpes had given a fig while she was alive – who few of them would even have been aware existed – had become, in death, a pivotal topic of conversation. For a brief while Becky Goforth was elevated from the lowest tier on the household scale of importance to the highest.

Even a death, however, was not enough to derail the Christmas festivities at the castle. All said and done, Goforth had still been just a scullery maid. Few would have noticed her absence, save certain members of the domestic staff who, already stretched thin by the demands of so many extra guests, were having to pick up the slack caused by her absence.

Nor was anybody aware, aside from Holmes, me, and Thaddeus and Shadrach Allerthorpe – and, of course, her killer – that Goforth had died in sinister circumstances. Thaddeus insisted to everyone that she had met her end through misadventure. All seemed satisfied with that, and no one felt moved to leave Fellscar. Even the parents of small children, who might have been expected to show concern for their offspring's tender sensibilities, chose to remain rather than go home. The youngsters, anyway, were not unduly distressed. Indeed, from what I saw, they were eager to learn the full gory details of Goforth's demise, fascinated to the point of ghoulishness, and it was a disappointment to them that no adult was willing to satisfy their curiosity. Death is an alien concept to the juvenile mind, so far removed from its understanding as to be all but meaningless.

Where Eve Allerthorpe was concerned, I myself was the one who informed her about Goforth. I broke it to her gently, at her bedside. I told her that the scullery maid had broken her neck in a fall but omitted to mention where the fall had taken place.

All things considered, she took it well. "The poor girl," she said. "We must notify her next of kin."

"Everything is in hand. Your father has charged Trebend with making the necessary arrangements. What you must concentrate on is yourself. Save your energies for Eve Allerthorpe, no one else."

"I am so tired, Doctor," Eve said, yawning.

"You are still groggy from the chloral hydrate. I recommend bed-rest for the remainder of the day."

"This place is cursed." Her speech was slurring. She was dozing off again. "We are doomed never to be happy."

"Not in the least, Eve. Your family has had a run of bad luck, that is all. Now sleep."

Shortly thereafter, Holmes and I found ourselves in Fellscar's main library, a room of truly gargantuan proportions, filled with enough books to keep any bibliophile occupied for years. Alongside novels and collections of plays and poetry there were atlases, encyclopaedias, almanacs, histories, bound volumes of magazines, and countless other works of reference, all sitting in rows, resplendent in their gilt and leather finery, like guardsmen on parade. It behoved me, as an author, to look for my own work amongst the multitude, but a cursory inspection turned up nothing. I consoled myself with the thought that my literary career was still in its infancy. The time would come, surely, when the name John Watson MD was a fixture on every bookshelf.

Our purpose for being in the library was not books,

however. Rather, it was to have a private audience with Kitty Danningbury Boyd, which Holmes had engineered by means of a politely phrased note, conveyed to her by a footman. When the lady arrived, she took her seat across from us with a sullen pout, as though she would prefer to be anywhere but here.

"Mrs Danningbury Boyd," said Holmes, "it is kind of you to spare us your time."

"I have no idea why you wish to speak to me," replied she. "Nor why your note stipulated that I come alone, without my husband. Without my husband – you were quite specific about that."

"For good reason, as you shall see. First, let me assure you that everything we say in this room today is in the strictest confidence. Matters of some delicacy are involved, and they pertain, as you may well have inferred, to Mr Danningbury Boyd. Hence I requested that he not be present."

Kitty Danningbury Boyd bridled at that. "You are on dangerous ground, sir," she hissed, her eyes narrowing to slits. "Take great care where you tread."

Her reaction was so disproportionately scathing that I wondered whether it was born of guilt. That was when it crossed my mind that this woman might, after all, be the one who murdered Goforth. She could have donned men's shoes, padding them out so that they fit her feet, in order to give the impression that the culprit was male. But then would she have known that the footprints in the tower room would be so readily interpretable by Holmes? And was she sufficiently calculating to try and throw us off the scent through this deception? If so, it pointed to malice aforethought, and that did not tally with Holmes's assertion that the crime was spontaneous rather than planned.

Holmes maintained an air of purest suavity in the face of Mrs Danningbury Boyd's ire. His smile did not falter in the slightest. "Your marriage is not a contented one," he said.

"How dare you."

"I do not think I am speaking out of turn. Watson and I witnessed the aftermath of your little row with Eve Allerthorpe the night before last. We know that you accused your cousin of flirting with your husband."

Mrs Danningbury Boyd made a token attempt at denying it, but Holmes forged on regardless. "Mr Danningbury Boyd seems to have a reputation as a ladies' man. He is inarguably handsome. His eye wanders, he is free with his affections, and you have accommodated yourself to that, even if at times resentment gets the better of you. Yet in Eve's case, I saw with my own eyes that she was not returning his attention. She was, at best, enduring it, and your allegations against her were unfounded and unjust."

"So you say. You know nothing. I have seen secret looks pass between them before now. Whatever act Eve may have been putting on for your benefit, in the past she has led Fitzhugh on. He is the victim here, not she. Can he help it if he is so irresistible to the opposite sex? If they fawn over him?"

I have seldom seen someone exhibit such a blatant disregard for the obvious facts. Kitty Danningbury Boyd was hardly fooling herself. She was definitely not fooling Holmes and me.

"It strikes me," said Holmes, "that in the area of looks, you and he are somewhat mismatched. Mr Danningbury Boyd could have married any of the world's great beauties. Instead he settled for you, a lady of, to be blunt, modest attractions. But I daresay your maiden name Allerthorpe, with its connotations of wealth, enabled him to overcome any qualms he might have had."

At that, Kitty Danningbury Boyd leapt to her feet, her eyes flashing. "Now you go too far!" she shrieked. "I have never been so insulted in my life!"

I must say I had to agree with her. Holmes had overstepped the bounds of civility.

"Calm down, madam," he said coolly, "and sit down. These displays of outrage are all very well, but you and I both know I am telling the truth."

Stiffly, her face still puce with rage, Mrs Danningbury Boyd resumed her seat. "If it isn't to cause offence, what, pray, are you hoping to achieve with these insinuations?"

"Firstly, to establish to both our satisfaction that I am in full possession of the facts regarding your relationship with Mr Danningbury Boyd. Secondly, to extend my sympathies. It cannot be easy being married to a man who is unfaithful in thought if not also in actuality. Every day you are on your guard. Every one of your female peers is a potential threat. You live in fear that one day he will commit adultery, or do so again if he has already, and you as the cheated-on wife will become an object of scorn and derision."

Emotions warred in Mrs Danningbury Boyd's face. She was furious with Holmes, but his abrupt switch to compassion had touched a vulnerable spot in her. I realised, now, that he was manipulating her. His initial cruelty was designed to make her more receptive to the blandishments that followed, whereupon she would be more pliable.

"It would drive even the saintliest woman to distraction," he went on. "She would be apt to do something, anything, to keep her husband from straying. Something desperate. Something drastic, even."

Again it occurred to me that Kitty Danningbury Boyd was Goforth's murderer. Holmes seemed to be hinting as much. But again I rejected the idea. Apart from anything else, it wasn't plausible that a woman who was not much larger than Goforth could have overwhelmed the scullery maid and ejected her from the window. Moreover, in a straight fight between the two of them, the younger and wirier Goforth, toughened by a life of hard graft, less pampered than Mrs Danningbury Boyd, was far more likely to have been the victor.

"Now tell me," Holmes said, "is that why you gave Becky Goforth your diamond necklace? The companion piece to the bracelet you wore last night?"

Kitty Danningbury Boyd looked astonished, then aghast. "That is not... How can you...?"

All at once, she crumpled. Covering her face, she fell to sobbing, a picture of utter dejection.

"You cannot possibly understand," she wailed. "You cannot know what it is like. The humiliation I must undergo every time Fitzhugh and I go out. Every dinner party and ball we attend. The hunt meet. The theatre. Bridge evenings. He does it right in front of me, blatantly, as if I am not there. Women are drawn to him like iron filings to a magnet, and he not only encourages it, he revels in it. I knew what he was like even before we were wed, of course. My every instinct was telling me ours could never be a happy union. But when he turned his gaze upon me... And he was so zealous in his pursuit. So insistent. How flattering it was to be courted by Fitzhugh Danningbury Boyd, the handsomest man in all Yorkshire. How thrilled I was when, scarcely a month into our courtship, he proposed. I could not have said no even if I had wanted to."

"He has no money, of course."

"None to speak of. A modest annuity from a trust fund set up by his grandfather was enough to keep the wolf from the door in his bachelor days, but still he counted on the charity of friends and lovers."

"Marriage brought an end to his relative penury, but no alteration to his Lothario ways."

"Much though I hoped it might. For a while I turned a blind eye. I put up with his unexplained absences from home, periods for which he would offer no excuse other than that he had been 'busy' elsewhere. Two, three days without sign of him, without word, not so much as a telegram. 'Busy'! Then he would come back and he would tell me he loved me, and I would believe him and would persuade myself that all was well. But the longer I let him get away with it, the bolder he became, until at last…"

Mrs Danningbury Boyd's hands tightened into fists.

"Until at last…?" Holmes prompted.

"Under this very roof," she said, her knuckles whitening. "Right under my nose."

"You are speaking of Eve?" I said.

"No, Doctor. Fitzhugh regards Eve as… practice, I suppose you could call it. He would never dream of actively wooing her. She is pretty, a convenient toy for him to sport with when no one more suitable is around. I lied just now when I spoke of them sharing looks. They do not. In that respect Eve is in no way culpable, and it was quite wrong of me to chastise her the other day. My temper got the better of me. I scolded her instead of the person I should have scolded."

"Then if not Eve, who…?"

"Come, Watson," said Holmes. "Try not to be so dense. Mrs Danningbury Boyd is clearly talking about Goforth."

"Oh," I said. "Ah!" Suddenly, albeit belatedly, things were starting to make sense.

"That – that little trollop," Kitty Danningbury Boyd said. "No better than she ought to be. Flashing those cow eyes at him. Leading him on. No," she corrected herself. "Again, I am being unfair. I have developed the habit of blaming the woman when really it is my husband who is at fault. I do it to protect my own dignity. The moment Goforth joined the kitchen staff – it was in March, as I recall – I could see she had taken Fitzhugh's fancy. She was good-looking, in a coarse country way. He had taken her fancy, too, but then that is hardly surprising. He kept finding excuses to visit the kitchen. He might return a dish to Mrs Trebend, asking if she could cook the meat a little more, doing this personally rather than have one of the staff do it for him, or he might simply say he wished to pay his compliments to her on her latest culinary masterpiece; but I knew he was angling for a chance to peer in through the door to the scullery and speak to the room's occupant. One time, I caught him in the scullery itself, conversing with

Goforth. She had her arms up to the elbows in suds, scrubbing away. He was leaning over her, closer to her than propriety normally permits, and he was using his special smile, the one he reserves solely for his conquests. The one he used to use on me. When I caught him at it, all he did was shrug, as if to say there was no law that forbade a gentleman from talking to a scullery maid. And of course there is none, save the law of decorum."

The corners of her mouth turned down as though there was a sour taste on her tongue.

"I am being far too candid," she said. "I know full well where your line of enquiry, Mr Holmes, is leading. I had an inkling, when I received your note, that you would be asking me about Fitzhugh and Goforth. To be honest, it is something of a relief to get this out in the open. It feels like lancing a boil, painful but necessary. The thing was, Goforth was doing little to discourage Fitzhugh, and I could see it all unfurling. He would chase her. There would be more of these 'chance' encounters between them. He would perhaps think that nothing would come of it and it was just a bit of harmless fun. Then, though, the moment would arrive. The inevitable would happen.

"And so it did. I cannot say precisely when the fling began, but sometime around the end of April, early May, Fitzhugh took to staying up late, much later than normal. I would retire, and he would promise to follow soon, but he would not come to our room for at least another hour or two afterward. That was when I knew."

"He even used my aunt's death as an excuse for the change in his routine. 'I am grieving for dear Perdita,' he said to me once. 'I miss her very much. You go up to bed, Kitty. I shall have a last glass of sherry and sit alone with my sad thoughts for a while, if I may.'

"In hindsight, I should have worked it out sooner than I did. A part of me simply did not want to believe that he would stoop so low. A scullery maid! Before then, Fitzhugh had at least had the decency to confine himself to women from his own station in life. Now he was carrying on with a member of staff? It felt like a slap in the face. It showed just how little he thought of me and of our conjugal vows."

"How long did it go on for before you took action?" said Holmes.

"A few months. Perhaps longer. I was eaten up inside with rage and jealousy. Eventually I could stand it no more, and so one morning – October, I think it was – I got Goforth alone and confronted her. I said, 'Listen to me, my girl. I can see what you are up to.'

"She, this little chit of a thing, had the nerve to play the innocent. 'I don't know what you can mean, ma'am.' Spoken with an impertinent twitch of the lips, for she knew exactly. 'Why ever are you in such a state, Mrs Danningbury Boyd? I have done nowt wrong.'

"I don't mind telling you, Mr Holmes, I nearly struck her. Only the fact that I am a gentlewoman, and she my inferior by some degree, prevented me. It would not have been seemly. I demanded that she stay away from my husband, to which she replied, obtusely, that she could not help it if their paths should happen to cross. 'It is a big castle but not that big,' she said, adding, 'And who am I, a mere kitchen girl, to say where Mr Danningbury Boyd does and doesn't go?'

"Well, I called her all manner of names in response to that, the kindest of which was 'saucy hussy', and she maintained her air of blithe insolence throughout. I accused her of being a thief as well."

"A thief for stealing your husband?"

"No. Not metaphorically. An actual thief. There have been some strange disappearances around the castle recently, you see. Things have been going missing. Small items, nothing too significant. I had a porcelain ring tree on my dressing table that vanished one day, a pretty little thing with a periwinkle pattern. There was no jewellery on it at the time. I scoured my bedroom, thinking the ring tree might have fallen behind some piece of furniture. I even looked further afield. However, in a building this large, finding something that's lost, especially an object of no great size, is a futile task. I have heard servants remark that the odd item of silverware has gone astray, too. The assumption is that someone on the staff is pilfering. It happens in stately homes all the time, and it tends to be regarded as just the price you pay for employing menials. With regard to the ring tree, I decided Goforth was as likely a candidate for the crime as any, and said so to her. In hindsight this may seem petty, but it is a mark of how much I detested the creature."

"How did she take it?"

"She vehemently denied the accusation, of course, and without proof, how could I pursue the matter further? Finally, as a weapon of last resort, I threatened her with the sack. Her answer to this was that even if she was no longer resident at Fellscar, she and my husband might easily find themselves in Yardley Cross at the same time, or Wold Newton, and who could prevent them from ever-so-unintentionally bumping into each other there? It was then, when I realised that neither insult nor intimidation was having any effect, that I decided upon another course."

"Bribery."

Mrs Danningbury Boyd nodded. "The carrot rather than the stick. 'What would it take,' I said to Goforth, 'to make you break it off with Fitzhugh?' At that, her eyes lit up and I knew I had found the key to solving my problem.

"'I am sure, ma'am,' she said, 'that you can make it worth my while.'

"'Name your price,' I said.

"She deliberated a moment and said, 'I've seen that rather splendid diamond necklace you wear, Mrs Danningbury Boyd. The one that often forms part of your evening attire, with the bracelet to match. I've admired it greatly. It's the kind of necklace that'd leave a lass feeling like a millionaire if she were wearing it.'

"I was astounded. The avarice! The sheer effrontery! I had been thinking that a few pounds might do, but my necklace? I had bought it for myself at Asprey and Garrard, when I was last down in London. I was in a funk at the time – over Fitzhugh, what else? – and it cheered me. The necklace alone is worth a small fortune, never mind the accompanying bracelet, and I told Goforth I would not dream of parting with it; but she was adamant it was what she wanted. 'The necklace and nowt else,' said she.

"What else could I do, gentlemen, but accede to her demands? 'If I let you have it,' I said, 'will you give me your solemn vow that you will end your affair with Fitzhugh? You will never so much as look at him again?'

"'Upon my life, Mrs Danningbury Boyd,' said she, crossing her heart.

"'And a further condition,' I said. 'You do not tell him about any of this.' For if Fitzhugh were to find out how I had bought her off, I would never hear the end of it. He might even force Goforth to return the necklace to me and then would resume the affair as before.

"'As you wish,' said Goforth.

"I went straight to my room and fetched the necklace. Handing it to her, I said, 'Should you break your promise, I will see to it that you are fired from your position and you will never work in any respectable household again.'

"'On what grounds might you have me fired?'

"'I will claim that you have stolen that very necklace.'

"'Like I stole your ring tree, you mean?'

"'Yes, but in this instance it will be demonstrably true. Then where will you be? Not only jobless but jailed too, most likely.'

"'Well, you need have no worry on that account, Mrs Danningbury Boyd. I wouldn't do owt that'd part me from this beauty.'

"So saying, Goforth proceeded to drape the necklace around her neck. I had to show her how to work the clasp. Can you imagine? The girl had never worn anything like it before. Pearls before swine, as the saying goes. Or rather, diamonds.

"'I shall keep it on me at all times,' she said to me. 'Hidden, so that no one can see it, but I will know it is there, and so will you.'

"'Then let it be a constant reminder of our agreement, Goforth,' I said, 'and be sure that you do not go back on your word.'

"She, fingering the necklace lovingly, once again

assured me that she would not, and as far as I am aware she kept to that promise. I do not know how she broke it to Fitzhugh that their little dalliance was over. I do know that he did not take it well. He was irritable for days. Women do not jilt Fitzhugh Danningbury Boyd, you understand. He jilts them. He even began muttering to Uncle Thaddeus about Goforth, intimating that she was no good at her job and should be got rid of. But Thaddeus was having no truck with that. Fitzhugh could give him no specific reason why she should go. He was just being vindictive, and Thaddeus seemed to sense it, even if he had no idea what inspired the vindictiveness. I, anyway, sang Goforth's praises to my uncle, and he listens to me more than he does to Fitzhugh. Frankly, I don't think he has much time for Fitzhugh. So Goforth stayed."

"Why would you want that?" I asked. "You must have loathed the girl."

"True, but I did not loathe how her continued presence made my husband feel. It would remind him every day of this thing he could no longer have. Whenever he looked at her he would see one of his rare failures, a woman who had deserted him rather than the other way round. You may think me petty, but it was a satisfying victory. Worth every penny, in fact, of the necklace's value."

"Would I be right in thinking," said Holmes, "that Goforth made her assertion about encountering a ghost in the east wing not long after she and your husband began their clandestine liaisons?"

"That is so, Mr Holmes."

"You do not see a connection?"

"No."

"I do. I would suggest that their trysts took place in the self-same east wing. I would suggest, furthermore, that Goforth invented the ghost as a means of ensuring the two of them had complete privacy."

"My God." Mrs Danningbury Boyd's hand flew to her mouth. "I never thought of that, but it fits. The devious little madam. You know, I almost admire her."

"Yes, it is quite a cunning ploy," Holmes said. "The east wing already had bad associations, thanks to Mrs Allerthorpe's death. Few would go there as a matter of course. Around July, after Goforth and your husband had been consorting with each other for perhaps two months or so, the girl decided to put the seal on it by spinning a yarn about ghostly happenings. Now it was guaranteed that no one would venture into the east wing after dark, leaving the way clear for her and Mr Danningbury Boyd. Superstition and credulity would keep potential interlopers at bay, and the lovers were even less likely to be discovered."

"And Mrs Trebend inadvertently helped," I said, "with her own sighting of the ghost subsequent to Goforth's."

"Mrs Trebend certainly carried on the good work," Holmes said.

"Even though there was never any ghost, only a scullery maid's scaremongering."

"Have we not already established that Mrs Trebend fell prey to her own suggestibility?"

"She still does not strike me as the suggestible sort."

"I agree."

I expected Holmes to expound further on this statement, but he did not. Instead, he turned back to Mrs Danningbury Boyd, saying, "You must realise that all of this casts your husband in a very dim light."

"You do not mean his infidelity. You mean regarding what has happened to Goforth this morning."

The woman was looking more shrewdly confident now, more like her usual self. She had got a great deal off her chest over the past ten minutes. Her storm of passion had scoured her clean and she was better for it.

"Yes," she continued, "I am minded to think that there is more to Goforth's so-called 'accident' than Uncle Thaddeus let on. Why else would you have been asking me about the necklace and about her and Fitzhugh? You are of the opinion that her death was a consequence of villainy and that my husband may have been responsible."

"It is not hard to find a possible motivation for murder in Goforth's rejection of him," Holmes said. "In the weeks since, he may have stewed over it. A blemish on his heretofore pristine record where women are concerned. Perhaps he could no longer bear the thought of the girl continuing to live in the castle after subjecting him to such ignominious treatment, and if he could not persuade your uncle to fire her, he would have to take matters into his own hands. He demanded that they meet and entreated Goforth to hand in her notice. She refused. Driven into an uncontrollable frenzy of thwarted rage, your husband killed her. Either that or he wished to convince the girl to change her mind and become his mistress again, and when she declined, the red mist likewise descended, with the same result."

"That is all very well, Mr Holmes, but I know for a fact that Fitzhugh cannot be her killer."

Holmes canted his head to one side. "Really? You do not think that any man may resort to murder, with the right provocation?"

"Whether I think that or not is irrelevant. The simple fact is that I am my husband's alibi. He was in bed beside me the entire night."

"You are quite certain?"

"I would know if he had got up during the small hours and left the room. I would have awoken."

"Can you honestly say, Mrs Danningbury Boyd, hand on heart, that Mr Danningbury Boyd, practising the utmost stealth, could not have slipped out from between the sheets, gone to the east wing, and come back and resumed his place beside you without your knowledge?"

The lady nodded but seemed markedly less sure of herself now. "I grant you it is possible. I am usually a light sleeper. Last night, however, I did have a bit to drink. We all did, didn't we? My goodness. How appalling. Would he – *can* he have committed cold-blooded murder? Fitzhugh? Is it possible?"

At that moment, the library door burst open and who should step in but the man himself. Fitzhugh Danningbury Boyd did not look best pleased.

"Kitty," he growled. "It was rumoured that you were meeting Mr Holmes here. What is going on? Why, Mr Holmes, are you talking to my wife? And why without me to chaperone her? Kitty has nothing to say to you that she cannot say in front of me."

Mrs Danningbury Boyd answered before Holmes could.

"Fitzhugh," she said. There was iron in her voice. "Look me in the eye. Tell me you did not kill Becky Goforth."

Danningbury Boyd's face paled. He cast a panic-stricken look at the three of us.

Then, all at once, he turned and fled.

Chapter Nineteen

A GOOD ARM AND A GOOD EYE

Holmes and I leapt up and gave chase.

Danningbury Boyd had a head start on us, however, and was fleet of foot. More to the point, he knew the layout of Fellscar Keep better than we did, its twists and turns, its shortcuts. Sherlock Holmes was fast, and I had a decent level of stamina, attributable to my regular rugby playing. All the same, we soon lost sight of him.

"Let us split up," Holmes said. "I shall hunt through the castle. You, Watson, make for the front gate. If he attempts to leave the premises, you can waylay him. Whatever you do, keep hold of him. He must not escape."

I hastened towards the main courtyard, pausing only to enquire of anyone I passed whether they had seen Danningbury Boyd. No one had.

Then, just as I arrived in the central hallway, I spied the man from a window. He had scavenged a bicycle from somewhere and was pedalling furiously across the courtyard.

A bicycle might seem wholly unsuited to the wintry conditions. However, the numerous ruts left by the comings and goings of coaches created channels of hard-packed snow which a cyclist could follow with his wheels, like a train along tracks. Somebody wishing to effect a speedy departure from Fellscar could do worse than use this mode of transportation.

Danningbury Boyd was already closing in on the gate, which stood wide open. Uttering a cry of dismay I dashed outside. As I emerged onto the courtyard, my dismay turned to elation, for Holmes was there. My friend, having arrived in the courtyard from a different entry point than me, was on course to intercept our quarry.

He made a grab for Danningbury Boyd, attempting to unseat him. The other fended him off, and Holmes lost his footing in the snow and stumbled to his knees. Danningbury Boyd continued onward, wobbling somewhat on the bicycle but swiftly regaining equilibrium.

I hastened to my friend's side to help him up.

"Not me, Watson!" Holmes said, batting my hand away. "I am fine. Get after Danningbury Boyd!"

The fellow was through the gateway by now and onto the causeway. I scurried off in hot pursuit. At a sprint, I thought I might just be able to catch up with him and force him to dismount, as Holmes had been attempting to do.

It was no good. Danningbury Boyd threw a glance over his shoulder and pedalled all the harder, gaining speed. The gap between us widened, and by the time I was halfway across the causeway, he had gained the far end.

Then, from behind, I heard Holmes call out, "Watson! Duck!"

Without thinking twice, I crouched down.

Holmes was back on his feet and poised just inside the castle entrance, his right arm drawn back, his left extended forward, much in the manner of a spear thrower. With a mighty effort he launched an object from his right hand. It sailed the length of the causeway in a smooth, low parabola, and I gasped in bemusement.

It was a snowball.

I watched the snowball begin its arc of descent, on a perfect collision course with Danningbury Boyd. It struck the fleeing felon on the back of the head with a hearty *smack* and a small explosion of snow. He toppled from the bicycle to the ground, limp as a mannequin. The riderless conveyance rolled onward for a few yards before it, too, keeled over.

I expected Danningbury Boyd to get up again. It was, after all, only a snowball that had hit him. Yet, oddly, he did not stir.

"Come along." Holmes strode up beside me, brushing off his palms. "The fellow looks to be out for the count. He will need a doctor."

"A splendid throw, Holmes," I said, as we fell in step together, crossing the causeway towards Danningbury Boyd's inert form. "A bullseye at forty yards."

"At school, I captained the cricketing first eleven two years in a row. You knew that, didn't you? I had a good arm then, and a good eye. I am glad to learn that neither faculty has diminished since."

"But how could a mere snowball have such an impact?"

"I took the liberty of inserting a stone into the middle of it," came the reply, accompanied by a sly chuckle. "The snow packed around that projectile will have cushioned its force, rendering the blow a stunning one rather than a potentially lethal one."

And so it proved. Fitzhugh Danningbury Boyd was out cold. I gently palpated the back of his skull and found that a swelling had formed over the occipital bone. There did not appear to be any cranial fracture. His breathing was shallow but even. He had suffered a concussion but there would be no lasting damage.

Holmes took his arms, I his legs, and between us we carted him indoors. Thaddeus and Shadrach Allerthorpe were in the central hallway as we entered.

"What is all this commotion?" Thaddeus barked. "People

haring around the castle. General mayhem. You had better have a damned good explanation, Mr Holmes."

"Is that Fitzhugh?" said Shadrach. "Is he all right?"

"Gentlemen," said Holmes, "please tell me there is somewhere we can put Mr Danningbury Boyd where he will be confined but comfortable."

"Confined?"

"You see before you," I said, "the murderer of Becky Goforth. We have apprehended him."

Thaddeus gaped. "The…?"

"A room with only one way in or out," Holmes went on. "Ideally on an upper floor. The door lockable from without, of course. Come along. Hurry. He is not getting any lighter."

After some further chivvying by Holmes, the brothers led us to a third-floor bedroom, one of the very few in the castle still unoccupied. It was a narrow, mean little chamber. The bed upon which we laid out the unconscious Danningbury Boyd was hardly more than a cot. The window was the merest slit. Overall, the place had a monastic feel and something of the gaol cell about it too, both of which aspects were, I thought, ironically apposite.

"Yes, this will do nicely," said Holmes. "Slim though Danningbury Boyd is, even he cannot fit through that window; and anyway, the forty-foot drop to the ground ought to deter him from trying."

"Are you quite certain Fitzhugh killed the scullery maid?" said Thaddeus. "It is hard to credit. I mean, the man is a slave to self-interest, I am under no illusion about that. But capable of murder?"

"In my experience, Mr Allerthorpe, self-interested people are the ones to watch out for. They are callous to a sometimes dangerous degree."

"But what can have compelled him to commit murder?" said Shadrach.

"Thereby hangs a sorry tale," said Holmes, and he proceeded to relate the history of Danningbury Boyd's affair with Goforth, all the way to its fatal conclusion. "It is my belief that he arranged to meet her in the east wing tower, with a view either to persuading her to quit her position in the household or to rekindling the flame which his wife had so effectively dowsed. Goforth went along to the meeting, perhaps thinking she might use it as leverage against Mrs Danningbury Boyd. It would enable her to extort more valuables, or maybe this time just plain cash. 'Your husband met me in secret last night,' she might say. 'Ask him yourself. See if he can deny it. Nothing happened, but next time I might not be so unforthcoming…' But alas, there was a spat. Danningbury Boyd ran to the window and opened it. I imagine he was threatening to throw himself out. 'If I cannot have my way, I shall kill myself.' A mere ruse, this, but Goforth fell for it. She went over to remonstrate with him, whereupon he sprang his trap. He grabbed her and shoved her out."

"Ghastly," said Thaddeus, agog.

Shadrach Allerthorpe was even more shocked. "My poor Kitty. She never let on. All this time. It must have been unendurable for her. Married to such a monster. A maniac!" He shot a venomous scowl at his supine son-in-law. "I always thought she was too good for him. I only wish I could have warned her off him. But he seemed to make her happy…"

"And for Fitzhugh to comport himself so shamelessly under my roof," Thaddeus added. "The scoundrel."

"You know, in hindsight, I ought to have recognised that necklace on Goforth as being Kitty's," said Shadrach.

"In my experience, most men are not adept at identifying jewellery on females," said Holmes. "One trinket adorns a woman as well as any other. It is all much of a muchness to our sex. Whereas to the acquisitive eyes of a girl on the make like Goforth, that necklace would have been outstandingly and irresistibly alluring. She would have been drawn to it like a magpie."

"Well," said Thaddeus, "this is unquestionably a police matter now. I shall instruct a man to fetch a constable from Wold Newton forthwith."

"A capital notion," said Holmes. "I would advise you to hold off from sending for the authorities, however, until Danningbury Boyd has regained consciousness. The police do not have the wherewithal to look after someone in his present condition properly."

"How long do you think it will take him to recover?"

"Watson is better placed to enlighten you about that than I. Watson? It is unfortunate that Danningbury Boyd sustained a blow to the head during his capture. Sometimes an injury like his can render a man insensible for a good twenty-four hours, don't you think?"

My friend had a meaningful glint in his eye, which I picked up on. "Twenty-four hours at least, I would say," I replied. "Of course I shall tend to him in the meantime, until I judge him well enough to be taken into custody."

Holmes gave me a barely perceptible nod, to indicate that I had performed just as required. "There you have it, gentlemen," said he to the brothers. "The opinion of an expert."

"We must at least let the police know about Goforth's murder," said Shadrach. "To delay informing them would be immoral as well as illegal."

"If it is your desire to contact them, by all means do so. I am sure, however, that a day here or there will not make much difference."

The Allerthorpe brothers debated the issue between themselves. Shadrach remained in favour of bringing the police in as soon as possible. Thaddeus, the more bullish of the two, agreed with Holmes that a day's delay would not hurt.

"It might look as though we were covering something up," Shadrach argued.

"We are Allerthorpes, respected throughout the county," said his brother. "Throughout the *country*. Nobody would dare suggest there was anything underhand going on. Nobody of any consequence, at least."

"If it comes to it, blame me," said Holmes. "Tell the police that you were following Sherlock Holmes's advice. My reputation at Scotland Yard has earned me some latitude within the crime-investigation fraternity."

That settled it as far as Thaddeus was concerned. "We shall wait until tomorrow. The police can come then to collect Fitzhugh, and at the same time Goforth's body. Now, Shadrach, I don't know about you, but I could do with a good stiff drink. Mr Holmes? The key to the room is in the lock, as you can see. I am entrusting Fitzhugh to your and Dr Watson's care. Frankly I want nothing more to do with the blackguard. I wash my hands of him."

"Seconded," said Shadrach, with feeling.

The brothers departed, leaving Holmes and me alone with the insensible Danningbury Boyd.

"Now then, Holmes," I said, "perhaps you'd explain why you had me pretend it will take him so long to come round. You know as well as I do that unconsciousness lasts a quarter of an hour at most. He will surely begin to revive soon." Already Danningbury Boyd's fingers were beginning to twitch, a sign that his senses were returning.

"You have caught me out in my little subterfuge. What I need you to do is keep him in a comatose state for as long as you safely can. Have you brought a sedative with you to Fellscar?"

"No, but Eve has a plentiful supply of chloral hydrate. I can borrow some of hers. I strongly caution against this course of action, though. Apart from anything else it is highly unethical."

"I would not have you behave in a way that contradicts your Hippocratic oath, Watson. All I am asking is that you bend the rules a little."

"What for? I don't understand your rationale. Here he is. A murderer. We have him bang to rights, as the saying goes. You have solved the mystery of Goforth's death in record time. What is to be gained by keeping the culprit on the premises and tranquillised? The sooner he is in police hands, the sooner you and I can go back to London. Unless…"

"Yes, Watson? Unless…?"

"By thunder, Fitzhugh Danningbury Boyd is not the murderer after all!" I declared.

"A touch louder, old fellow. I don't think the entire castle heard you."

Somewhat more softly I said, "You want everyone to believe he is the murderer in order to make the real murderer think he has got away with his crime scot-free."

"The sight of comprehension dawning in your eyes is one that never palls. I hope I shall continue to see it for many years to come. It is immensely gratifying."

"You know, come to think of it, I did find your analysis of Goforth's meeting with Danningbury Boyd somewhat curious. Would the girl really have tried to blackmail Mrs Danningbury Boyd further, when that would have violated the terms of their pact and brought about undesirable consequences for her?"

"It was a plausible fabrication," said Holmes, "sufficient to convince Thaddeus and Shadrach. I am just glad you refrained from voicing your doubts at the time."

"But why do you wish to lull the real murderer into a false sense of security?"

"Go on, old fellow. Keep those cogs turning."

"It is so that he will become overconfident and make some crucial mistake that gives him away."

"But the fact is, I already have a fair notion who the killer is. I do not need him to identify himself."

"Then you are leaving him at liberty for another reason."

"Namely?"

I racked my brains. "It cannot be in order to allow him to kill again. You would not be so cavalier with the lives of others. He is up to something else. That would imply that Goforth's death was not a crime of passion but rather a calculated effort to cover up another crime. Can it be that the murderer is also the Black Thurrick? The two things are somehow connected?"

"Yes and no," said Holmes. "You have come so far, yet you are still unable to piece together the evidence into a coherent whole. But no need to be downhearted. There remain gaps in my own understanding of events here at Fellscar. I need this extra twenty-four hours to accumulate the final few scraps of data that will tie everything up neatly. But look. Danningbury Boyd's eyelids are fluttering. Time is short. Fetch that chloral hydrate, would you? And make it quick. There's a good fellow."

Eve was still sleeping. I took the bottle of sedative from her bedside table and hurried back.

Fitzhugh Danningbury Boyd was awake by the time I returned.

"My head," he moaned thickly. "It aches something awful."

"And I have medicine that will help with that," I said.

"What is it?"

"Paregoric."

I felt ashamed as I administered a heavy dose of the chloral hydrate – and with good cause, for I was betraying dearly-held principles. I consoled myself with the thought that, although not a murderer, Danningbury Boyd was a thoroughgoing reprobate. For his mistreatment of his wife, if for nothing else, he did not deserve my sympathy.

"Bitter," he said with a cough. "Are you sure that is paregoric?"

"One of the lesser-known proprietary brands," I replied, masking the label on the bottle with my hand lest he should see it.

"You – you attacked me, Mr Holmes." Through the pain and the fog of concussion, Danningbury Boyd was slowly regaining his wits. "It's coming back to me now. You came after me and tried to assault me. Tried to push me off that bicycle."

"You fled, Mr Danningbury Boyd," said Holmes. "Remember? After your wife enquired about Goforth and the possibility that you killed the girl, you turned tail and ran like a startled deer. Can you blame us for giving chase? Your actions were patently those of a guilty man."

"But… I am not guilty. I did not kill Becky. That is, Goforth."

"Then why abscond? An innocent man would have stood his ground and argued in his own defence."

"I wasn't thinking clearly. When I heard at breakfast that the girl was dead, my mind was a maelstrom. It is apparent that you know that she and I… we used to be…"

"We do."

"So you can imagine how I felt."

"Relieved. No longer was there this young woman in the castle, carrying around the secret of your affair with her. No longer was there a human bomb waiting to go off and destroy your life."

"Somewhat relieved, yes," Danningbury Boyd allowed. "Now there was no chance Kitty would ever find out about the two of us. Mostly, though, I felt devastated. Becky was a lively lass. I was fond of her still, even though it was over between us. It appalled me that she had met her end in such a cruel and arbitrary manner. And then I learned of your private appointment with my wife. Coming hard on the heels of Becky's death – well, it looked to me as though the much-vaunted Mr Sherlock Holmes was unearthing the truth about the situation after all. I raced to the library in the hope of forestalling you, before you revealed all to Kitty, but I was too late. The accusing look Kitty gave me. The loathing in her eyes. And, worse, her imputation that I had committed murder. The shock was enormous. It was too much. All I could think was that I must get out of there, by whatever means necessary."

It seemed absurd that someone so debonair could look quite so pathetic.

"I don't know what you must make of me, gentlemen. I am not a good person, that is certain. A good husband neither. I am aware of my deficiencies but incapable, it seems, of amending them. Nevertheless, please believe me when I say that I... I do not have Becky's blood on my... my hands."

Danningbury Boyd was becoming disorientated, his words faltering. The chloral hydrate was taking effect.

"I am suddenly very tired," said he. His eyelids drooped. "I think... I think I shall... rest."

His head sank back onto the pillow and soon he was snoring.

Holmes and I stole out of the room, locking the door behind us.

Chapter Twenty

LORD OF MISRULE

At lunchtime, Erasmus Allerthorpe shambled into the dining hall, looking haggard and more hollow-faced than usual.

His father, glancing round at him, said sharply, "The prodigal son returns. And where have you been all this time, Raz?"

"Yardley Cross."

"I presumed as much. The clear implication of my question was what you have been up to?"

"Ah."

"And?"

"Nothing much. This and that."

"I see. 'Nothing much'. How very forthcoming." Thaddeus's voice was rising, and with it the colour in his face. "You should have been here, boy. You assured us yesterday that you would be back in time to meet our guests as they arrived. To fail to do so was exceedingly rude."

"It wasn't my fault," Erasmus said. "I was… unavoidably detained."

"Were you, now? And what could be more important than your familial obligations? No, don't bother answering. I have no wish to know. I imagine you found somewhere amenable to stay the night."

"The Sheep and Shearer. The rooms above the bar are perfectly acceptable. Now please, Father, I have just walked five miles through the snow. I am famished. Might I be permitted to sit and eat a bite?"

Erasmus had the chapped cheeks and fingers to show for his long, cold journey. He sported a black eye, too. He was trying to disguise this by allowing a lock of his hair to fall in front of it, but it was all too conspicuous.

"Not until you tell me how you came by that," Thaddeus said, indicating the bruise.

"I slipped. Slipped in the snow and fell and banged my face."

His father harrumphed. "While drunk, most likely."

Erasmus disregarded the comment, as though it were beneath him to respond. Instead, he swept his gaze across the other forty or so of us seated at the dining table.

"Well, well, well," he said. "Look who's here. Allerthorpes

galore, and sundry in-laws and outlaws." He seemed to be including Holmes and me in the last category. "Greetings, all. Nice to see you again. Great-Aunt Maud, your hair is looking lovely. I swear it was greyer last year. And Cousin Theobald. *Your* hair is corresponding more and more with the latter portion of your name. And is that young Timothy? My, how you've grown, lad. Not necessarily in the right direction."

These barbs elicited mutterings and a few furtive giggles.

"Raz!" his father snapped. "Address your kin with courteousness or not at all."

"I'm sorry, I'm sorry," Erasmus said with an exaggerated bow of remorse. "I am just being mischievous. You know me. A twinkle in the eye. A ready quip. That's Erasmus Allerthorpe. It is delightful to have you all back under our roof, making merry, after what has been such a difficult year. A difficult few days, indeed."

"You don't know the half of it," said Shadrach.

"What's that, uncle?"

"Have you not heard? No, I don't suppose you can have. Overnight, there has been a death in the castle."

Erasmus's eyebrows shot up in alarm. "Whose? Is it Eve? I do not see her here. My God. Surely not Eve." His voice quavered. "Please tell me she is well."

"Your sister is fine," said Thaddeus. "A little overwrought but in no danger. Is that not so, Dr Watson?"

"It is, Mr Allerthorpe," I said. To Erasmus I said, "Eve has taken to her bed. I am looking after her."

"Thank heaven," said the young man with a deep, earnest sigh. "If Eve were dead, I should not know what to do with myself. Die too, probably. But if it is not her that has perished, then who?"

"The scullery maid. Goforth." Briefly Thaddeus described how the kitchen girl had met with an accident, to which Erasmus responded with astonishment and an appropriate level of consternation. "You should also be made aware that Fitzhugh is…" He threw a glance in Holmes's direction. "Indisposed."

"Ill?"

"Touch of brain fever," said Holmes. "Sudden and quite unexpected. Watson and I were obliged to pursue him through the castle. He was beside himself and we needed to corral him, for his own good. It all culminated in him falling off a bicycle on the causeway."

No one save for Holmes and me knew precisely how Danningbury Boyd's unsaddling had been brought about. There had been no other witnesses to the event.

"Cycling?" said Erasmus. "In the snow? Old Fitzhugh really must have lost his marbles."

"I'm sure it is only temporary," Holmes said. "Don't you agree, Watson?"

"These things pass," I said. "It can happen to anyone."

Kitty Danningbury Boyd was not present, otherwise she might have had something to contribute to the conversation. She was at this moment up in her room, being attended to by her mother.

"Honestly," Erasmus said. "I am away for one night, and everything goes to pot. Good thing it wasn't longer. Who knows what calamities might have befallen then?"

The lad took his place at table, and the conversations that had been interrupted by his arrival resumed. The mood in the dining hall was a strange mixture of perturbation and excitement. For the houseguests, this Christmas, with its alarums and excursions, was turning out to be a Christmas like no other. I suspected that some would remember it with a sombre shudder and others with a measure of fond bewilderment, but none would ever forget it.

After the meal ended, the Allerthorpes decamped en masse to the castle's music room. There, they sang carols to a piano accompaniment.

I, meanwhile, took a bowl of beef consommé up to Eve, which she supped gratefully. Then I looked in on Fitzhugh Danningbury Boyd. He was still in the arms of Morpheus, dead to the world. My third and final port of call was Kitty Danningbury Boyd's room.

Olivia Allerthorpe responded to my knock. She had appointed herself her daughter's gatekeeper as well as nurse.

"Kitty is not taking visitors right now, Doctor. She has no desire but to be left alone."

"I understand, madam," I said. "I merely wished to enquire whether there was anything I might do to help."

"Who is it, Mama?" a reedy voice called out from within.

"Dr Watson. I have told him you will not receive him."

"No, you may show him in. He knows full well my situation. I have nothing to keep from him."

Mrs Danningbury Boyd sat in bed, propped up on pillows. She looked listless and wan.

"You are kind to call on me, Doctor."

"Not in the least. How are you feeling?"

"Wretched. I am not sure I will ever be quite the same."

"Might I suggest a spoonful or two of laudanum? You have had a trying time of it."

"Trying?" She gave vent to a bitter laugh. "You have some knack for understatement. My life is in upheaval. My marriage is in tatters. No drug is going to make any difference. I have just one query. Is Fitzhugh behind bars yet?"

"As good as."

"Good. I hope he hangs for what he has done."

I wondered if she meant for killing Goforth or for the tribulations he had put her through as her husband. Either seemed as likely.

I left her to wallow in her misery. For some patients, that can be as efficacious as any patent medicine.

Holmes and I had agreed to reconvene in the library, and that was where I found him. The sound of carol singing filtered through to us from next door. The Allerthorpes were in the midst of a rousing rendition of "Good King Wenceslas".

"Finished with your rounds, eh?" Holmes said. "A pity you are not getting paid for your professional services here."

"I know. It would be proving quite a lucrative few days otherwise. What is our next move?"

"Yours, my friend, is to go to your room and get some rest. You look worn out."

"Two wakeful nights in a row will have that effect on a person. But I am prepared to forge on regardless."

"No, I would much rather you caught up on your sleep, for another wakeful night looms."

"I'm not sure I like the sound of that."

Holmes chuckled. "Your querulousness may not be misplaced. Tonight you and I are going to keep vigil in the east wing."

"How delightful. Watching for ghosts, I presume." I said this with a lightness of tone which hitherto I might not have been capable of mustering. I was now satisfied that the Fellscar phantom was nothing more than a figment of Mrs Trebend's imagination, built upon Becky Goforth's spurious invention.

"Ghosts and other things that go bump in the night,"

said Holmes. "Speaking of which, what did you make of our spectre at the feast earlier?"

"Erasmus? Made quite an entrance, didn't he? I presume he was out carousing in Yardley Cross last night. He may even still have been drunk when he got home, or if not, then terribly hung over."

"He certainly seems to have embraced the yuletide role of Lord of Misrule. What about that shiner of his? How do you think he came by it?"

"The state he was in, I would not be surprised if he sustained it in exactly the way he claimed. A trip and a fall."

"Yet in gaining a black eye, he appears to have lost something else."

"His dignity? Not that he had much of that to begin with."

"Lack of sleep has not blunted your pawky sense of humour, Watson. No, I am referring to a gold signet ring, the one he has previously been wearing on the fourth finger of his right hand."

"I must confess I did not notice he had a ring."

"Just as well one of us is observant, then. Until yesterday, when the family departed for church at Yardley Cross, Erasmus was the possessor of a signet ring imprinted with the Allerthorpe coat of arms. His father and uncle each has one to match. Although it is hard to distinguish real gold from fake by sight alone, I would stake my reputation on all of the rings being the genuine article. Would an Allerthorpe even dream of owning a gilt counterfeit?"

"I strongly doubt it."

"More likely the rings are made of twenty-four carat gold – nothing but the best – and therefore worth a pretty penny. So we must ask ourselves how come Erasmus no longer has his and why he has not seen fit to refer to its absence. One answer is that he has mislaid it."

"He might have lost it while inebriated, I suppose. It slipped off, or he removed it and forgot where he put it."

"But," said Holmes, "rings seldom simply fall off the finger, and one does not tend to take off certain kinds of ring, especially signet rings, without good reason. They are a more or less permanent fixture on one's hand."

"Could it have been stolen? Mrs Danningbury Boyd told us various trinkets have been going missing. Erasmus's ring might just be the latest."

"But those thefts have all happened around the castle. Erasmus was wearing his ring when he left yesterday. He is not wearing it today. But he has not, as far as we know, been present at Fellscar in the interim."

"Good point. Then it was taken from him. By force."

"A much more plausible scenario, and one which would account also for his injury."

"He was attacked and robbed in Yardley Cross," I said.

"Precisely."

"But then why did he not mention that when Thaddeus asked him about his black eye?"

"Embarrassment. Shame. A reluctance to cause upset."

"We are still talking about Erasmus Allerthorpe, aren't we?"

Holmes laughed. "Quite so. None of the qualities I just enumerated can be ascribed to him. But supposing he neither mislaid the ring nor was robbed. What does that leave?"

"He parted with it voluntarily."

"Yes."

"Why? As a gift?"

"Consider this. What if Erasmus was not in Yardley Cross all this time? What if it was him in the tower room in the east wing last night?"

"There with Goforth? He is her killer?"

"On the face of it, the evidence supports that possibility. Erasmus's feet are size eight, for one thing. And before you ask, I know because a size eight shoe is ten and one eighth inches long from heel to toe. The floorboards throughout the castle are five inches wide precisely. I measured them with a ruler after lunch, just to be sure. I have seen that Erasmus's foot spans two of the boards with an eighth of an inch to spare. It is a simple computation."

"Then his supposed overnight stay in Yardley was only a cover story," I said. "He came back to Fellscar in secret at some point yesterday. He met up with Goforth during the small hours, murdered her, then hid somewhere in the castle until lunchtime in order to make everybody believe he had been away all that time."

"There are plenty of places in a vast, rambling pile like this where a man might conceal himself without fear of discovery."

"And the black eye – he received that from Goforth during their struggle in the tower."

"It is clear the girl was more of a hellcat than we first thought. She did not go to her doom meekly."

"But what about the signet ring? How does that fit into this?"

"Erasmus may have proffered it to Goforth before they fought," said Holmes.

"What for?"

"I must acknowledge that I can only speculate as to a reason. Might it be that he was tendering it as some kind of bribe or peace offering? If so, in either case it did not meet the requirement. Goforth balked. She slapped the ring out of Erasmus's hand, or else took it from him and hurled it into a corner of the room. Erasmus snatched it up afterwards, pocketed it and forgot to return it to his finger. That or he left the room in such haste that he neglected to retrieve it."

"But we did not see the ring there, and we surely would have. You," I amended, "surely would have."

"Which suggests that it could have fallen between two floorboards or into a crack beneath the wainscot. Erasmus could not collect it because it was beyond recovery."

"Or, alternatively, Goforth did accept the ring after all and it was in her possession when she fell from the window," I said. "In a pocket of her dress, perhaps."

Holmes nodded. "That is a possibility. Inspection of the body would settle that question one way or the other."

"But if all of this is true, what was Erasmus's motivation for killing her? What connects the two of them?"

"Erasmus may have learned of Goforth's and Danningbury Boyd's affair. His purpose in meeting her was much as I outlined to Thaddeus and Shadrach in respect to Danningbury Boyd's assignation with her. He wished to convince her to leave the Allerthorpes' service. He tendered her his signet ring to sweeten the deal. When that did not work, he resorted to more extreme measures."

"In that case I am surprised Goforth did not accept the ring. She had no qualms about dunning Mrs Danningbury Boyd out of her diamond necklace."

"Yet," Holmes said, "all of this paints Erasmus in a rather noble light. Too noble."

"Murdering Goforth?"

"Not that. Stepping in to rid the household of a stain on its reputation. Making a well-intentioned – but, as it turned out, disastrous – attempt at protecting his cousin Kitty's honour. Erasmus Allerthorpe, after all, is a young man who cares about no one except himself."

"Himself and Eve. When he feared that she was dead, his relief upon learning to the contrary appeared entirely genuine. She, I believe, is the only member of the family for whom he feels any kind of affection. It is perhaps his only redeeming feature."

"You may be right about that," said Holmes. "Moreover, were he Goforth's killer, he would have known immediately that it was her death to which Thaddeus referred. He would not have made the assumption it was his sister's. Unless, of course, his misapprehension was feigned. But I think, like his reaction to the news that Eve was safe and well, it was genuine."

"Could Erasmus have been conducting a clandestine affair with Goforth too?" I posited. "She, having acquired a taste for handsome, wealthy young men with Fitzhugh Danningbury Boyd, fixed her sights on him, with a view to profiting financially from it in the end. Where one act of extortion had been so successful, another might."

"Quite the Machiavelli, our young slavey."

"Too scheming for her own good, as it transpires."

Holmes shook his head and clucked his tongue. "No. It's a nice idea, Watson, but it does not add up. None of it does. The more I think about it, the more I feel we are trying to force Erasmus into being the culprit, as though dressing him up in a suit that simply does not fit him. He has something to hide, mark my words, but I have a fair notion that it does not pertain to Goforth's death."

"Then this entire exchange has been redundant," I said somewhat ill-temperedly.

"Not so. You have proved to be, as usual, an excellent sounding board. But here is another collaborator, with whom I hope to spend a profitable afternoon."

The door that joined the library to the music room had just opened, letting in the strains of "Once in Royal David's City" and also Shadrach Allerthorpe.

"Thank you for agreeing to come and assist me with some research, Mr Allerthorpe," Holmes said. "You are done with carolling for the time being, I take it."

"I am hardly in the mood for a singsong," said Shadrach, closing the door behind him. "I endured it as long as I could, but all I can think about is Fitzhugh and his appalling acts. I've half a mind to strangle the miscreant."

"You would do better to restrain yourself."

"No jury on earth would blame me if I killed him."

"No jury on earth would acquit you, either. Let us channel that passion of yours into something more useful. I have need of you both as an historian and as a resident of Fellscar Keep. You must be familiar with this library."

"More than. It is a marvellous resource to one such as me. I have whiled many a happy hour in here."

"Whereas to me, it is dauntingly well-stocked. It might take me ages to locate a particular book. With your assistance and experience, however, the task will be made considerably easier."

"Will this help convict Fitzhugh of murder?"

"It will not hinder my investigations," Holmes said.

I could tell, even if Shadrach could not, that my friend was choosing his words with care. Since I knew that Holmes did not reckon Fitzhugh Danningbury Boyd to be the murderer, his reasons for conducting research in the library must lie elsewhere.

"And you, Watson," he said to me, "are surplus to requirements. Please take this opportunity, as I proposed, to rest and refresh yourself. You have earned it."

In my room, I lay down on the creaking, unforgiving bed, not expecting that sleep would come my way. In the event, I was out like a light the moment I closed my eyes, and I did not wake up until shortly before supper.

Chapter Twenty-One

THE DEVIL WORSHIPPER
AND THE HELL STONE

I ate with gusto that evening. One could hardly not do so when presented with such fare as calves' foot jelly, pork griskin, stewed cardoons and potted lampreys, all cooked to Mrs Trebend's usual high standard.

At Holmes's insistence, however, I restricted my alcohol intake to a single glass of wine. He had told me I would need my wits about me later that night. I would also, he had said, need my revolver.

Trebend did not make it easy. He kept plying me with splendid wine after splendid wine, and I, with the utmost regret, kept having to refuse.

"You are missing out on this superb Château Cos d'Estournel," he said at one point, holding the bottle of Médoc under my nose like a trophy.

I replied that it pained me greatly but I must abstain.

"You and Mr Holmes both, it seems," Trebend said. "What a temperate pair you are this evening."

I offered him a doleful smile, which he mirrored before moving on.

After the meal, it was time for parlour games. These included a few energetic rounds of Blind Man's Buff that had the children squealing at near-deafening levels. The youngsters were no less enthused by the violent combat of Are You There, Moriarty?, which they and the older generations engaged in with glee.

As Holmes and I watched pairs of blindfolded opponents lie on the floor and wield rolled-up newspapers like clubs, each guided to his target by the sound of the other's voice alone, my friend remarked pithily that "Are you there, Moriarty?" was a question he often posed to himself. I had only the vaguest inkling what he meant, for by 1890 I had heard him mention that particular surname just once or twice, and then only in passing. I had no idea of the full extent of Professor James Moriarty's evildoing, nor could I have predicted the significant and terrible role the Napoleon of crime would come to play in our lives just a few months hence.

Holmes excelled at being the "guesser" in a game of Pass the Slipper, for nobody could hide the item of footwear behind their back without him instantly being able to tell who it was. Some tiny tic or quirk, invisible to most but obvious to his keenly penetrating gaze, invariably gave it away. Likewise, a memory game proved no challenge to him. Every time, without fail, he was able to identify which of a score of trinkets on a tray had been removed when his back was turned. Because he was so adept at these pastimes and so incapable of disguising his disdain for them, invitations to participate soon ceased.

Bedtime arrived for one and all. Holmes and I took to our respective rooms, waited an hour, then sallied forth through the sleeping castle to the east wing.

"What exactly are you expecting to come of tonight's enterprise?" I asked as we went.

"A manifestation."

"Not a ghostly one, surely."

"In that case I would have suggested you exchange your Eley's No. 2 rounds for a brand of ammunition capable of inflicting damage upon ectoplasm. In the absence of such advice, you must be able to infer that the prey we are hoping to roust is all too human."

"Human but still dangerous."

"In as much as practically every human being can be dangerous, not least one surprised during the commission of illicit deeds, then it is as well to be prepared."

"I have been meaning to ask. How went your labours in the library this afternoon with Shadrach Allerthorpe?"

"Our researches turned up some very interesting data."

"Care to elaborate?"

"All in good time. I have managed to clarify much that was opaque to me, and dot a few i's and cross a few t's into the bargain. Fellscar Keep has a fascinating, albeit chequered history. For instance, did you know—? No, you cannot possibly, so I shall tell you. This castle is not the first such edifice to have been built upon the island, you see. So I discovered today. Prior to Fellscar, there was another castle here, erected during the fourteen hundreds. Shadrach was aware of this fact but was unclear on many of the details until he and I dug a little deeper into the library's archive. The former castle, it transpires, fell into rack and ruin at the turn of the century, in consequence of a devastating fire. The island remained unoccupied from then until it and the land around it were purchased in 1835 by Alpheus Allerthorpe."

"Shadrach's and Thaddeus's father."

"Correct. Alpheus was the son of Roland Allerthorpe, who founded the Allerthorpe coal-mining and wool empire. Roland may have established the family business but it was Alpheus who built it up into a colossal, moneymaking machine. Work began on Fellscar Keep in 1838, the castle being designed and constructed to reflect Alpheus's own sense of self-worth."

"Which, it seems safe to say, was rather high."

"Ha ha. Judging by the enormity of the place, I would

agree. Alpheus was not even deterred by the somewhat sinister reputation the island had accrued just a few decades earlier. Or, I should say, the island's previous occupant had accrued. For he, Sir Mansfield Allerthorpe by name, was not only a notorious rake and libertine but, by all accounts, a devil worshipper too."

"Sir Mansfield… Allerthorpe? A direct ancestor of our Allerthorpes?"

"Yes, and if you think that the current crop have their flaws, they are nothing compared with him. It is said that he and likeminded cronies would hold wild orgies at his castle where Satan himself was allegedly in attendance, presiding over the revels. They would steal sheep and cattle belonging to nearby villagers and smallholders and sacrifice them to their dark lord in hideous rituals. They would abduct young women from their homes and subject them to the worst kind of depredations. Eventually the locals had as much of this as they could stomach, and there was an uprising. They stormed the castle and burned it to the ground, and Sir Mansfield with it. He died heirless and intestate, and his estate passed to the Crown. The island, the lake and the surrounding property were designated common land, and the locals merrily grazed their livestock there for the next few decades, some compensation for the abuses inflicted upon them by its former owner. That was until Alpheus came along."

"Alpheus cannot have bought the island and made it the family seat once more out of sympathy for his ancestor, can he?"

"On the contrary. He did it in order to expunge the stain left upon the family name by Sir Mansfield, who was his second cousin twice removed. Where 'Allerthorpe' had come to be associated with the misdeeds of his forebear, and likewise the island, Alpheus was determined to erase the past and write the family history anew. Allerthorpes would, he hoped, be remembered thereafter not for Sir Mansfield's depravity but for a respectable grandeur, symbolised by Fellscar Keep."

"Fascinating though I'm sure this all is, I don't see the relevance."

"I am coming to that. Let me tell you about the Hell Stone."

"The what?"

"You will recall Eve Allerthorpe's account of a meteorite that fell to earth at Wold Newton."

"Yes. She said something about a stagecoach whose passengers fell unconscious as the meteorite flew overhead."

"It happened in 1795," said Holmes. "Sir Mansfield Allerthorpe, still alive then, took an immediate interest in the meteorite, in no small part because of the queer effect it had reportedly had upon those people in the stagecoach. He judged this visitor from the skies to have infernal connotations. The meteorite was, in his view, an omen – nothing less than a sign from Lucifer, who himself fell blazing from the heavens and to whom Sir Mansfield had, as I have mentioned, pledged his fealty. He went to Major Edward Topham, the playwright and newspaper proprietor who owned Wold Cottage Farm where the meteorite came down, and asked to buy it from him. Topham had plans to profit from the rock by exhibiting it to the public, but being a good businessman was amenable to the idea of selling Sir Mansfield, if not the whole thing, then a portion. The meteorite, which is the type known as a chondrite and weighs the best part of sixty pounds, resides today in the British Museum. Shadrach Allerthorpe showed me a lithograph of it in an East Riding guidebook, and while the majority of its surface area is pitted and uneven, with a dark colouration, one side is perfectly smooth and light-hued, as though part of the meteorite has sheared off. Purportedly the rock broke in two mid-flight, the lesser segment coming to earth miles from where the majority landed, never to be found. The truth is that Topham and Sir Mansfield arranged for a stonemason to chip away a slab of the meteorite, for which Sir Mansfield parted with the princely sum of fifty guineas. This became his Hell Stone."

"And what, dare I ask, is a Hell Stone?"

"Sir Mansfield engaged the stonemason to carve into the piece of meteorite an oath of loyalty to the Prince of Lies, which he himself had composed in Latin. He then gave the slab the name Hell Stone and had it embedded in one wall of his castle, with the inscription facing out for all to see."

"That demonstrates a rare commitment to unchristian values," I remarked.

"Sir Mansfield was, it would seem, quite brazenly shameless. His so-called Hell Stone signalled his defiance of convention and the Church. And it was the final straw as far as the locals were concerned, providing the catalyst for the uprising I mentioned earlier. When word got around about the Hell Stone's existence, outrage finally spilled over into action. People roused themselves to form a mob and march on the castle."

"Serves him right, I'd say."

"To answer your question, finally, the relevance is this. When the residual heat of the conflagration at the castle had cooled, Sir Mansfield was buried amidst the rubble. Needless to say, he did not receive a Christian interment. Those responsible for his comeuppance simply dug a shallow grave and tossed his charred remains in it. The Hell Stone was smashed into pieces and interred along with him. Now then, Watson, where on the island do you think his gravesite might be?"

I had a fairly good idea, but Holmes's enquiry was rhetorical.

"Beneath Fellscar's east wing," he said.

"Of course it would be," I said. "Where else? And if there were a ghost haunting the castle…"

"Watson, really."

The fresh piece of intelligence regarding the devilish Sir Mansfield Allerthorpe and his Hell Stone had awoken in me fears I thought I had put to bed. "But if there were a ghost," I persisted, "who is it more likely to be than Sir Mansfield? His wretched soul is surely not at rest and roams the part of the castle built over the spot where his body lies."

"I have already made it clear that the east wing ghost was never anything more than a lie promulgated by Goforth," Holmes said testily, "in order to ensure that her and Fitzhugh Danningbury Boyd's trysts would go undiscovered."

"But what if, after all, she did not fashion it out of whole cloth? What if she genuinely did experience something uncanny and simply embroidered upon the event? Then Mrs Trebend's own ghost sighting becomes that much more explicable. Nothing to do with suggestibility, everything to do with –"

"Hush, Watson. Not another word. You are lapsing into credulity, and I will not have it. Stiffen your sinews, or I shall ask you to turn around and go back to your room. I cannot conduct a night-long surveillance with someone who is going to be jumping at shadows and seeing non-existent wraiths everywhere."

We continued on in silence – in my case a somewhat sullen silence – until we arrived at our destination. We were in the same ground-floor corridor where we had fetched up the night before, drawn by Goforth's dying scream. Holmes ushered me into the bathroom halfway along, which was to be where we would lie in wait.

For what? Beyond stating that he anticipated a "manifestation", my companion still had not vouchsafed why we were there, and when I attempted to press him on the subject he gave me very short shrift.

"No more talking," he hissed. "We must be quiet as monks from now on."

We settled down, I on the floor with my back to the claw-footed bath, Holmes beside the door, which he left open a crack. I drew my revolver.

Time crawled. In spite of Holmes's ardent rationalism, I could not dispel thoughts of Sir Mansfield Allerthorpe from my mind, try though I might. Perhaps all along it was he, rather than Perdita Allerthorpe, whom Becky Goforth and Mrs Trebend had variously encountered; his shade that had moaned at and breathed upon the former, and had brushed the latter's arm with icy fingers before allowing her a brief glimpse of his spectral self. Miserable sinner that he had been in life, why should he not continue to promote fear and upset even in death? I pictured his ghost, a hunched, tatterdemalion thing, still bearing the marks of immolation, groaning and muttering malevolently as it slouched along the castle's corridors.

Once this image became lodged in my brain it was hard to pry loose. I sought comfort from my revolver. The weapon had stood me in good stead many times in the past. With it in my hand, I normally had little to fear.

Yet on this occasion its hefty metallic solidity was not so reassuring. Holmes had joked about ammunition that could damage ectoplasm, but just then I rather wished there *was* such a thing. Against ghosts, a Webley Pryse top-break was unlikely to be effective. One might as well try to ward off a marauding lion by dancing.

Minutes became hours, and Fellscar Keep bombarded us with its nocturnal panoply of creaks and whispers, rustles and sighs. The bathroom's water pipes ticked and gurgled softly. A man in a nearby bedroom cried out in his sleep, pleading with someone in his dream, "Don't leave me! Give me another chance! I love you!"

Holmes remained attentive at the door. Outwardly he appeared calm but there was discernible in his eyes a fierce, glittering intensity. I thought of a cat outside a mousehole, poised to pounce the moment a twitching nose showed itself.

Midnight came and went. I shifted position in order to ease a cramp in one leg, then the other. My state of tension did not diminish with the passage of time and the uneventfulness of the vigil. It only increased, like a bowstring being drawn ever more taut. I speculated – and rather hoped – that this was to be our final night at Fellscar. Holmes and I would at last lay hands on Goforth's killer, and Holmes would then produce an explanation that tied together the murder, Jocasta Keele's will, the Black Thurrick's birch twig bundles, the mystery of Erasmus's missing signet ring, and much else besides, showing how each element dovetailed immaculately like the best Chippendale joinery. Not only was I looking forward to a satisfying resolution to this adventure, I was eager to return to London, see my Mary once more, and put behind me the Allerthorpe family, their castle, and the turbulent past and present of both.

Then the night air was rent by a bloodcurdling scream.

Chapter Twenty-Two

MRS TREBEND'S TERROR

It was not a short, truncated scream like Goforth's. It was long, drawn out, and it echoed piercingly through the castle, being repeated once, then twice, before dwindling into a series of ever fainter wails.

I was frozen in place, stupefied by the suddenness and unexpectedness of the initial scream. It was as though every sinew in my body had been shocked stiff, along with every hair on my skin. I daresay it would have taken me a good minute to stir myself to move, had Sherlock Holmes not darted from the bathroom while the sounds still continued. His swift response galvanised me into action. I hurled myself after him. He dashed through the castle, and I trailed in his wake, gun in hand.

Around us a hubbub grew. Doors were flung open. Various Allerthorpes emerged from their rooms in their nightwear and descended staircases, blinking dazedly. Several of them threw queries at us as we passed, but Holmes rushed on, heedless, and I followed his example.

The hue and cry was loudest in the servants' quarters, and that was where we found the source of the screams. It was Mrs Trebend, who lay sprawled on a first-floor landing, with her concerned husband bending over her and various other servants looking on.

One glance told me the woman was in a dire state. Her face was extraordinarily pale and coated with a sheen of perspiration, and she was trembling all over. Pocketing my revolver, I felt her wrist and discerned that her pulse was racing. With my ear to her sternum, I registered an erratic heartbeat.

"Mrs Trebend," I said, and then, more forcefully, "Mrs Trebend."

There was no response, so I patted her cheek. Her eyes rolled in their sockets, found mine and gained focus.

"Dr… Watson?"

She could speak. That was something. Her voice was faint but her speech was not hampered, nor was there a slackness to her mouth. I picked up her left hand, then her right, requesting that she squeeze my own hand with each. She managed to do so.

"What has happened to her, Doctor?" Trebend asked. His customary inexpressiveness had been replaced by a rictus of anxiety.

"She has not had a stroke, that much I can tell you," I replied. "A heart attack, however, remains a possibility."

"My goodness. She only stepped out of the room for a moment, in order to go to the kitchen. She remembered she hadn't put the bread away in the breadbin, she said. She was worried the mice might get to it."

By now a sizeable crowd had assembled around us, made up not only of servants but of Allerthorpes too, including Thaddeus and Shadrach. I entreated them to back away and give Mrs Trebend some room.

"Everyone, you heard Watson," said Holmes in an imperious tone. "If you have no good reason to be here, kindly return to your rooms. Not you, of course, Mr Allerthorpe," he added somewhat more deferentially, addressing Thaddeus. "Nor your brother."

As the throng began to disperse, Mrs Trebend said something.

"I'm sorry, I didn't catch that," I said.

Her voice was a husk of its usual self. "I saw… it, Doctor. Again."

"Saw what, Mrs Trebend?"

"The ghost. It was… there." She raised a quivering forefinger. "Right there."

She was indicating the corner of the landing by the window.

Beside me, Holmes gave a very audible tut of exasperation. I shot him a reproving look. His answering look conveyed a distinct lack of remorse.

"Its eyes," Mrs Trebend said. "Oh, its eyes. The emptiness… in them. The despair."

"Please, madam, do not talk," I said. "You must not tax yourself."

"So lonely. So angry. It… despises us. It wishes we were none of us here."

Those few servants still within earshot murmured amongst themselves. I saw one man make the sign of the cross.

"Let us get you to your bed," I told Mrs Trebend.

"A capital idea," said Holmes. "The fewer who hear this twaddle, the better."

"Holmes!"

My friend was allowing his contempt for belief in the supernatural to overmaster his natural compassion. Yet he was unrepentant. "Every utterance about a ghost serves only to foment superstition and sow unrest, and at this juncture that is something we can sorely do without."

With aid from her husband, I helped Mrs Trebend to her feet. Between us, he and I bore her to their room and laid her down. I made a cold compress out of a washcloth and draped it across her brow. For the next hour I watched over her, regularly taking her pulse and monitoring her breathing. Little by little her condition improved. Her heartbeat strengthened and stabilised, and my concern that she had suffered a coronary thrombosis abated. Her face regained some colour. Soon she was well enough to sit up and take a sip of lime cordial.

Yet she remained in an enfeebled state, and I resigned myself to yet another wakeful night of supervision.

Trebend, however, volunteered to look after her.

"Margery is my wife," said he. "I can do no less."

I consented to leave her in his care, with the proviso that if she took a turn for the worse he was to fetch me immediately, whatever the hour.

When I returned to my room, Holmes was waiting for me there.

"The gallant medic now has a fourth invalid to tend to," said he wryly. "And how is Mrs Trebend after her latest brush with a hideous ethereal apparition?"

"Much better. But do you know, Holmes, this cynicism of yours is becoming dashed tedious. The woman was in a very bad way. Her heart was arrhythmic and tachycardic, resulting in acute hypertension. For a time I feared she might not pull through. You cannot tell me that so severe and adverse a physical reaction was triggered by some mere trick of the eye or mind. Mrs Trebend must have seen *something* – something truly frightening."

"You detected, no doubt, a strong odour of oranges about her? No? I did."

"I was more preoccupied with her wellbeing than how she smelled. What of it, anyway? She makes marmalade. Obviously she had been preparing a fresh batch shortly before she went to bed, and the oranges' aroma still clung to her."

"Obviously. That must be it." Holmes yawned. "Well, I shall leave you to your rest, old friend. One thing you should know. We depart from Fellscar tomorrow morning."

"Depart…?"

"For good. London calls. We have done all we can here. Nothing is to be gained by staying."

"What?" I exclaimed. "But Goforth's murderer is still at large. And what about Eve? The will codicil? The Black Thurrick? Erasmus's ring? The ghost, even? You cannot let all these things go unresolved."

"I can if I want."

"This is not like you at all, Holmes."

"Perhaps you hold me in too high esteem. My powers of ratiocination and logical analysis are useless here, too mundane to prevail against otherworldly creatures. I yearn for a good old burglary or blackmailing, something commonplace without any fantastical folderol attached, and London offers an abundance of those. Yes, back to the Great Wen you and I shall go in the morning, Watson. My mind is made up. Nothing you can say will dissuade me."

Chapter Twenty-Three

DEPARTURE FOR LONDON

I went to sleep fuming and awoke fuming. How could Holmes be so capricious? So pig-headed? There was work still to be done at Fellscar Keep, and he was simply walking away?

I resolved to have it out with him before breakfast. Now that he had had a chance to sleep on his decision, which seemed to have been made in the heat of the moment, perhaps he might be more willing to recant.

He was not in his room, however. I found him downstairs in the dining hall, where it was clear that he had just formally announced his intention to leave.

Thaddeus and Shadrach Allerthorpe were both present, and neither man appeared any too bothered. They were under the impression that it was the imprisoned

Danningbury Boyd who had slain Becky Goforth. As far as they were concerned, Sherlock Holmes had more or less fulfilled his remit at Fellscar. The main matter, the murder, had been dealt with. Any other business, ghostly manifestations included, was of minor consequence.

"I will have Winslow prepare the brougham and horse," said Thaddeus. "He can get you to Bridlington in time to catch the nine-fifty train to York."

"Thank you," Holmes said. "You may feel free to summon the police at any time, to take Mr Danningbury Boyd away. Here is the key to his room."

"I heard him stamping around in there a short while ago," said Shadrach. "It would seem he has at last regained consciousness. He sounded disgruntled, to put it mildly. Thumped on the door a few times. Uttered a few choice oaths."

"He will almost certainly protest his innocence when the police come. Pay no attention."

"I shall have no problem doing that," said the man's father-in-law firmly.

"But there is Eve to consider," I interposed.

"The girl is doing well," said Thaddeus. "Erasmus has taken it upon himself to bring food up to her in her room. He was even reading poetry to her yesterday afternoon. For all his shortcomings, Raz is a good brother."

"And don't forget," said Holmes, "there is always Dr

Greaves if proper medical attention is called for."

"Which Mrs Trebend may require, if no one else. In fact, since Dr Watson is leaving, I shall have Greaves brought here as soon as possible for that very reason. Would you believe it, I found her in the kitchen when I came down this morning. She was working! I sent her back upstairs to bed straight away. I wasn't having any of that, not after what happened last night. I have given her the day off. We can ill afford her absence, with so many mouths needing to be fed, but the mother of one of the footmen is, by all accounts, a competent cook with experience of working in large households. She lives nearby and he has gone to fetch her. With luck, we shall be able to muddle along without Mrs Trebend until tomorrow."

"There." Holmes sounded satisfied. "All seems to be well in hand, eh, Watson? Nobody at Fellscar will miss us."

Knowing that further protest was futile, I settled down to eat. The food was as good as always, although perhaps lacking the finesse Mrs Trebend would have brought to it had she been able to give it her full attention.

Thereafter it was simply a matter of packing my case and waiting with Holmes in the central hallway for Winslow to bring the carriage round.

"Should we not tell Eve that we are going?" I said. "She deserves to hear it from us rather than someone else. It was at her request that we came here in the first place, after all.

We should explain to her why we are forsaking her."

"Forsaking?" said my friend. "You do have a tendency to overstate things, Watson. It is the writer in you."

"How else would you put it? Eve wanted to know why someone is leaving birch twigs around the castle in the manner of the Black Thurrick. She engaged you to investigate. You are signally failing to hold up your end of the bargain."

"Sometimes there are mysteries in life that must forever remain mysteries. Eve Allerthorpe is not too young to learn that lesson. Her constitution is more robust than perhaps you give her credit for. She will get over the disappointment."

"I am going to say goodbye to her, regardless."

I made for the stairs, but Holmes forestalled me. "The brougham is pulling up. We must hurry. If we miss the nine-fifty, there won't be a York train for another two hours."

So it was that I, feeling more than a touch frustrated and aggrieved, boarded the brougham, along with Holmes. Winslow lashed the horses and we trundled out of Fellscar Keep and across the causeway. As we entered the woods, I took a look back at the castle. The rising sun tinged its encrustations of snow a glowing red, so that it seemed almost to be afire, just like the castle which had been razed to the ground at the same spot almost a century ago.

An hour later we jounced to a halt outside Bridlington railway station and disembarked. Winslow handed down our bags and bade us farewell.

A bitter, dismal wind was whistling in off the North Sea, and Holmes and I ducked inside the station building for refuge. It was half past nine, but my friend seemed in no hurry to purchase tickets.

"Yonder café should provide us with a warming, restorative cup of tea," he said. "And then we shall go about the task of finding ourselves some form of transportation."

"What do you mean? I thought we were catching the train."

"We are not. We need to hire a dog-cart or similar. I imagine the stationmaster will assist us in that endeavour."

"I don't understand."

"Oh, Watson, Watson, Watson." Holmes shook his head. Suddenly, having been presenting a taciturn, rather grim demeanour, he was all smiles. "You surely have not been fooled by my little masquerade? 'London calls.' 'You may feel free to summon the police any time.' 'Nobody at Fellscar will miss us.' Honestly?"

"If it was just an act," I grumbled, "it was a most convincing one."

"Once again I feel I have missed my true calling. I should have gone into the theatre. I could have been one of the great tragedians of our times. But really! As if I would abandon the case just when it is ripening to fruition."

I was flummoxed. "So we are not going home?"

"Hardly. We are going to Yardley Cross. There, we shall

find temporary lodgings – the local inn is the Sheep and Shearer, if I remember rightly – and use that as a base from which to pursue this affair from a somewhat different angle. All being well, everything should be cleared up in time for Christmas Eve tomorrow and, by the same token, Eve Allerthorpe's twenty-first birthday."

"That is splendid news." I had been looking forward to seeing Mary again that afternoon. It would have been a welcome consolation after the disappointment and shame of leaving Yorkshire with the case unresolved. However, I could accept deferring the pleasure of a joyous reunion with my wife by one day if it meant, as Holmes was promising, that the many dangling loose ends at Fellscar were to be tied up.

Chapter Twenty-Four

A COSTLY COMRADESHIP

A dog-cart and driver were provided, and Holmes and I travelled back the way we had lately come, diverting from the route only when we came to the junction with the signpost for Yardley Cross.

The town was not much more than a large village, situated at the confluence of two roads and home to perhaps three thousand souls. It had a church, post office, pub, blacksmith, a decent smattering of shops, and the aforementioned inn, whose sign depicted a docile ovine being relieved of its wool by a beaming, smock-clad rustic. I wondered if the farmers hereabouts, well aware of the actual sweat and toil involved in agricultural work, enjoyed seeing their livelihood portrayed in this romanticised fashion or resented it.

The innkeeper was only too happy to rent us a room. "Thah'll be needin' it just the one night, sirs?"

"Perhaps not even that," replied Holmes.

At this somewhat cryptic answer, the fellow could only scowl and say, "Well, thah'll be paying the full daily rate, never mind 'ow long thah stays."

To me, the implication of Holmes's statement was all too clear. We had another busy night ahead of us.

He confirmed this after the innkeeper's wife had shown us to the room and left us to make ourselves at home. "It would be a good idea, Watson, to take a nap now, if you can. Tonight holds out little prospect of sleep, I fear."

I duly removed my hat, coat and boots and stretched out on the bed, which, to the inn's credit, was markedly more comfortable than the medieval torture rack I had been subjected to at Fellscar Keep.

To my surprise, Holmes did not do likewise. Rather, still dressed in his Inverness cape and ear-flapped travelling cap, he headed for the door.

"You are not staying?" I said.

"There are certain avenues of investigation I must pursue in Yardley. The shops are about to close for lunch, and there is one in particular I should like to visit."

"I shall come with you."

"There is no need. I'm perfectly content to do this on my own. You rest."

With that, he was gone.

I slept for a solid two hours and awoke hungry. There was no sign of Holmes, but the bar served a passable steak and kidney pudding, which I ate perusing a copy of the *East Riding Clarion*.

Thereafter I took a turn about the town, noting that the air temperature had risen a notch or two and there was something of a thaw underway. Tree branches dripped. Snow on roofs was melting, turning into crystalline arrays of icicles on the eaves, while the snow underfoot was becoming slush.

The church was a sizeable and very handsome specimen of ecclesiastical architecture. Just in front of its lychgate lay a frozen-over pond with an island in the middle and a duck house upon that. I was reminded of Fellscar Keep – here was a representation of both lake and castle in miniature – and my thoughts went back to the death of Becky Goforth. Conniving and immoral she may have been, but few deserved to perish in such a horrible manner, and so young, too. It pleased me to think that, in the very near future, Sherlock Holmes was going to bring her assassin to justice.

A familiar voice intruded upon my musings. "Watson! There you are."

"Holmes." It was as though I had magically summoned my friend merely by thinking about him.

"I have been looking all over for you." He cast an eye at the church. "Does that not strike you as inordinately large for a town this size? One can only assume that, like many a church in the north of England, it was built by some industrialist wishing to curry favour with the Almighty. That way he would avoid the fate traditionally reserved for the rich man desirous of entering the kingdom of Heaven. 'It is easier for a camel to pass through the eye of a needle', and so forth."

"Anything to report?"

"Plenty. What say we avail ourselves of the pub and a pint of something foamy and thirst-quenching, and I shall unburden myself of all I have learned."

"It sounds like an excellent plan."

The Carpenters Arms was a dark, low-ceilinged hostelry, the walls of its saloon decked out with horse brasses and framed etchings of farmyard animals. Ensconced in a snug, Holmes and I supped brown ale while around us a handful of other patrons chatted in low voices about hay baling, coy milkmaids and the rising price of cattle feed. At one table a game of dominoes was in full swing; at another, a game of draughts.

"Yardley boasts, amongst its many amenities, a pawnbrokers," Holmes said. "We passed it on the way into town. You saw the three golden balls hanging out front, I am sure. It was there that I called in after leaving you at the inn.

After a spot of artfully contrived browsing, I told the proprietor I was in the market for gold – jewellery, cigarette cases, watches, you name it – and was willing to pay top price. The fellow, a Mr Dobbs, said he had a few suitable items in stock, in the safe in a room at the rear, and invited me back to look. Lo and behold, one of them happened to be…"

He left it to me to complete the sentence. "Erasmus Allerthorpe's signet ring."

"None other. It was not for sale yet. However, Dobbs agreed that if it had not been redeemed by the end of the contractual period, a fortnight hence, it could be mine. 'Strictly between thee and me, sir,' he said, tapping his nose, 'I strongly doubt the owner will return for it. He's 'ocked a fair few bits and pieces with me over time, and has yet to buy owt back.'"

Holmes's approximation of a Yorkshire accent was spot on. But then his talent for vocal mimicry, which formed an essential part of his disguises, was well-honed.

"I expressed a keen interest in purchasing the ring and enquired the price," Holmes said. "'Thirty pound,' I was told."

"Seems rather steep," I said.

"I imagine it would have been lower had I not been a southerner and so obviously affluent. At any rate, I proffered Dobbs a couple of pounds. 'Consider this a down payment,' I said, adding, 'Non-refundable.'

"The pawnbroker licked his lips. 'Mine even in the event the ring is redeemed?' he asked.

"'Yes.'

"'Spoken like a true appreciator of the finer things in life, sir,' said he as the money vanished into his breast pocket. 'I may as well tell thee, thah has a good eye. Purest gold, that ring is, and it has a most excellent provenance, what's more. I shan't reveal the owner's name – for reasons of discretion, like – but it mayn't surprise you to learn that he's landed gentry. The ring isn't the first thing I've bought off him, either, and I doubt as it'll be the last.'

"I pretended, of course, not to have the faintest idea whom he was talking about. I appeared amused and intrigued, however, which had the effect of encouraging Dobbs to enlarge upon his subject.

"'Of late, he's been comin' in once a month, sometimes twice, with some dainty little trinket he's keen ter "pop",' he said. 'Silver paperknife, tortoiseshell fountain pen, porcelain ring tree, and suchlike.'"

"The very kind of things Mrs Danningbury Boyd said had been going mysteriously missing from Fellscar," I said. "Right down to her ring tree."

"The very kind of things," Holmes said, "that one might pilfer unobtrusively, slipping them into one's pocket when nobody is looking."

"But what would Erasmus need to steal them and pawn

them for? Surely he does not need the money?"

"Dobbs aired the very same sentiment. 'Now,' he said, 'thah might be askin' this'sen why a young man as comes from a well-to-do background would need ter visit a pawnbroker for ter mek a little ready cash. Thought's crossed my mind more than once. But it's not for the likes of me ter enquire. I just offer him what I consider a reasonable price, and he seems more than 'appy ter tek it.'

"I speculated whether the fellow in question might have got himself into debt – the sort of debt he could not service without recourse to selling off the odd valuable. 'Perhaps,' I said, 'he has exhausted his existing financial reserves and is having to seek alternative means of funding.'"

"At that, Dobbs's expression turned sly. I could tell in an instant that he knew something, something he was eager to share but ought not. Remembering the alacrity with which he had accepted my two pounds, I was fairly confident that a little further expenditure would loosen his tongue.

"'Tell you what, my good fellow,' I said. 'I don't believe I gave you nearly enough to secure that ring for me. Here's another couple of pounds.'

"The notes vanished as swiftly as the last two had, and Dobbs was now my very best friend in all the world."

"A costly comradeship."

"Yet worth the outlay, I reckon. 'I shouldn't tell thee this – but what's the harm?' he said. 'Thah seems a dependable sort, if thah knows what I mean. It's my opinion that the young man I'm talking about is a gambler and has landed his'sen in a spot of bother with some local toughs. One or two occasions now, I've seen him out and about in town, consortin' with a pair of ne'er-do-wells, the Dawson twins. The Dawsons – Neville and Nigel – are the ones ter go ter, sir, if thah has a brace of pheasant that thah's poached and are wantin' ter sell, or if thah has some stolen goods as needs fencing. They also run card games in an upstairs room at the Sheep and Shearer, and in this case the inn's name could not be more fitting. If thah's the kind of fool who's easily parted from his money, then cards with the Dawson twins and their cronies is as good a way as any ter go about being fleeced.'

"'They cheat, I presume,' I said."

"'If what's tantamount ter barefaced robbery can be called cheating, then aye, they cheat. Pity the mug who sits down ter play euchre or lanterloo with 'em and expects ter leave the table the richer. Then there's the altercation as 'appened in the street just the day before yesterday.'"

"'Sunday?'"

"'Aye. Late Sunday evening. Now, I didn't see it me'sen, mind, but I've heard about it since from several sources, all of 'em reliable. The fine young gent whose name I shan't reveal got inter a bit of a barney outside the Sheep and Shearer with one of the Dawsons – Neville I think it were.

Squawkin' and skriking, they were, like two angry crows. The lad was protesting about how he'd be able ter make good his losses, and Neville Dawson was refusing ter let him play cards any more unless he first paid back all he owed. It came ter blows. Or, I should say, *blow*. Dawson struck him a good 'un in the face, and the youngster went down and didn't get up again in an 'urry. Dawson's parting words ter him were, "And don't thah darest show thah face in Yardley again until thah's got our brass.""'

"Quite the gossip, your Mr Dobbs," I remarked drolly.

"Oh, once he'd started, I couldn't stop him," said Holmes. "'The very next morning,' he went on, 'who should come in through my shop door but the aforesaid gent, sportin' a nice juicy black eye. "How much for this here ring?" he asked, tekkin' it off his finger. Well, I offered him a few shillings.'"

"A few shillings!" I exclaimed. "Hardly the soul of generosity, this man."

"Show me the pawnbroker who is. 'The young fellow mithered and griped,' he said. 'He telt me he were desperate. In the end, after some 'aggling, we settled on the figure of three pound ten. He went away, and I have no doubt that every last penny of that three pound ten has wound up in the Dawsons' grubby paws.'"

"Well," I said, "that clears that up, then. We now know who the Fellscar larcenist is. We also know what Erasmus Allerthorpe was up to in Yardley yesterday and how he came by his injury. I feel a certain grudging sympathy for the lad, as it happens."

"And a certain grudging kinship too?" said Holmes. "You yourself are fond of the turf accountant and the card table."

I huffed in indignation. "I have never got myself into arrears through wagering. It is my brother I am thinking of. My gambling habit knows limits. His was egregious." A thought occurred to me. "In light of this fresh intelligence, could it be that Erasmus is Becky Goforth's murderer after all?"

"What makes you say that?"

"I know you exonerated him from blame. You said you thought that he had something to hide but that it did not pertain to Goforth. However, I put it to you that Goforth learned of his gambling and his association with the Dawson twins. She might even have seen him committing one of his acts of petty theft around the castle. What might she do then, a girl like her, but try to blackmail him? And what might Erasmus do in return but kill her in order to ensure her silence?"

"Well now, that is a turn-up for the books."

"You mean to say you hadn't thought of it?"

Was it possible? Could I, for once, have beaten the great Sherlock Holmes to the solution of a crime?

I should have known better.

"What? Oh no, Watson," said he. "I wasn't referring to

your theory. It is wholly unsound. I was referring to the pair of gentlemen over there who are even now making their way towards us."

I turned my head to follow his gaze.

Two rough-hewn bravoes were approaching our snug with a purposeful gait. Each was practically the spit of the other, right down to the collar-length hair, the earring in the left ear, the bulbous nose and the eyes that were rather too close-set.

These could only be the notorious Dawson twins, and it seemed they had a bone to pick with Sherlock Holmes.

Chapter Twenty-Five

THE IDEAL MURDER WEAPON

"Art thah the southern toff what's been goin' around town askin' too many questions?" said one of the twins. "Thah matches the description right enough. High forehead. Big, beaky snout."

Around us, the room had gone rather quiet. The other patrons were all of a sudden very interested in their beers and not so much in conversation. The domino players laid down their tiles with none of the banter that had hitherto accompanied their game, while the draughts players studied the board intently as though it held the secrets of the universe.

"Mr Neville Dawson, I presume," said Holmes in a somewhat sardonic tone. "Or is it Nigel?"

"I'm Neville," the same fellow said. He jerked a thumb at his brother. "He's Nigel."

"The handsome one," said Nigel Dawson with a leering grin.

"And the younger one."

"Only by five minutes."

"Thah should've been quicker off the mark, then."

"And thah shouldn't've pushed in front like thah always does."

This had the air of a rehearsed routine, humorous to them if to nobody else.

"'Appen as the Lombard came ter us not an 'our ago," said Neville Dawson, "with a story ter tell about a London gent who seemed ter think our business were his business."

"The Lombard?" said Holmes. "Ah yes, the slang term for a pawnbroker. You must be referring to Mr Dobbs."

"Stanley Dobbs, aye."

"I presume he volunteered this information to you in exchange for money?"

"He said he had something we might want ter hear. We paid him a bob or two for it."

"He has somewhat mischaracterised our exchange, I must say," said Holmes. "Until I met him, I did not have the slightest idea you two fine fellows even existed. But I suppose a pawnbroker isn't above distorting the truth if he thinks he can turn a profit on it."

"Be that as it may," said Nigel Dawson. At least, I thought it was Nigel. They were so hard to tell apart and spoke with such unanimity that I had lost track of which was which. "The fact remains, me and my brother weren't too chuffed ter learn somebody were pokin' his nose where it don't belong. We don't tek kindly ter that sort of thing. We don't tek kindly ter it at all."

"We've come ter deliver a spot of friendly advice," said Neville, if it was Neville. "In a spirit of northern charitableness, like. There's nowt for the likes of you in Yardley Cross. You and your friend would do well ter leave town at the earliest opportunity."

Holmes rose from the table, drawing himself to his full height. He had a good three inches on the Dawsons, and he leaned over them, smiling a smile which, while superficially genial, conveyed a certain wolfish menace.

"Do you not think we should take this discussion outside?" he said. "Where there are fewer eyewitnesses?"

"Don't see why not," replied Neville, or Nigel, with a shrug.

As the four of us trooped out into the street, I foresaw this interaction going one of two ways. Either there was to be a fight, or Holmes would use his wits to extricate himself and me from trouble. The Dawsons certainly seemed open to the former outcome. One might even say they were spoiling for it.

We stood on the pavement in front of the pub, Holmes

and I facing the twins. There were perhaps half a dozen pedestrians in sight, but none appeared too curious about our mismatched little quartet. They were concentrating more on negotiating a safe path through the slush.

"Now," said a Dawson twin, "thah have a choice. Thah can go, and there'll be an end of it; or thah can stay and continue to be a nuisance, and then thah'll learn the true meaning of trouble."

"If thah start walking that-a-way," said the other, "thah could be in Wold Newton by sundown."

"You are labouring under a misapprehension," said Holmes. "I can honestly say that I do not give two hoots about the pair of you. My companion, I would aver, feels much the same."

"And dost thah know what I reckon ter that? I reckon that's a lie. I reckon thah were sent by a certain nob of our acquaintance what's lookin' ter mek things square after I lamped him one yesterday."

"You think that we are in the employ of Erasmus Allerthorpe? That we are some sort of enforcers?"

"There's about the sum of it, aye."

Holmes chortled. "Do we not strike you as a little too genteel to be professional bullyboys?"

"A ruffian's a ruffian, 'owever posh he talks."

"In that case, there seems only one way to settle the matter."

"I were rather hopin' thah'd say summat like that."

One Dawson twin produced a clasp knife from his pocket, prising the blade out from the haft. His double did the same.

I cursed myself mentally for having left my revolver in our room at the Sheep and Shearer. I hadn't dreamed I might need it. Yardley Cross had seemed a rather peaceful little town.

I lofted my fists and circled them in the air. Knives notwithstanding, the Dawson twins would not find me an easy mark.

Holmes, for his part, reached behind him to the portico above the pub's front door. Deftly he snapped off two of the foot-long icicles that hung from the eave and brandished them in his gloved hands like a pair of rapiers.

"Before we go any further," he said, "I should have you know, Messrs Dawson, that I am now holding two specimens of the ideal murder weapon."

"Oh aye?" said one Dawson, cocking an eyebrow.

"Is that a fact?" said the other, cocking an eyebrow too.

"Observe the icicles' tips. I have seen blunter stilettos. Now imagine one such tip being thrust between your ribs, into the soft tissues of your body. I could impale you with a single thrust, like so."

He jabbed the icicle in his right hand forward. Both Dawsons flinched reflexively and took a step back.

"So cold is an icicle," he continued, "and so very, very sharp, that you might not feel it enter you. Not at first. The pain would hit within a few seconds, however, and it would be a fierce pain indeed, like none you have known before. You perhaps might attempt to pull the icicle out, but you would fail. Not only would it be stuck fast, but you would have difficulty maintaining a grip on its slippery surface. At best you might succeed only in snapping the end off."

The Dawson twins were eyeing the twin shafts of frozen water with somewhat greater circumspection now.

"The marvel of it is," Holmes said, "that as you collapsed to the ground, breathing your last, you would understand that your assailant – me – had just pulled off a remarkable feat. For soon the icicle would melt. The heat of your body would turn it to water, and within an hour's time, possibly less, there would be nothing left of it but a wet stain on your clothing. I would, of course, perforate the two of you simultaneously. I am quite capable of the feat."

As if to prove it, he made a spearing motion with both icicles at once. Again the Dawsons flinched.

"Do you know what all of this means?" he said.

The Dawsons shook their heads in dumb unison.

"It means, crucially, that there would be no way of proving I killed you. The police would be unable to fathom why each of you had this perfectly round hole in his body that did not match the hole in his brother's body. They would be quite baffled. Even if they attempted to prosecute me, I could simply ask them to show how I slew you with two completely different stabbing implements, and what those stabbing implements were, and, indeed, what had become of them. The case, I submit, would not even reach court."

The Dawsons exchanged glances. All at once they were not looking anywhere near as smugly confident as they had been. The clasp knife each held was wavering.

"So then." Holmes looked from one brother to the other. "What are we to do? Are we to do battle, or are we to call it quits?"

A moment passed, and then Neville Dawson folded his clasp knife shut and stowed it back in his pocket. Nigel Dawson followed suit.

"There's no need for anybody to die today," Neville said. He looked cowed. "We were nobbut mekkin' a point, that's all."

"Aye," Nigel chimed in. "That's right. Nobbut mekkin' a point."

"In which endeavour I would suggest we have all been successful," said Holmes. "Farewell, gentlemen. This has been a most invigorating meeting. I am glad we have managed to bring it to an amicable conclusion."

The Dawson twins sidled off down the road, frowning. The swagger they had previously exhibited was all but gone. They were defeated but didn't seem quite to know *how* they had been defeated.

"Well," I said, letting out a breath I hadn't realised I was holding. "That was quick thinking on your part, Holmes. Who knew an icicle was so potentially lethal?"

"Not me, for one," came the merry reply.

"I don't understand."

"You so rarely do. There is a prevalent myth, Watson, that an icicle is, as I just put it, the ideal murder weapon."

"The reasons you provided to justify that epithet were very convincing."

"And one hundred per cent bogus. The Dawsons might be able to bamboozle Erasmus Allerthorpe across the baize, but against an inveterate bluffer like me they didn't stand a chance. All that nonsense about the wounds not matching and the police being unable to prosecute. When there are passers-by who would be quite willing to testify they saw me commit the deed?"

"I did wonder about that, and I am surprised that it did not occur to either of the Dawsons. They may not be the brightest of individuals, but nevertheless it seems glaringly obvious."

"Oh, I was quite prepared for one or other of them to raise the point. I had some marvellous fabrication prepared just in case, something about an icicle being invisible to the naked eye beyond a certain distance. However, there is a larger, indeed crucial flaw in my strategy which neither Dawson was likely to have intuited, namely that killing someone with an icicle is quite impossible. Allow me to demonstrate."

Without further ado, he drove one of the icicles at my chest like a lance. The instant it struck, it shattered into a dozen pieces.

"Ouch," I said, rubbing the spot. "That hurt."

"But are you dead? No," said Holmes. "Is there even a hole in your garments? I may have overstated the case somewhat when I compared the icicles' tips favourably to those of stilettos. They can seem that way until you look at them up close, when their roundedness becomes apparent. The penetrative power I boasted of is sorely lacking. Not only that but an icicle is a fragile thing, as brittle as spun sugar. If I had aimed for your eye, I might well have maimed you for life; but still, not a fatal blow. The trouble with the Messrs Dawson is that neither is as smart as he believes. Plus, of course, as with all bullies, they are cowards at heart. All it took to outwit them was a little bravado and a little browbeating. Now then." Tossing the other icicle aside, he consulted his watch. "It is gone three. We have an hour, at best, until we lose the light. I propose we have sandwiches made for us at the Sheep and Shearer, to take with us as iron rations, and thereafter we should commence our journey."

"Journey? Where to?"

"Where else? Fellscar Keep."

Chapter Twenty-Six

A FROZEN PURGATORY

With the thaw came a mist. It began to build just as the sun was setting. Swirls of vapour rose from the ground, thickening into a gauzy miasma of white. It was not long before one could scarcely see a hand in front of one's face. The white of the mist merged with the white of the snow, creating a world of overall whiteness. Trees and drystone walls were mere grey shadows. The sun itself was no brighter than a cue ball on a snooker table.

Holmes and I followed the road out of town that led to the junction with the fingerpost. There we took the Fellscar track. Before leaving Yardley Cross, I had fetched my revolver from the inn. Holmes had not had to suggest this. After our little contretemps with the Dawson twins, I was not going to be caught unarmed a second time.

Our footsteps sounded muffled, as did our breathing. The mist deadened all noise like the dampers on a piano.

"Holmes," I said. My voice carried a weird, tight echo. "Before we were so rudely interrupted by the Dawsons, we were talking about Erasmus potentially being Goforth's killer."

"Were we? So we were."

"You said my theory was unsound."

"Well, it is."

"Why? It seems to me that it holds water."

"Then a sieve would seem to you to hold water. It takes but a moment's thought to spot the fundamental flaw in your idea. Assume Goforth were to threaten Erasmus with blackmail. 'I will tell your father you have been stealing valuables from the castle in order to fund your gambling habit', or words to that effect. Erasmus, if he had any sense, would simply call her bluff. 'Go ahead. Tell him. I shall deny it. See who he believes. A mere scullery maid, or his own son and heir.' Her word against his. There would be no contest."

"Even if Thaddeus and Erasmus do not see eye to eye?"

"They are still kin, and what is that saying about blood being thicker than water? Simply by accusing Erasmus of theft, Goforth might put her job in jeopardy, and she would be canny enough to know that."

"Oh. Yes, I suppose so."

"A valiant effort, Watson, but you are on a hiding to

nothing with this one. By no means should we disregard Erasmus and his gambling debts, but they are not germane in this particular context."

"Are they germane to the Black Thurrick?"

"Now there," said my friend, "you may be on to something."

The sun slipped from view, to be replaced by the moon, whose glow infused the mist with a fainter, more nebulous effulgence.

Presently we entered the woods adjacent to the lake. When we emerged on the other side, the castle would have been in full view were it not for the mist. All we could see were the lights of its windows, shimmering like rows of candle flames suspended in mid-air.

Holmes put finger to lips. From here on, there was to be no more conversation.

Passing the end of the causeway, we followed the perimeter of the lake round. We finally came to a halt on the side furthest from Fellscar. Somewhere to our backs, I judged, lay the copse where we had discovered the layer of soil which Holmes had suggested was deposited there by the Black Thurrick. Immediately in front of us was the lake bank and, just visible beyond, a rind of ice marking the edge of the lake itself. At this distance the lights of the castle showed as an indistinct lambent haze, like some polar aurora.

Now, in the lowest of voices, my companion said, "Nerve yourself and stay vigilant, Watson. You and I must tap our reserves of patience and endurance like never before. For tonight, unless I am sorely mistaken, we shall be meeting the Black Thurrick himself in person."

What can I say about that long, cold watch? Shall I mention how the frigid air seemed to seep through my muscles into my bones and made them ache? Shall I relate how the silence filled my ears as though it had actual substance? Shall I talk about the continual, stealthy shifting of feet and wriggling of fingers that was required in order not to lose all sensation in my extremities?

What about the way that time, as though made torpid by the cold, crawled by? Or the way the mist writhed and coiled around us, thinning and thickening in response to the vagaries of barely perceptible breezes, so that sometimes I could see Holmes beside me, clear as day, and at other times he was all but hidden from view?

It was all these things and more, that vigil. It was, indeed, one of the most trying, enervating tests of resolve I have ever undergone, and that is taking into consideration the many hardships I endured during my time in the army, the many arduous medical challenges I have faced as a doctor, and of course the many similarly adverse situations in which I have found myself as part of my adventures with Sherlock Holmes.

Holmes himself stood rigid throughout the ordeal, as motionless as a statue. But for the regular puffs of vapour from his nostrils as he exhaled, one might have thought him dead. His gaze was fixed unwaveringly upon the lake.

Accordingly, I kept mine upon it too, as best I could. The longer I strained my eyes staring into the mist, however, the more I began to glimpse shapes in it – things that resembled faces, or monstrous figures, or huge gnarled hands reaching for me. Each was there for a fleeting instant, then gone again.

It was a kind of madness. Time and again I told myself the shapes were illusions, yet still they manifested. It was as though the mist was not only alive somehow but malevolent.

It came as some considerable relief when, around eight o'clock, Holmes produced from his pocket the sandwiches that had been prepared for us by the innkeeper's wife at the Sheep and Shearer. He unwrapped the wax paper around them, carefully so that it did not make a crinkling sound, and handed me one. The sandwich consisted of a thick slab of ox tongue between two no less thick slices of butter-lathered bread. My half-frozen fingers could scarcely hold it, and my jaws felt so immobile that I could chew only small morsels at a time. Still, the sustenance was warming and welcome, as were the nips of brandy I took from the hip flask that Holmes offered me.

The meal provided respite, but then we were back to staring into the mist, and soon enough the chill was worming its way ever deeper into my bones and I was once more seeing those flitting, hallucinatory shapes and feeling that horrid sense of disorientation and oppression.

Gradually the far-off glow from Fellscar Keep dwindled. The Allerthorpes were going to bed. By ten, there wasn't a light left burning at the castle, and the mist seemed to revel in this fact, as though it had won some kind of victory. It grew denser and teemed with evanescent humanoid forms in still greater number. When they became too abundant, too overwhelming, I found myself having to close my eyes for short periods. This would dispel them, at least for a while.

Time continued to drag by, and more and more the feeling was creeping up on me – the certainty, in fact – that I had become trapped in limbo. It seemed I had been standing there amidst that numbing, cloudy nothingness since the dawn of creation and would continue to do so until the end of days.

It was then, just as my thoughts were commencing a spiralling descent into out-and-out existential panic, that Sherlock Holmes plucked at my sleeve. He nodded towards the lake.

Out there on the ice I descried a dim silhouette. A moving figure.

At first I was convinced it was just another of the mist's mirages. I blinked a few times. The figure was still there. It was moving closer, hunched, lumbering. It was spindly and dark. It had a sack slung over its back.

The Black Thurrick was here.

Chapter Twenty-Seven

FRAGILE ICE

Holmes motioned me to crouch down. He was excited but doing his best to suppress the emotion. I was excited, too, but with reservations. The figure on the frozen lake remained just a dim outline. I knew it must be a human being, but my mind was still partly adrift, unmoored from reason. My thoughts had become a jumble of ghosts, demons and dead souls. At that particular moment, it would not have surprised me if the thing slouching towards us turned out to be a fiend from folklore after all.

Holmes lay a hand upon my shoulder. His grip steadied me, anchoring me back in reality. I reached into my pocket for my revolver.

The silhouette of the Black Thurrick was becoming sharper and clearer by the second. His garb was purest black. His face was a pale oval speckled with dark blotches, somewhat like a brindled cat's.

As quietly as I could, I cocked the hammer on my pistol.

The Thurrick reached the edge of the lake and rested his sack upon the bank, preparing to clamber up.

"Now, Watson!" Holmes cried, springing upright.

The Thurrick's eyes widened in startlement. His mouth gaped.

"Got you!" my friend declared.

He lunged for the Thurrick, seizing him by the arm.

The Thurrick backpedalled and, with a desperate, mighty wrench, tugged himself free of Holmes's grasp. Holmes lost his footing and slithered down the bank onto the ice. The Thurrick turned and began to run.

"Watson, a warning shot, if you will," Holmes said.

I fired just over the Thurrick's head, so close to my target that I fancy he must have felt the round waft his hair as it hurtled by. Certainly he would have heard it buzzing past him like some angry hornet.

"The next one goes into you," I said. "Don't think that I did not miss deliberately just now."

The Black Thurrick, still just visible through the mist, came to a halt.

"The game is up," Holmes said. "Watson has remarkable aim, as you have discovered. Had he wanted to fell you, he could have easily. He is also a medical man, and knows where to put a bullet so that it may incapacitate without doing lasting harm. Not that that matters much. The severity of an injury is ultimately meaningless to one who has an appointment with the hangman – as you do, Mr Trebend."

The Thurrick bowed his head in submission, then turned back round.

I had been expecting Erasmus Allerthorpe, but in fact it was that very person whom Holmes had addressed by name, Trebend. The butler's features were eminently recognisable for all that they were besmeared with what looked like dirt or soot.

"I should have known you would try something like this, Mr Holmes," he said. His expression was rueful and embittered. "When you said you were leaving the castle and returning to London, I thought it was too good to be true. Yet I dared hope you had given it up."

"So that you would be able to resume your nocturnal activities as before," said Holmes. "That was exactly what I wanted you to think."

"A nice trap."

"I like to think so."

"But I am left in something of a quandary," said Trebend. "You are right. Now that you have me at your mercy, my quest to obtain what is rightfully mine is over. I've nothing to look forward to except the scaffold and the noose. Why, then, should I care whether you take me alive or not? The ice on the lake is noticeably more fragile tonight than it has been over the past few days, what with the slight warming in the weather. On my way across I came upon patches where it felt perilously thin indeed. I hear that drowning in freezing-cold water is one of the more pleasant ways to go. You just sort of… fade."

With an abrupt, surprising turn of speed, Trebend spun on his heel and started to run again. I was taken aback, and in the split-second it took me to collect myself, the butler had disappeared into the mist. I fired, more in hope than expectation of hitting him.

"Dash it all!" Holmes said. "But we can still catch him."

"You heard what he said, Holmes. The ice is thinner than before, and he is slight, whereas both of us are larger and heavier. It would be unwise to give chase."

"So he wishes us to think. He could quite easily make it to the other side of the lake and get away scot-free. After him!"

Holmes hastened off in pursuit of Trebend. I lowered myself gingerly down the bank and onto the ice, and began to run too. Straight away, one foot skidded out from under me and I almost fell flat on my face.

I set off again at a somewhat more measured pace. In no time, I could no longer see the bank behind me. A little further on, I realised I had entirely lost my bearings. I did not know where I was on the lake, where the bank was, where the castle was. All I could see was mist and ice.

I forged onward. Several times the ice sagged suddenly where I trod, a web of fissures radiating outward from my foot. Each time I leapt backward, my heart in my mouth; then I would make a detour around the damaged area, giving it a wide berth, and carry on.

Still nothing but mist and ice. No sign of Holmes or of the Thurrick.

Eventually, in desperation, I called out to my friend.

"Over here, Watson," came the reply. The mist made it hard to tell how close he was. He could have been ten feet away or a hundred.

I ventured in the direction of his voice, my revolver to the fore. All at once there came a loud, splintering *crack* from somewhere up ahead, followed immediately by a mighty splash. I made a beeline towards the sounds, praying they signified that Trebend had fallen through the ice and not Holmes.

The mist billowed, becoming more impenetrable than ever.

"Hullo?" I said. "Holmes? Are you there? Holmes! Please tell me you are all right."

All of a sudden, two strong arms encircled my waist in a powerful hold and threw me roughly to one side. I reeled to my feet, lifting my gun. My assailant loomed before me. It could only be Trebend. My finger tightened on the trigger.

"Please don't shoot, Watson," said Sherlock Holmes. "I cannot imagine the agonies of guilt you would suffer, knowing you had slain your greatest friend. Not to mention," he added archly, "the tremendous loss my death would be to the world."

I lowered the revolver. "Good Lord, man! That was a close thing. But why did you attack me? Did you mistake me for Trebend?"

"Not in the least. And it was not an attack. It was a rescue. Look there. Just to your left."

I peered and was able to make out a jagged, roughly circular hole in the ice, mere inches from my left foot. The hole was a yard in diameter. Dark water lapped and swirled within its circumference.

"You were walking straight for it," Holmes said. "Another step and you might have plunged in."

"Dear God in Heaven. I didn't even see it. If you had not intervened…"

"Well, quite."

"And Trebend? Is it safe to say…?"

"You heard the splash. What do you think?"

"I think," I said, eyeing the hole, "that he got his wish. He cheated the hangman, and this marks his final resting place."

"I concur," said Holmes. "Our Black Thurrick has gone to a watery grave."

"And I would prefer not to share his fate. Our work here on the ice is surely done. The sooner we get off the lake, the happier I shall be."

As we trudged off towards what I hoped was the nearest bank, I asked Holmes what Trebend had meant when he had spoken of a quest "to obtain what is rightfully mine".

"If you can bear the suspense a little longer," he replied, "all will be revealed."

Chapter Twenty-Eight

THE LESSER OF TWO EVILS

Holmes pounded on the main door to the castle, yelling loudly. At last, after several minutes, a footman came. He peered out through a peephole set into the wicket gate.

"Mr Holmes?"

"Jennings, isn't it? Kindly let us in, Jennings."

"It is very late, sir, and the household are all abed."

"And my friend and I are frozen to the bone and losing patience. It is important. I would not be knocking at this hour if it was not."

Reluctantly Jennings opened the gate to let us in. He was wearing slippers and dressing gown.

As we entered the courtyard, Holmes said to him, "Awaken the family, would you? There's a good fellow. No need to trouble the extended Allerthorpe clan. The permanent residents of the castle – the inner circle, as it were – will do. Tell everyone to meet us in the drawing room."

"At this hour of the night?"

"Believe me, they will want to be up for this. You would do well to rouse Mrs Trebend, too."

The footman blinked in confusion. "Mrs Trebend?"

"Don't ask questions, Jennings. Just do as I say."

By now we were indoors, in the central hallway. The embers in the enormous hearth were still giving off plenty of residual heat, and I paused a while to warm my hands until, at Holmes's insistence, he and I made for the drawing room. Jennings, meanwhile, had gone upstairs to discharge his orders.

Ten minutes later, nightwear-clad Allerthorpes began filing into the drawing room. Thaddeus was first, followed shortly by Shadrach and Olivia, her hair pinned up beneath a silk nightcap. Eve was next, then Erasmus, yawning hard, and finally Mrs Danningbury Boyd.

Thaddeus Allerthorpe was livid bordering on apoplectic. "Mr Holmes, it is half past one in the morning!" he thundered. "What is the meaning of this? You aren't even supposed to be here. Winslow dropped you at Bridlington station. You should have been back in London hours ago."

Holmes answered this choleric tirade with a phlegmatic smile. "A necessary subterfuge, Mr Allerthorpe, as you will see. I shall make everything clear in due course, and you will, I trust, be satisfied that I have not got you out of bed for nothing."

"Am I wrong," said Shadrach, "or did I hear a couple of gunshots somewhere outside not so long ago? I could have sworn I did, but Olivia said I must have imagined it."

"You are not wrong. I shall account for that, too." Holmes turned to Eve. "Miss Allerthorpe. May I be the first to wish you a happy birthday, and many happy returns."

She looked bemused. "Yes. I suppose it is Christmas Eve, technically."

"Twenty-one years of age. Congratulations on achieving such a milestone. And on successfully coming into your legacy." Now Holmes turned to Mrs Danningbury Boyd. "Your husband, madam, is not in a position to join us, I take it."

"He is presently in police custody," said the wronged wife, with some satisfaction.

"It may surprise you to hear that I shall be wiring the police station in the morning to recommend his release."

"What?"

"Mr Danningbury Boyd remains an adulterer and, to that extent, despicable. He more than deserves a night on a wooden cot in a police cell. But he is not a murderer. My accusation was false. Another necessary subterfuge. Ah! Last but not least, here is Mrs Trebend."

All eyes fell upon the cook, whose usual formidable demeanour gave way to something akin to alarm as she entered the room and spied Holmes and me. She seemed to understand that we bore news of her husband and that it was not good – or so I assumed.

"Don't be shy, my good woman," said Holmes. "Your presence is required at this little gathering as much as anyone's."

"I can't imagine why."

"Oh, but I think you can. No, don't cringe so. It ill befits you. Come over here." He beckoned to her. "Take a seat beside me. That's it. Everyone else should make themselves comfortable too. I have something of a tale to tell and it may take some time."

His tone brooked no refusal, and the various Allerthorpes acceded to his request either out of curiosity or through a grudging complacency. Even Thaddeus set aside his outrage, for the moment at least, and sat. Erasmus helped himself to a glass of Madeira, then joined Eve on a sofa. He reached for his sister's hand and clasped it. Mrs Trebend fixed her face in an impassive expression, staring off into the middle distance.

Holmes put his palms together as though in prayer, bent his head, then raised it again.

"This has been an unusual case," he said, "by turns fascinating and frustrating. It had so many disparate facets that, in the initial stages, I was having trouble reconciling them all. Until, that is, I realised I was dealing with two discrete but intertwined sets of events rather than one – two threads braided around each other so tightly, it was hard to distinguish each from the other.

"But to begin at the beginning. In town, young Miss Eve Allerthorpe came to me in a woeful state. She told me about her plight. A tragic suicide, a sizeable legacy, a creature from folklore, a haunted castle, with herself at the heart of it all, a maiden so beset with fear she was starting to question her own sanity. Material there to gladden the heart of any writer of penny dreadfuls.

"Agreeing to take her case, I proceeded from the premise that all of the aforesaid supernatural elements were to be taken with a pinch of salt. I am pleased to say that events have borne out that assumption. There is no ghost. Nor is the Black Thurrick real. Having eliminated these two impossible creatures from my thinking, I was left with the somewhat more probable notion that the handiwork of both could be ascribed to human agency.

"To take the Thurrick first, whose actions appeared to have no goal other than to terrify Eve. What was to be gained by frightening this girl other than to leave her so bereft of reason that it would invalidate the codicil of her Aunt Jocasta's will? If she did not inherit the money, it was to be divided up between family members of the same generation. Each of them would receive monies worth in the region of four thousand pounds. That includes both Mrs Danningbury Boyd here, and Erasmus."

"But I had nothing to do with it!" Kitty Danningbury Boyd declared.

"You cannot say you have not shown jealousy towards your cousin."

"Only as far as Fitzhugh's behaviour regarding her was concerned, and I deeply regret that. I am sorry, Eve, that I slandered you in front of everyone the other night. It was unwarranted and unkind. I was just so infuriated by Fitzhugh. I was teetering on a precipice already, and seeing him pay court to you, in his usual unctuous manner, tipped me over the edge. Can you forgive me?"

"I can," said Eve.

"Thank you, cuz." To Holmes, Mrs Danningbury Boyd said, "As to Eve's legacy, I am pleased for her. She is a lucky woman, and I wish her nothing but the best."

"I am sure that is true," said Holmes. "If only the same were true of her brother."

Erasmus Allerthorpe spluttered into his fortified wine. "What are you saying?"

"I am saying, quite simply, young man, that it is you who have been leaving bundles of birch twigs strategically placed around the castle in emulation of the Black Thurrick. The reason? Greed. No, perhaps greed is too strong a word.

Acquisitiveness. You were trying to drive your sister mad because you wanted a cut of Lady Jocasta's money."

"Well, that is about the absurdest thing I have ever heard."

"And that is about the most predictable response I have ever heard. Denial does not obviate the obvious."

"But what would I want the money for? I have an allowance."

"That is very true," said Thaddeus. "I am generous to all my immediate dependents, whose number comprises everyone in this room. You had better have something to back up this accusation, Mr Holmes."

"I do. What you may not be aware of, sir, is that your son has got himself into serious debt with a pair of local rogues, the Dawson twins of Yardley Cross."

Erasmus paled visibly. "I – I have no idea who you are talking about," he blustered.

"That is queer, Erasmus," Holmes said, "because they seem to know you rather well. As does a certain Stanley Dobbs, pawnbroker by trade, to whom you have hocked various trinkets appropriated from Fellscar. Mrs Danningbury Boyd's ring tree, for one. Your own signet ring, for another."

"His own…?" Thaddeus scowled at Erasmus's hand. "Goodness gracious, boy! Your ring. I hadn't noticed. Your mother and I gave you that ring for your eighteenth birthday. What has become of it? Is Mr Holmes right? You have pawned it?" He sounded appalled.

"No. I... lost it. It fell off by accident. Down a drain. I was going to tell you." Erasmus was growing more and more despondent and his refutations were becoming increasingly lacklustre. "And I don't know about Kitty's ring tree, or any paperknife, or anything."

"Paperknife?" said Holmes with quiet gratification. "I did not mention a paperknife."

"You did. I'm sure you did."

"He did not," said Thaddeus. "Tell us straight, Raz. Have you been thieving from the castle?"

Erasmus understood then that his little slip of the tongue had destroyed whatever last shred of credibility he thought he had. His defensiveness curdled into spite. "Very well. So what if I did pinch a few gewgaws here and there, and make some cash out of them? They were just lying around the place, doing no one any good. I needed money. That pittance you would have me live on, Papa, is a joke."

"Your allowance is more than enough for someone of your age and standing."

"Hah! You think so? My friends down in London laugh when I tell them how much it is. A paltry sum by their standards. Their parents are far more unstinting. I have asked you time and again to give me more, but you always say no."

"Your allowance might have sufficed," said Holmes to Erasmus, "were it not for the fact that you have been gambling at the Dawsons' makeshift card club upstairs at the Sheep and Shearer."

"Gambling as well?" said Thaddeus. "Oh, Raz. You young fool."

"The Dawson brothers are not above using physical coercion to get their way. It was courtesy of one Neville Dawson that Erasmus came by that black eye of his."

"You did not get it from a fall?" said Eve to her brother. "You were struck?"

Erasmus gave her a hangdog look. "There was a scuffle. I came off worse. That is all."

"You should know, Erasmus, that the Dawsons have been cheating," said Holmes. "The card games are rigged, and you have been their mark."

"No."

"Yes. That unscrupulous pair have been taking you for every penny they can. It has left you in a financial hole which even pawning valuables has not been able to get you out of all the way. That is why you hit upon the idea of masquerading as the Black Thurrick and trying to scare your sister out of her wits. That four thousand pounds would have come in very handy, would it not?"

"I don't believe it," said Eve. "Was it really you, Raz?"

"How could it have been me, sis?" he replied. "The second

set of birch twigs appeared outside my own window."

"Misdirection, plain and simple," said Holmes. "A good means of throwing off suspicion from oneself is to make oneself appear to be a victim. The same goes for the twigs you deposited outside Watson's window during the night. Eve was your principal target all along, but spreading your aim would make it appear as though she was not."

"You," said Eve. Her gaze was pinned upon her brother. Her voice was rising, more in dismay than anger. "You wanted me insane?"

"No, of course not."

"But do you deny you were responsible for the twigs? Look me in the eye and tell me you were not."

Erasmus Allerthorpe drew a deep breath and exhaled. All at once, what little fight remained in him was gone. He looked deflated, drained, bereft of spark. "There seems no point in pretending any more. All right, yes, it was me."

"My God." Eve snatched her hand out of his. "The person I trusted most in this world…"

"Hear me out, Eve. Please. I have been a frightful ass, I realise. I shouldn't have done what I did. I was desperate but I never meant to harm you. It seemed like my only chance, that's all. I could not go to Papa and ask him to bail me out. It would have meant explaining everything. You can imagine how well he would have taken it."

"Not well in the least," Thaddeus growled.

"I thought to myself, if I can get my hands on my portion of Aunt Jocasta's will, all my problems are solved. I can pay off the Dawsons and have plenty left over so that I can keep up with my London friends."

"At my expense?" said Eve. "If Dr Greaves had pronounced me mad, I might have been consigned to an institution."

"I thought that even if you did get locked up, it would only be temporary. You would soon recover and the doctors would judge you cured and you would come back home and all would be well. I... I didn't really think it through. I see that now. I was dazzled by the idea of easy money, and I turned a blind eye to your suffering. Until the day before yesterday, at least."

"What changed, the day before yesterday?"

"It was when I came back from Yardley to be told that somebody had just died at the castle. My immediate thought was that it was you. In that moment, it all hit home. I had pushed you too far. I had previously considered the business with the twigs to be... well, little more than a practical joke."

"A practical joke," Eve echoed hollowly.

"I saw how it was distressing you. It was meant to. I knew how the Black Thurrick had frightened you as a child, and I was playing upon that. But all at once the game seemed to have turned deadly serious. You cannot imagine my relief at being told that it was Goforth who was dead, not my beloved sister. I resolved there and then to abandon the whole scheme. I would devote myself instead to your welfare. Hence I have been bringing you broth in your room and reading to you and…"

Tears brimmed in Erasmus's eyes. He slid off the sofa and prostrated himself before Eve.

"Sis, please forgive me," he implored. "I cannot apologise enough. I will spend the rest of my life making amends, if that is what it takes. Just say I am pardoned and all between us will be as it was before."

Eve gazed down at her brother. Tears were rolling down her cheeks too, yet she held herself with an imperious grace.

"Raz, you are an absolute blithering idiot."

"I am. I am."

"You have behaved atrociously."

"I have."

Her lofty demeanour softened just a fraction. "But you are my brother still, and I love you." She laid a gentle hand upon his. "Now, how much exactly do you owe these Dawson people?"

Erasmus raised his head. "In the region of a hundred pounds."

"As soon as Jocasta's will has gone through probate and the money is disbursed, I will pay them off."

He blinked at her in delighted disbelief. "You would do that for me?"

"What is the point in having wealth if I cannot use it to help those in need?"

"Great heavens. You are an angel, Eve. An angel!"

"There is one condition."

"Name it."

"You do not gamble any more, with these Dawson people or with anyone. Swear?"

"I swear."

"And you start taking instruction from Papa on how to run the estate and the family finances."

"I swear that, too."

"And drink less. Much less."

"Those are three conditions, not one."

"It is a single condition in three parts. Would you argue with me? Or will you accept my terms?"

"I accept."

"Then we have a deal," Eve said. "Up you get. Off your knees."

Erasmus leapt to his feet and showered his sister with kisses. It was a touching sight, and while a sceptical part of me wondered whether Erasmus would keep his side of the bargain, a less sceptical part very much hoped he would.

"Daughter, I am proud of you," said Thaddeus gruffly. "Your mother would have been too. With you, on the other hand, my son, I shall reserve judgement. If you hold to your promise and truly do turn over a new leaf, then I am prepared to put your history of misdemeanours behind us."

Sherlock Holmes likewise seemed content with the outcome. "So we have unpicked one of the two interwoven strands of the investigation. I would call the Black Thurrick the lesser of the two evils at work in Fellscar. For it was not Erasmus whom Eve saw crossing the lake that night some two weeks ago. Erasmus confined himself to the twigs. He did not carry his imposture any further than that."

"But I did see someone?" Eve said. "I did not dream the whole thing?"

"You did not. Here is where the one mystery impinges upon the other. You might call it the point at which the lesser evil and the greater overlap."

"If not Raz, then who was it?"

"A pretender. But not in the sense of one who impersonates. More in the sense of one who aspires to usurp."

"Whatever is that supposed to mean?" said Thaddeus.

"This," said Holmes. "Within your household, Mr Allerthorpe, you unwittingly harboured a man who desired to claim the Allerthorpe lands for himself, and his name was Robert Trebend."

Chapter Twenty-Nine

THE GREATER OF TWO EVILS

"Trebend?" said Thaddeus. "What on earth are you talking about? Trebend is a capital fellow. A man couldn't ask for a better, more attentive butler. Where is he, by the by? You had Mrs Trebend join us here but not Trebend himself. What has become of him?"

"I regret to inform you that Trebend cannot be with us," said Holmes. He turned to Mrs Trebend. "It falls to me to be the bearer of bad tidings, madam. Your husband—"

"He is dead, isn't he?" said she. Her features contorted in sorrow and vindictiveness. "I knew it. I knew it the moment I saw you and Dr Watson here. I could read it in your faces. Did you kill him, you devil?"

"It was pure mishap. He fell through the ice on the lake."

"And you did nothing to save him, no doubt."

"I would have if I had been there to witness the event. As it was, I arrived too late at the scene to be of any use."

At this, Mrs Trebend let loose a torrent of most unladylike oaths, after which, her spleen vented, she collapsed in a swoon.

"Watson? Can you be of assistance?"

I administered smelling salts and slowly she came round.

"Perhaps, madam," Holmes said, "you would like to repair to your room. We can continue this in the morning, when you have recovered."

"No," said she with bitter resignation. "May as well get it over with."

"Very good. Your resilience does you credit. I had my first intimation that there might be more to Trebend than met the eye when I observed the shield above the mantel in the central hallway. The Allerthorpe family coat of arms consists of three golden bars angled downward to the right on a red background, with a lion above. In heraldry, a bar is known as a bend, while the heraldic term for 'three' tends to occur as the prefix 'tre-', as in the three-leafed trefoil; the tressel, a three-legged frame supporting a table; and the tremoile, which comprises a trio of hearts. By putting 'tre-' and 'bend' together... Well, I hardly need to spell it out for you."

"Good grief!" Thaddeus declared. "You mean to say Trebend was one of us by birth? Some distant, unacknowledged relative?"

"I feel, as an historian, that I ought to have known the names of the symbols on the crest," said Shadrach, "and ought to have made the connection with Trebend."

"There is no need for self-recrimination, sir," said Holmes. "Unless one has a keen interest in heraldry, one tends to take a coat of arms, even that of one's own family, at face value. It is just a set of patterns and images. In Trebend's case, there is grimly pleasing applicability in the fact that when a bar goes from the top left corner of the shield to the bottom right, it is known as a bend sinister. And Trebend was, without doubt, a sinister character."

"My Robert was a good man," Mrs Trebend piped up. "A wronged man but a good one."

"We shall see about that," said Holmes. "It is clear to me that Trebend already knew, when he entered your employ, Mr Allerthorpe, that he was in some way related to your family. His humble origins notwithstanding, there was Allerthorpe blood running in his veins. I suspect his widow can enlighten us as to how he arrived at that knowledge, but we shall come to that in a moment. First, I must explain how Trebend was mistaken by Eve for the Black Thurrick.

"Put simply, Trebend was carrying out excavations beneath the east wing. He had been doing it for some while. There is a door at the far end of the ground-floor corridor that opens onto a cellar which was once a cold store or a root cellar but which has since fallen into disuse. During the small hours of yesterday morning, I conducted a thorough survey of it. This was after Mrs Trebend's unfortunate, rather noisy episode in the servants' quarters which had the effect of bringing us all running.

"Once everyone had returned to bed, I took myself back to the east wing, where Watson and I had earlier been keeping lookout. Watson himself is unaware I did this. He, too, went to bed, but I decided that the night should not be a complete loss, and so I gained access to the cellar by lowering myself into it. The stairs leading down have partly collapsed, but by dint of hanging by my hands from the remainder, I was able to drop to the floor below safely. Similarly, I was able to jump up and catch hold of the bottom riser and haul myself back out. Neither feat of athleticism was too taxing.

"I had taken the precaution of lowering a dark-lantern down into the cellar beforehand on the end of a length of string. And what did I discover down there by its light? Only that the heap of planks that had been the broken staircase were being used to conceal the entrance to an adit – a horizontal tunnel, dug out by hand and propped up at intervals by timbers. Along this adit, its dimensions just large enough to accommodate a man on his hands and knees, I crawled a short distance. At the end I emerged into a broad chamber – again, hand-dug – which was dotted about with the remnants of old masonry.

"With Shadrach Allerthorpe's assistance earlier in the day, I had learned that the ruins of an older castle lay beneath the foundations of Fellscar Keep. The sorry saga of Sir Mansfield Allerthorpe is perhaps familiar to you. It is a dark chapter in your family history, all the way to its fiery, fateful conclusion. That chamber demonstrated that someone had been busy uncovering the long-buried rubble, in secret, and not for reasons of archaeological enquiry, either."

"Trebend," said Thaddeus.

"Trebend," said Holmes. "I was looking at many months' worth of diligent nightly labour, conducted by your butler after he had discharged his normal household obligations for the day. This was the source of the various indistinct thuds, scrapes and bangs noted by other servants; the groans, too, which may be attributable to the grunting of someone exerting himself. The work would have necessitated the removal of significant quantities of earth, of course. And where, I asked myself, could all that earth have gone?

"The answer must be: into the lake. Trebend would fill a sack with the excavated earth – the spoil or overburden, as it is known in mining parlance – which he would hoist back up to the corridor and thence dispose of its contents into the water. Rather than tip the spoil out of a window, however, which might leave telltale traces of soil on the rocks below, he was obliged to do something a little more involved. The only safe way down to the lake's edge would be by fastening a rope around a window mullion. I said as much to you, Watson, when we were discussing how to reach Goforth's body. Trebend could lower the sack down onto the rocks and lower himself after it. Then he could simply dump the spoil straight into the water.

"Repeated use of the rope, with the weight of a man hanging from it, had progressively caused the base of the iron window frame to warp outwards. That was one of the clues that led me to deduce the nature of Trebend's activity. Another was the fact that the hinges and latch of the cellar door, a door which supposedly had not been used in a long time, had been oiled so that they did not squeak."

I recalled Holmes opening and closing the door and now realised that he had been testing the smoothness and noiselessness of its operation.

"But what can the fellow have been looking for down there?" Olivia Allerthorpe asked.

"All in good time, Mrs Allerthorpe. Until the end of autumn, Trebend's system of spoil disposal would have presented no problem. With the onset of winter, however, the lake froze over and so he could not continue to get rid of the earth as before. Now, perforce, he had to resort to the more arduous measure of walking across the ice and emptying his sack in the copse that lies just beyond the far bank, the nearest place where the ground is free of snow. It was while he was conducting this task that Eve, looking out from her window late one night, spotted him and took him for the Black Thurrick."

Eve's hand flew to her mouth. Comprehension dawned in her eyes.

"Picture it," Holmes said. "A man dressed in dark clothing. A man who has been digging underground so that his face and hands are dirtied, blackened like a coalminer's. He has a sack slung over his shoulder. As he picks his way across the ice, he turns to look back at the castle. Perhaps he is merely checking that he is unobserved, or perhaps, in that uncanny way that a person knows instinctively when he is being watched, he senses another's gaze upon him."

"His eyes," Eve said. "I told you they seemed to glow. I remember that distinctly."

"The moon was up and full. You were looking northward, so that it was at your back. I am of the view that Trebend's eyes caught and reflected the moonlight. This, and the contrast between their brightness and the darkness of the rest of his face, is what made them appear to shine in such an eerie fashion. Your mind, Eve, did the rest. It synthesised the various factors into a whole, assembling them in the image of a folkloric Christmas monster that had had such a profound influence on your imagination in childhood. Where someone else might have seen only what was there, you saw the dreaded Black Thurrick."

Eve was on the point of crying again, but this time the tears, when they came, were tears of relief. Erasmus stroked her arm comfortingly.

"You were already primed to see the Thurrick," Holmes continued, "thanks to your brother's endeavours with the birch twigs. Alas, together the twigs and your sighting of Trebend served only to exacerbate your anxieties and take you to the brink of madness."

"Did Trebend have something to do with Goforth's death?" Thaddeus asked.

"Not something," replied Holmes. "Everything. Becky Goforth was conducting an illicit affair with Fitzhugh Danningbury Boyd. I trust Mrs Danningbury Boyd will not mind me stating it so boldly."

"In this company it can hardly matter," said the lady, with a certain sourness. "Practically everybody knows by now."

"By great mischance, the two of them were meeting up in the same part of the castle where Trebend was carrying out his excavations. As far as Goforth and Danningbury Boyd were concerned, the east wing was ideal. No one else went there, especially not after the sad demise of Mrs Perdita Allerthorpe, and there were plenty of vacant rooms. Goforth even took the precaution of claiming to have had a ghostly visitation in the east wing, in order to ensure their privacy. Mrs Trebend then went and compounded it by saying that she, too, had encountered a ghost. Her reasons were not dissimilar from Goforth's."

"She knew what her husband was doing, then?" said Thaddeus. "She wished people to stay away from the east wing to lessen his chances of discovery? She was his accomplice?"

Mrs Trebend's curl of the lip was tantamount to a yes.

"It appears to be the case," said Holmes, "that at some point Goforth's and Trebend's paths crossed. Goforth fathomed that Trebend was up to something in the east wing – something clandestine and nefarious – and being the kind of girl who thought nothing of extorting a diamond necklace out of a paramour's wife, she spied an opportunity to profit from it. Do I have it right, Mrs Trebend? Did Goforth get it into her head to blackmail your husband?"

Another lip curl gave him the answer he sought.

"Trebend invited her to the tower room to discuss the matter. His intention, no doubt, was simply to convince her to keep her silence. Perhaps he promised her that once he had proved he was an Allerthorpe and gained a more elevated position in life, he would share some of his newfound prosperity with her. Mrs Trebend? A simple nod will do. There. It is affirmed. Goforth, however, must have stuck to her guns. She wanted money immediately, not at some unspecified future date. Trebend therefore felt he had no alternative but to get rid of her, and did the deed promptly and cold-bloodedly."

A silence settled over the drawing room as the Allerthorpes contemplated Trebend's heinous act.

Holmes resumed his monologue. "He must have realised, however, that the murder would have repercussions, especially with Sherlock Holmes a guest on the premises. All at once he had graduated from mere duplicity to a far more serious crime. He also needed to be able to pursue his excavations uninterrupted. One must presume that my presence, and his act of murder, served as a spur. He perceived that his time might be limited, and if was to complete his task it were best done as soon as possible, rather than delayed. Mrs Trebend, you may be able to confirm whether or not this was his thinking."

"Robert was feeling some greater urgency than before," said she. "He also believed he was close to achieving his ultimate aim, and after so long, so much effort, he would not be denied it. It may have been rash of him to carry on, not least with the east wing occupied by guests, but he would not be deterred. Nowt I said to him, at any rate, would convince him otherwise."

"No. Rather, you and he together concocted a scheme that you hoped would deflect my attention away from the east wing. You would fake a heart attack, and do it in such a way that you would even fool a trained medical practitioner, namely my friend Dr John Watson."

"But her symptoms…" I began.

"The consumption of orange peel in significant quantities is known to cause palpitations, sweating, an irregular heartbeat," Holmes said, "and orange peel is something that a maker of excellent marmalade would have in plentiful supply. I remarked at the time of her collapse that Mrs Trebend smelled of oranges, did I not, Watson?"

"You did. Dash it all."

"I have been considering for a while penning a short monograph on the toxicity of certain everyday foodstuffs and condiments if consumed in excess. Orange peel will undoubtedly rate a mention."

"It was quite a risk to take," I said.

"Yet, as Mrs Trebend has just admitted, the times were desperate, and so desperate measures were called for. Trebend, you see, had observed at supper that evening that Watson and I were more or less abstaining from drink. He would have guessed that we needed to be sober and alert because we were intending to stay up late. He would have assumed that we were ghost-watching in the east wing and thus he would be hindered from digging. Mrs Trebend elected to provide a distraction so that we would be drawn away from there and possibly spend the rest of the night investigating her professed sighting of a ghost in the servants' quarters. Doubtless she and Trebend hoped we would thereafter not bother with the east wing, so that he could continue his labours, regardless of the guests occupying that part of the castle. I went one better than that and announced that Watson and I were leaving Fellscar altogether. The Trebends must have been overjoyed at the news. Now Trebend had carte blanche. His great work could begin again, all fear of discovery gone. What is more, I had identified Fitzhugh Danningbury Boyd as the killer of Becky Goforth. Trebend had got away with murder. Or so he thought."

He addressed himself once more to Mrs Trebend.

"There remain a few gaps in my understanding, madam," said he. "Would you, for the benefit of us all, care to fill them in?"

Chapter Thirty

THE TRAGIC HISTORY
OF THE TREBENDS

S lowly, haltingly, Mrs Trebend began to speak.

"My husband only wanted what was due him," she said. "His great-grandfather, Tobias Allerthorpe, was a cousin of Sir Mansfield Allerthorpe. Sir Mansfield's closest living relative, in fact, and a Yorkshireman as well. By all accounts, though, he had little in common with that notorious devil worshipper. Quite the opposite. He was a rector, pious and honest, well loved by his flock.

"But Sir Mansfield's sinful behaviour was bringing shame to the Allerthorpe name. My husband told me that his great-grandfather tried several times to persuade his cousin to change his ways and embrace the message of the scriptures. Sir Mansfield repeatedly rebuffed him.

"Eventually, renouncing all association with his cousin,

Tobias quit Yorkshire. He moved south and started over in a London parish. He married a local woman and, in order to wipe the slate completely clean, changed his surname. The name he adopted instead of Allerthorpe was Trebend. He knew a thing or two about heraldry, did Tobias, and the word was taken from the family coat of arms, as you say, Mr Holmes.

"When the news reached him that Sir Mansfield had met his end in a fire, Tobias journeyed back up to Yorkshire. He wished to pray at the site of Sir Mansfield's demise, begging the Lord to have mercy on his cousin's soul. He found the crude grave in which the body was buried. He also found, beside it, a triangle-shaped chunk of charred stone with an inscription on it – words in Latin."

"Part of the Hell Stone," said Holmes.

"Just so. Tobias knew of the Hell Stone, the thing that Sir Mansfield had had made from a segment of meteorite in order to seal his compact with Satan. It was supposed to have been broken into bits and buried with Sir Mansfield's body, but it seems a fragment had been overlooked. Tobias took the fragment away with him. A sort of souvenir, I suppose."

"Or a memento mori. To remind him of the fallibility and frailty of man."

"Maybe," said Mrs Trebend. "At any rate, when Tobias died, the fragment ended up in the possession of his son, my husband's grandfather. It was passed on from there to my husband's father, Thomas. Over the three generations the Trebends' circumstances declined. Thomas Trebend was reduced to eking out a living as a casual labourer. He was a drunkard, a profligate and a bully. He was free with his fists, too, and it were his wife and child who bore the brunt.

"His son, my Robert, grew up in poverty, with a savage brute for a father and a burning yen to improve his lot. When Thomas Trebend died – jaundice, of course – he left behind little in the way of worldly goods. A few worthless knick-knacks, or so it was thought. But amongst them there was one thing of value, even though it might not have appeared as such. The Hell Stone fragment.

"My husband had known nowt about the fragment until he happened upon it while emptying out his father's cupboards. Thomas himself must have had no idea what the piece of stone signified. It had become just a piece of family junk, a meaningless heirloom. He'd probably have sold it if he'd thought it would fetch a decent price.

"Robert, though, was intrigued by it, and began researching its origins. The trail led to Fellscar Keep and the Allerthorpes.

"It was child's play for him to insert himself into the household. A butler position was advertised, after the previous butler, Lapham, took ill and retired. By then Robert had several years' experience in service and an exemplary record. He came highly recommended by his previous employers."

"That is very true," Thaddeus admitted. "I considered myself fortunate to be able to hire him."

"He even married the cook," said Holmes, "thereby further entrenching his position as a loyal servant."

Mrs Trebend clucked her tongue disputatiously. "Robert is — was — an admirable specimen of manhood through and through. We were a good match, him and me. A very good match." A hoarseness entered her voice as she uttered these last words, and I was reminded that only a few minutes ago did she learn she had been widowed. Her composure under the circumstances was remarkable, evidence of a strong will; but it was fragile, too.

"Did you learn of his Allerthorpe roots before or after you were wed?" Holmes asked.

"After. It wasn't a consideration in my marrying him, if that's what you're implying. We'd been husband and wife for many a week before Robert took me into his confidence. He told me he'd identified which area of the castle was built over the old castle. He said he even thought he knew how to gain access to the ruins below. He showed me the Hell Stone fragment. 'This,' he said, 'is my proof. It will reveal the truth about my heritage.'"

"I see. He believed that if he could unearth the other fragments of the Hell Stone and match his part of it with them, this would put the matter of his ancestry beyond question."

"It would confirm that he, and nobody else, was the lawful owner of these lands," said Mrs Trebend. "Never mind that Alpheus Allerthorpe had erected his own castle on the island. All of it belonged to my husband, fair and square, and once that had been established, he'd claim the place for himself and evict these folk who wrongly thought it theirs. He would become the lord of the manor, and I the lady. And so he commenced his digging."

"Astonishing," said Thaddeus. "To think that for two years that – that *snake* was pouring my wine, overseeing my pantry, serving my guests, and all the while quietly plotting to oust me."

"And I loathed every minute of it," said a sneering voice.

All eyes turned to the doorway.

There stood none other than the man himself, Trebend.

He was holding a double-barrelled shotgun.

There were gasps of alarm from the Allerthorpes.

Mrs Trebend gasped too, but hers was one of joy. "Robert! You're alive!"

"Very much so, my dear Margery," said he, "and now that everything is out in the open, it is a relief to have to play the meek, unflappable underling no more. All those months kowtowing to my master." The emphasis he placed on the last word was more than a little sarcastic.

"Recompense for what was stolen from me is long overdue. I have come to collect."

"Trebend…" said Holmes.

"No, sir." Trebend levelled the shotgun at my friend. "I have been listening at the door. You have talked enough. Now it is my turn."

Briefly holding the gun with one hand, he delved into a pocket and produced a chunk of stone. It had roughly the size and shape of a set square from a child's geometry set. I glimpsed letters carved into its scorch-marked surface. One word stood out: DIABOLUS.

"Here is Sir Mansfield Allerthorpe's Hell Stone, the little of it my great-grandfather retrieved. When I locate the other pieces – and it is only a matter of time before I do – there will be no dispute. Fellscar Keep and its estate will be mine. I have worked long and hard, exhausting myself night after night, in pursuit of this goal. After all that, I will not be denied my inheritance." He returned the chunk of stone to his pocket.

"You are hardly likely to be granted ownership of the land even if you were given the chance to find the other pieces of the stone," Holmes pointed out. "You are a criminal now. You have committed murder."

"And I will do it again!" Trebend declared, tightening his grip on the weapon. His eyes, staring from his soil-stained face, were wide and wild. "I will murder you all if I have to."

"Just calm down, Trebend," said Shadrach. "Put the gun aside. Let us discuss this rationally. I am sure we can come to some sort of accommodation."

"Never," snarled the other. "I have endured enough. Being manhandled by Mr Holmes and shot at by Dr Watson was the final indignity. I knew that by stamping a hole in the ice of the lake and slapping the water beneath hard with both hands, I could give the impression that I had drowned. That left me free to steal back to the castle and remove this weapon from your gunroom."

"But what now, Trebend?" said Holmes. "You have sprung your ambush. You have the upper hand. You are in a position to make demands. What are they? Mr Allerthorpe is right. We can surely arrive at some sort of compromise, can we not?"

Trebend was preoccupied with Holmes at that moment. He was paying no attention to me. My hand crept to my pocket where my revolver nestled.

"I will concede nothing at gunpoint," said Thaddeus to Trebend. "I am prepared, however, to negotiate with you, provided that you cease to threaten me and my family."

"At present this gun is all that's keeping me from being overpowered by the various men in the room," Trebend said. "I may be a snake but I am no fool. The likes of you people are forever trying to keep down the likes of me, and I won't have it any more. The gun is my one advantage, an equaliser of imbalances, and I shall not throw it away."

I had my revolver in my grasp. All I needed to do now was draw it.

Before I could, however, Erasmus propelled himself off the sofa, diving at Trebend. He managed to seize hold of the shotgun by the twin barrels. There was a ferocious struggle. The shotgun went off.

The report was deafening, and was followed by a peal of frightened screams. I scanned around the room. A framed mezzotint on the wall now lay on the floor in pieces, but by great good fortune, nobody had been hit.

Out came my revolver, but Erasmus and Trebend were still locked together, vying for control of the shotgun. I could not get a clear shot.

Rising to my feet, I took three swift paces forwards. My plan was simply to place the pistol's muzzle against Trebend's temple. He would surely then realise that the game was up and would surrender.

In the event, Trebend spotted my move. With a sudden surge of effort, he wrested the shotgun out of Erasmus's grasp and swung it towards me. Before I could do anything, he squeezed the second trigger.

Next thing I knew, I was on my back and there was an intense, burning pain in my upper leg. The room reeled around me. I caught blurred glimpses of Sherlock Holmes snatching the now empty shotgun out of Trebend's clutches and then performing some intricate double-handed manoeuvre, a baritsu technique, which brought the other man helplessly to his knees. Thaddeus, Shadrach and Erasmus then took over, seizing Trebend and wrestling him to the floor, where he writhed and protested, to no avail.

Now Holmes was bending over me, a look of horrified concern upon his face.

"Watson. Watson! My God, man. I pray your wound is not a mortal one. I could not bear to be without my Watson."

I tried to reassure him that I was fine, but the words would not come out. Everything began to cloud over, as though the mist that surrounded the castle was leaking indoors and filling the room. The last thing I was aware of was Holmes demanding that someone must fetch a doctor. Absurdly, I wanted to remind him that *I* was a doctor. There was no need to pester anyone else.

Then all went black.

Chapter Thirty-One

A CHRISTMAS MIRACLE

D r Greaves, the Allerthorpes' family practitioner, turned out to be a grizzled fellow in his sixties, with the kind of voice that instilled faith and the air of someone for whom no illness or injury came as a surprise.

I had passed out from the shock of being shot. When I came round a couple of hours later, Greaves was already bandaging up my leg. Although he had been roused from his bed and driven from Yardley Cross to Fellscar in the dead of night, he seemed unruffled. He was the kind of seasoned senior medic I hoped I might become.

"I have picked out as many of the shotgun pellets as I could with my tweezers," he told me. "Some have gone deep into the quadriceps and will either work their own way to the surface in time or else will remain where they are in perpetuity. I'm afraid this may cause your leg to ache, especially in cold weather. But I understand from Mr Sherlock Holmes that you already have a bullet lodged in your shoulder, so you will perhaps be used to the discomfort."

"Used to it? No," I said, essaying a laugh. "Resigned to it? Yes."

"That's the spirit. Of course, you must not move for several days, to give the affected area time to heal properly. The Allerthorpes are only too happy for you to remain their guest while you recuperate. Thaddeus Allerthorpe insists upon it, in fact. He is immensely grateful for what you have done for his family – you and Mr Holmes both – and for your personal sacrifice."

"Out of the question."

"Doctor's orders."

"Which do not apply when directed at a fellow doctor. I must get home. Tomorrow is Christmas Day. I cannot miss it. Forget about Trebend and his shotgun – Mrs Watson will kill me if I am not there. She is an understanding woman, but wifely benevolence only goes so far."

Dr Greaves studied me in a measured fashion. "I can see that nothing I say will dissuade you. Very well. Against my express recommendation, go."

So it was that Holmes and I departed from Fellscar Keep not long after daybreak. The entire Allerthorpe clan, all forty-odd, turned out to wave us off. Thaddeus shook our hands hard enough to hurt. Shadrach saluted us. Erasmus huzzahed. Eve kissed us warmly upon both cheeks and said we had saved her. She promised to write more poems about us.

It was a wearisome, at times excruciating journey. I could barely stand, let alone walk. But I bore it as best I could. The end goal would make it all worthwhile.

Long, arduous hours later, Holmes helped me across the threshold of my house. Mary rushed to greet me, smothering me in an impassioned embrace. It was only when I hissed in pain that she realised I was injured.

"John! Good heavens! You look wrung out. What has happened?"

"A long story. I shall be only too happy to tell it to you, but first I must sit down before I fall down."

So relieved was I to be back home, and so delighted to be with Mary again, that I did not notice Sherlock Holmes quietly withdrawing, without so much as a goodbye. When at last I thought to look for him, he was gone.

Christmas Day dawned. I awoke to the delicious smell of roasting goose. Mary was hurrying about the house, making final preparations before her family arrived. Although she was an only child and both her parents had passed away, she had an uncle and aunt with whom she was on excellent terms. They, their children and grandchildren, a dozen bodies all told, would be descending upon us at midday. It might not be as large a family gathering as the Allerthorpes', but with that many Morstans added to it, our Paddington townhouse would seem, for a while, as populous as Fellscar Keep had been.

I was excused anything but the lightest of duties, thanks to my leg. Even the mere act of pulling my trousers on was a minor torture. As I waited for our guests, my thoughts turned to Sherlock Holmes. I pictured him alone in his rooms at Baker Street. He was no aficionado of Christmas, as I well knew. Still, I berated myself for not inviting him to join us, and resolved to do something about it.

Mary found me in the hallway, struggling to lace up my boots.

"And just where do you think you are going, John?"

"To fetch Holmes. Mrs Hudson is away visiting her sister in Farnham. I cannot wire him. The telegraph offices are closed. But it is not right that he should be on his own at Christmas."

"You shall do no such thing. Your leg is far too sore. You will get no further than the end of the street."

"But, my dear..." I protested.

My wife was the sweetest-natured woman in the world, but this belied a steely core. When her mind was made up, nothing anyone could say would change it.

The Morstans arrived in due course, and although I

felt morose about Holmes, I put on a smile and welcomed them in.

Just as lunch was being served, there came a knock at the door. Mary, making a puzzled noise, went to answer it.

Into the dining room swept none other than Father Christmas himself. He was dressed just as the Father Christmas at Burgh and Harmondswyke had been, in flowing dark green robe and mistletoe crown. His white beard was lustrously thick, his white hair long and wavy. Gold pince-nez spectacles perched upon his nose.

It was the nose, above all else, that gave it away. Only one man I knew had such a distinctive aquiline profile.

From a sack, he distributed presents to the younger generation – a set of tin soldiers here, a china doll there, a box of building blocks, some marbles, a kaleidoscope, all received with thrilled appreciation. There was a ruby brooch for Mary, bottles of vintage wine and boxes of cigars for the older Morstans, and for me, a hickory walking stick with silver knob and ferrule.

Mary knew as well as I did who Father Christmas really was. She had an extra chair brought to the table and cajoled him into sitting and partaking of the meal with us. Truth be told, he did not seem to need much persuading. He remained in character throughout, full of jollity, eating heartily, his voice booming. When pressed by the children, he told long, elaborate tales of the North Pole and his sleigh and his reindeer. As masquerades went, it was one of his finest.

Afterwards, I drew him aside.

"'Fatuous and tawdry'," I said. "Isn't that how you described Christmas to Eve Allerthorpe?"

"I have no idea what you mean," replied he. His grey eyes twinkled behind the spectacles. "Yuletide is the time we commune with our friends and loved ones. It is the time when we banish demons, lay ghosts to rest, re-establish bonds with those who are dear to us, and reaffirm the good in the world. Whoever told you it was fatuous and tawdry, that man could not have been I. I am Father Christmas, whereas he clearly does not have a festive bone in his body."

We pulled crackers, putting on the silly paper hats and reading aloud the even sillier mottos. Mary sat at the upright piano and we sang carols. She then proposed a game of charades, during which Father Christmas managed to slip unobtrusively out of the house.

A fortnight passed before my leg was strong enough to walk on. I made my way stiffly round to Baker Street, where I found Holmes at his acid-scarred chemistry bench, engaged in some noxious-smelling experiment.

"Many thanks for the walking stick," I said. "It is coming in very handy."

"What walking stick? Oh, I see. That one. It is a rather fine specimen. But why are you thanking me for it?"

"Come off it, Holmes. You know full well why. Christmas Day? My house? A certain unexpected guest? You went to a great deal of trouble. I can only assume you must have got to the shops just before they closed on Christmas Eve, to purchase the costume and the presents for everyone."

He eyed me blankly. "You will be pleased to hear that Trebend and his wife have been arraigned; he for murder, she as an accessory. Their trial commences in a month. I have been called upon to give testimony."

"That is good. But—"

"As for Fitzhugh and Kitty Danningbury Boyd, they are now living apart. According to the gossip columns, Danningbury Boyd has been seen squiring a wealthy young widow in York. I think it is safe to say he will fall on his feet. His kind always do."

"Again, that is good."

"Eve Allerthorpe has written to me. She does not have her money yet, but the Dawson twins have nonetheless been paid off in full. Her father dug into his own pocket for that. Meanwhile Erasmus Allerthorpe has, so far, been a model son and brother. I believe he has already begun learning the ropes at Fellscar, an attentive pupil to his father's teachings."

"Are you going to maintain the pretence that you did not turn up at my house on Christmas Day dressed as Father Christmas?"

"Why on earth would I do such a thing?" said Holmes.

"Because beneath that flinty, cerebral exterior there lurks a warm, even somewhat sentimental heart?"

Holmes merely laughed. "If, as you claim, Father Christmas paid you a visit in person, then if I were you I would regard it as a Christmas miracle."

I relented. Holmes himself was obviously not going to.

"A Christmas miracle?" I said. I could not help but smile. "Do you know what, old fellow? I think, all things considered, that is just what it was."

James Lovegrove is the *New York Times* bestselling author of *The Age of Odin*. He was shortlisted for the Arthur C. Clarke Award in 1998 and for the John W. Campbell Memorial Award in 2004, and also reviews fiction for the *Financial Times*. He is the author of *Firefly: The Magnificent Nine* and of *Firefly: Big Damn Hero* with Nancy Holder and several Sherlock Holmes novels for Titan Books.